INTO THE DUST
THE VIRGIN

A
BURNING MAN
STORY

This is a gift

from ....

to ....

INTO THE DUST
THE VIRGIN

A
BURNING MAN
STORY

JACK LYONS

This book is a work of fiction. Names, characters, places, and incidents do not depict any actual person, place, or event unless used by licensed agreement.

Cover design and illustration by Lisa Wachowicz – Paradox Fox Art

ISBN 979-8-9859457-2-0 (paperback)
ISBN 979-8-9859457-3-7 (e-book)
ASIN B09JQGLD9S (audio)

For sales, distribution, and more information about the book, visit www.IntoTheDustBook.com

This book is dedicated to my friends

John "Banjo Billy" Georges
A finer man never walked on the dust

Daniel Malone Mikkelson aka Ranger Nerf Herder
A kind and beautiful soul gone too soon

and Jesse Morrison
A peaceful warrior whose light touched many lives

ACKNOWLEDGMENTS

I would like to thank the following people for encouraging me and helping me write this book by reading and giving great feedback and support:

Nancy, Deidre, Fox, hawk hrdly, Weasel, Bob, Michele, Sarah Jane, Barry, and Dominique.

Special thanks to Joe Rogan. Listening to your podcast from the beginning inspired me to stop just thinking about writing and start writing for real.

Special thanks also to all the absolutely spectacular people and friends who contribute to the greatest experience on earth, Burning Man.

Thanks to Burning Man Project for their support. Without their hard work and dedication, this thing that we love would not happen.

A special apology, for ruining Burning Man.

It was better last year.

CHAPTER 1

Come all ye fractured souls, lonely children in adult skins,
Society's discarded broken vessels.
Bring your art, your love, and your wonder.
Find solace in the dust.

Diane Easting glared at her computer in frustration. She pushed her tinted glasses up to her forehead to keep her auburn hair from her face. Numbers, spreadsheets, customer complaints, and interdepartmental friction all seemed to land in her lap, the myriad problems of corporate structures and decisions, each of which seemed to require being done three times.

Rising from the sleek modern desk, she picked up her tumbler of tea and walked to the floor-to-ceiling windows that looked out on the city. Midafternoon sunshine warmed her face as she regarded her reflection. At forty-two, she was fit, accomplished, beautiful and, if she was honest, a bit bored.

Diane observed the street far below and the coffee shop where she had met Daniel, now her former boyfriend. A four-year relationship had started from a chance meeting and ended, though amicably enough, when it had run its course.

A chirp from her phone brought her out of her musings. Walking to her desk and glancing at the phone, she saw a text from her friend Stacy. Smiling as she picked up the device, she pressed the call button without reading the message.

"That's a change," Stacy said. "Since when do you return calls?"

"How have you been, my friend?" Diane asked.

"Busy as usual. Working to pay to play."

Stacy was her closest friend from college, her artistic lifestyle as diametrically opposed to Diane's as could be. She was a talented artist who eked out a living designing and making incredible artwork, while Diane had followed the corporate route. They had been inseparable in their school years. Stacy was a reckless and passionate wind into Diane's structured and calculated life. Diane was the stable touchstone to Stacy's sometimes chaotic existence.

"Same as always?" Diane asked.

"Bleh," Stacy said. "Anyway, what are you doing for the next two weeks?"

"Working, running . . ."

"Running the world, I'm sure. Disregard that. Come play with me."

Diane smiled, a common reaction to her friend's adventurous spirit.

"I can't just . . ."

"You can just hush and come with me. It's been forever. You need to play," Stacy said.

"And what, just asking from a place of curiosity, would that mean?"

"Two words," Stacy replied, then paused. She was always one for the dramatic.

Diane waited, letting the moment linger, buying time.

"I'm listening," she said, breaking the silence.

"Burning Man," Stacy said.

"Burning Man," Diane replied.

"Burning Man," Stacy repeated.

Diane recalled the various stories Stacy had described over the years as well as the articles she herself had read, the pictures she had seen.

"In the desert somewhere? Dirty hippies getting high in the desert?"

"Some hippies, yes, nice ones. Desert, yes. Getting high? Hmmm, you never know."

"Not interested," Diane said, taking a sip of tea.

"I know you better than that," Stacy said. "Besides, I bought you a ticket. You have to go."

"I'm too old. I don't want to run around with a bunch of kids."

"Most Burning Man attendees are over thirty," Stacy said.

Diane considered this information. If Stacy, who for all her talent had always struggled with money, had bought her a ticket, then it was a big deal.

"I don't really know anything about Burning Man. Stacy, I appreciate the . . ."

"Yes, yes, I know. *Too busy, what will I do, how*, and all that. Let me ask you this, Diane, my dear, a straightforward question. Are you happy?"

"Well . . ." Diane hesitated. "I'm doing well at work and—"

"Fucking boring!" Stacy's voice said through the phone. "Did I ask you how work was going, what money you have, or what fucking spin class you are into? Are . . . you . . . happy?"

Diane wanted to respond yes, to blow off this ridiculous conversation with her beloved yet crazy friend, but the words didn't come.

"Uh-huh. Your silence says volumes. So why don't you think it over and let me know by Monday? Buh-bye," Stacy said as she abruptly ended the call.

Diane took the phone from her ear and placed it on the desk, staring out the window as she considered. It was ridiculous. Just drop everything and take off? Not likely. Noticing her clock, Diane gathered her ledger book to take notes, walked down the hall to a meeting room, and took her seat at a long wooden table.

The meeting played out in its usual efficient fashion. Stella Worth, the CEO and Diane's mentor, kept a brisk pace, with little tolerance for unproductive people or cross talk.

"Diane? Do you have any input on this item?" Stella asked.

Diane looked up to see Stella staring with steel-gray eyes and a bemused look on her tanned, lean face. Diane could tell Stella knew she'd caught Diane daydreaming. Thankfully, they had enough of a history that a gentle nudge was all that was needed, even though Stella was putting her on the spot.

"I think Stephan covered the quarterly finances well," Diane replied.

Diane nodded at her lead team member, who she knew had been grinding on the figures for a week. She was glad for the chance to praise him in the public setting of the meeting and, more importantly, with Stella.

"What about on page seven, paragraph six? Capital outflows concerning South America and the refunds of monies from equipment returns and chargebacks? Have those funds actually settled, or are they in flux at the moment?" Stella asked.

"The monies have settled as of eight o'clock this morning. Stephan and I reviewed the banking transfers with our Zurich and Singapore accounts to release an accurate quarterly report," Diane said.

"Good. That's a wrap, then. Back to work," Stella said, closing her record book and the meeting. "Diane, meet me in my office in five, if you could."

Diane nodded and spoke briefly with her team, congratulating them on the presentation. Walking to Stella's office, she wondered what was up. It wasn't like Diane to drift off in a meeting, and she doubted a dressing-down would occur even though Stella was well known for taking subordinates to task for inattention during meetings.

Diane nodded to the two assistants in Stella's office lobby, both sharp-dressed young men.

"Go in, Ms. Easting," the taller of the two said with a smile.

"Darrell, close the door," Stella's voice came from within the office.

Diane walked into the large office, which had an even more impressive view of the city than her own. Stella was sitting with her knees crossed on the modern leather sofa in the sitting area.

"Sit, sit," Stella said, patting the couch beside her. "Would you like anything? Coffee?"

"No, I'm fine," Diane said. "Is this about the meeting?"

"The meeting?" Stella said with a mock smile. "Don't be ridiculous. Just keeping you on your toes. What's on your mind? A new beau?"

Diane grinned. "Nothing as exciting as that. A suggestion from a friend."

"Do tell."

"It's nothing, really . . ." Diane said.

"Come on, now," Stella replied, her gaze steady.

"A friend from college," Diane said. "She invited me to this festival coming up. It's a ridiculous idea, really."

"Is it Burning Man?" Stella asked, catching Diane off guard.

"Well, yes it is, actually," Diane replied.

"Hmmm," Stella said, then got up and walked to the window, looking out.

"I wasn't going," Diane said. "It was just a thought."

"Your friend Stacy painted that picture," Stella said, pointing at the large oil painting prominently displayed on the wall behind Diane.

Diane turned and looked at the painting. One side was an image of a young woman in dark blues and black shadows, reaching out to her mirror image in bold, bright colors and radiant hues on the other side. Stacy's talent was apparent in the beautiful painting. She had expressed so many emotions with oils upon canvas.

"Yes, that's her work. And yes, Stacy is the one who invited me."

Both women regarded the figure in the painting.

Stella abruptly broke the silence. "Is Stephan ready to take more responsibility?"

Diane took a moment to consider Stella's question. Stephan led her team and had done so for the past year. He was ambitious, hardworking, and smart. Diane also knew that the next step for him to take was the step she was already standing on.

"Probably."

"Yes or no?" Stella asked flatly.

"Yes, he is ready to be given more responsibility to season him. Do you have plans for him?" Diane asked.

"I have plans for you, my dear." Stella turned and regarded Diane. "You need to prepare for your next step, and that involves raising someone else."

"I see," Diane replied, excited but unsure of what that might mean.

Stella walked back to the window and looked out with her arms crossed, tapping her chin with the forefinger of her right hand. Diane waited and watched, knowing Stella was rolling scenarios, outcomes, and options through her formidable mind.

"Here's what I want you to do," Stella said finally. "Take the next two weeks and go to the Burn."

"I'm not sure when it . . ."

"I am very aware of when the Burn is as well as what it is," Stella said, turning to Diane. "You need to go—away, I mean. I want to throw Stephan into the deep end of the pool and see whether he can swim. And you need a break, as well as other things. Pack up and leave. Don't tell your team where you are going or when you'll be back. The quarterlies are done, and if you have prepared your team as well as I think you have, you taking a few weeks off shouldn't be an issue."

Diane stood stunned. She certainly hadn't expected this turn of events. At the same time, she realized with some amusement that Stella had done the exact same thing to her once. Thrown her into the deep end to see whether she could swim. She had.

Stella observed her protégé with a bemused expression. "Go have fun. Don't worry about this place. I'm jealous. You only get to be a Virgin Burner once."

"Well, okay then," Diane said, shaking her head.

Stella walked over to a curio cabinet in the corner. Diane knew the knickknacks there were memories of Stella's past, but

Stella had never shared what memories the objects represented. Stella unlocked a small drawer and withdrew an item.

"Wait," Stella said. "Here, take this."

Turning around, she handed Diane a leather belt with pouches, buckles, and hooks. A patina of dust, worked deep into the creases, covered the worn brown leather.

"You've been?" Diane asked, looking at the belt in her hand.

"I'll never tell," Stella said, smiling mysteriously. "Now go."

Diane looked at Stella in a new light. Despite all the years they had worked together, she didn't know that much about Stella's past. The wily CEO held her cards very close to the vest. Diane accepted the belt, shrugged, and walked to the door.

"One more thing, Diane," Stella said.

Diane looked back.

"Fuck your Burn."

CHAPTER 2

Wednesday, August 26, ten days until the Man burns

Diane looked out the window as the plane headed for Reno, Nevada. A whirlwind couple of days had been consumed gathering things on a list sent by Stacy. She'd bought a dust mask, goggles, and sleeping bag, along with all the other accoutrements and necessities for an extended stay out of contact from the world. All were carefully packed into a couple of bags. Stacy had written that she could provide a lot of the other items needed.

Diane had scoured the internet and watched several videos about preparing to go to Burning Man. They'd been very helpful, and she was both excited and apprehensive. The event had been around since the late eighties, starting in San Francisco. The organizers had just been a group of friends who got together on Baker Beach to burn a wooden effigy of a man. Rumors abounded that the man was a representation of the new lover of one of the founding members' ex-girlfriends. The party had grown year after year until it had to find a new home, the Black Rock desert in northern Nevada.

"Headed to Reno or Las Vegas?"

Diane turned from the window view to see an older gentleman with long gray hair worn in a braid down his back. He was dressed in a colorful tie-dyed T-shirt and brown shorts, and his eyes were blue and friendly in his craggy, tanned face.

"Reno," Diane replied. "Meeting some friends, camping."

"Playa bound?" the man asked.

"Playa? I didn't know there were beaches in Reno."

"The playa means Burning Man. The dust from the playa gets everywhere, and it's called playa as well. Deep playa is the large open area beyond the Man, out to the trash fence—which, by the way, is the outer limit of the site. You don't go past it. That's where dragons are, and a hundred miles of desolation. The city is a semicircle centered on the Man structure. That's where people camp. The city, I mean."

"Okay," Diane said, not really understanding. "Yes, I am headed to Burning Man."

"First timer?"

"Yes. It's a bit of a last-minute thing. My friend has been quite a lot."

"That's good," the man said, taking a sip from his cup. "To have an experienced friend, that is. Makes things simpler."

"You going?" Diane asked.

"Yes. I'm meeting up with my campmates, then heading out. My name is Badger, by the way."

He extended his hand. Diane shook it.

"Badger?" Diane said. "I'm Diane."

"Badger is my playa name. You might get one or might not. Most people who get a playa name go by that name when they're at the Burn."

"Did you name yourself?"

"That's not really how it works. You'll see. Someone else gives you the name. Though if you named yourself, no one would know or care. There is usually a story behind the name, and when someone names themselves, the story tends to be a bit lacking."

Badger signaled the flight attendant for more coffee.

"What do you do when you're not going to Burning Man, Badger?" Diane asked.

Badger took the coffee and took a sip. Then he turned back to Diane.

"When you're at the Burn, it's best not to ask people what they do in the default world. That way we can get away from it. Anonymity provides us freedom of expression, you see."

"Oh, I'm sorry. I didn't know . . ."

Badger waved his hand dismissively and smiled warmly at her.

"Not a big deal. It's just nice to meet people and not have labels on them. Start from just being humans and go from there," Badger said, adding, "This is my fifteenth time going in seventeen years. As clichéd as it sounds, the Burn has changed my life. Have you heard about the principles?"

"The ten principles? Yes. I can't say I remember or understand them all."

Badger ticked them off on his fingers. "Radical Inclusion, Gifting, Decommodification, Radical Self-Reliance, Radical Self-Expression, Communal Effort, Civic Responsibility, Leave No Trace, Participation, Immediacy."

"That's a few to remember," Diane said.

"Since you're a Virgin, your main job is to try not to die. Drink lots of water and do self-care. It can be very raw and difficult when you push yourself out there. Lots of people forget to sleep or drink and eat enough, and they crash, hard. Also, a lot of times, any emotions or trauma you have suppressed tend to come out, whether you want them to or not."

"Where did the principles come from?" Diane asked.

"Well, good question," Badger said, shifting in his seat. "There are a lot of opinions about when and where they happened. Some thoughts are they happened after the Burn of '96, when the thing got a little out of hand. Others are that they were always there but not written down. When Burning Man went from a party to a larger, well, movement, it had to have some guidance.

"The '96 Burn was a turning point. In order for the event to survive, there had to be rules. Some of them reportedly came from an earlier event called Rainbow Gathering, which still happens. That event's core principles are freedom from consumerism, capitalism, and mass media, along with love, peace, nonviolence, and environmentalism. The early Burners were, in essence, pioneers, and like the pioneers, they were tough and smart. They walked out onto a vast, desolate plain and decided they could do something out there.

"The Self-Reliance principle is a response to people showing up and just not being able to take care of themselves, expecting others to do it. Wooks aren't really embraced at Burning Man."

"What's a wook?"

"A wook is usually a young hippie—in appearance, anyway—who leeches off of others, not wanting to do any work or take care of themselves. A wook is what society may think of as a hippie, but in reality, most people who align with so-called hippie culture take care of themselves and others with an idealistic goal. I should know, because I consider myself in that category. The problem, you see, is that we as a species are hardwired to expect men to produce more than they consume. If someone does not meet that standard, they run the risk of being excluded."

"And Radical Inclusion?"

"Everybody is welcome, regardless of nationality, political alignment, and gender or sexual orientation. The guideline is 'Don't hurt yourself, don't hurt others.' Whatever you want to find, you can find there. If you want to rage to music and take sparkly things, you can. If you want to attend lectures on basically any subject, learn skills, do crafts, pray, volunteer, do performances, you can. It can be as wild or as mild as you want it to be. There is the gray area of shirt cockers and sparkle ponies, though."

"Shirt cockers?" Diane asked, amused.

"Men wearing only a shirt, not pants."

Diane laughed at the image.

"All nude is fine," Badger continued, "but with just a shirt? A lot of people don't like that."

"And sparkle ponies? Is that good or bad?" Diane asked.

Badger smiled at her.

"Good or bad is a flip of the coin. The term denotes being a taker instead of a giver. Sparkle ponies show up with costumes and entitlement. Usually, they expect others to do for them because they are busy being pretty and fabulous. They're taking pretty pictures, the kind of thing you see on the internet or in the media. Sparkle ponies are setting themselves outside the community instead of being part of it, and that goes against Self-Reliance. There are plenty of other people who show up and dress in fabulous costumes and take pictures, but they pull their weight. Anyway, a lot of Burners feel sparkle ponies misrepresent the culture and devalue their hard work. Sparkle ponies are accepted, but not everyone likes them. It is generally used as a derogatory term."

"The Self-Expression and Immediacy principles I kinda get. What about Decommodification?" Diane asked.

"Nothing can be sold or offered for sale except ice, coffee, and RV services. Are you staying in an RV?"

"No, a tent in a carport."

"Perfect. Your first time should be in the dust. If you had an RV, you could pay to get it pumped out and water-filled by the trucks that roam around. They only take cash.

"Gifting refers to a gifting culture that means people bring things to give to other people. That could be objects bought or made, food, drink, maybe a massage, a song, or just listening, holding space and being present for someone. It takes a while to realize that you don't have to give something back in return. It's not bartering. Gifts don't have strings."

"Participation and Immediacy?"

"Those are pretty well entwined. Being in the moment, being a part of something bigger than yourself. Not thinking about yesterday or tomorrow, just soaking it in and saying yes to life—or no, if you want. The ability and space to just be."

"That makes sense."

"Sooner or later it will," Badger said. "A wise man once told me, 'You don't experience the Burn, you *are* the experience.' How did you get your ticket?"

"My friend got it for me," Diane replied. "I'm not sure how that works."

"It's come a long way since you just drove out to the desert and paid cash to a guy in a car. He just sat there with a shotgun and a cashbox and pointed you in the general direction."

"Really?" Diane asked incredulously.

Badger laughed at her reaction.

"Really," he said. "Now, there are a few ways. You have to register on the Burning Man website, and then there are a few sales. First is FOMO . . ."

"Fear of missing out?" Diane asked.

"You got it," Badger replied. "Those tickets cost the most, almost triple regular tickets. Then there is the main sale on a specified date. Those go quick. There are reduced tickets for low-income Burners, and there is the OMG sale later.

"Established camps are allotted some tickets for their campers. That's a separate thing. People who volunteer the year before are given access to buy or be gifted tickets depending on how many hours they put in. Then there's the STEP sale, which is a way to purchase tickets for the Burn from people who return their tickets for whatever reason. STEP stands for secure ticket exchange program.

"And then there are the offline sales, people putting tickets up on scalping sites. Not only is that frowned upon, sometimes they are counterfeit tickets. If you show up to gate with a fake ticket, you are just out of luck. There are ticket sales where people buy just to resell at ridiculous prices. It is very frowned upon, and the Burning Man Organization takes steps to discourage it."

"Civic Responsibility?"

"We support the rules and means by which we exist in society. It's better to think of it as 'do no harm.' Not to ourselves, to the environment, to one another. Treat all of those with kindness. Communal Effort is just that as well. Help your neighbor, help yourself, be a part of something more than yourself, help to raise everyone."

"Thanks for all the information," Diane said.

"Then there is the eleventh principle," Badger added.

"What's that?"

"Consent," Badger said. "Consent to take someone's picture or to touch them, and especially for sex. You also need to be able to check in with your partner. Just because someone says yes at first, or at one time, doesn't mean that consent lasts forever. Say you were with someone, engaging in activities consensually, but then something changed. You need to be able to communicate, check in with your partner and ensure that everyone is still on board. Each person has the power at any time to give or withdraw consent. Each person has the responsibility to *both* check in *and* communicate, because assumption of an understanding takes away the other person's capacity and potential to be their best self. Consent is essential on the playa. Not everyone gets it at first."

Diane looked at him, blinking as she processed the large amount of information.

"You'll understand more as time goes on," Badger said.

"We are making our arrival at the Reno airport," announced a flight attendant. "We want to thank you for choosing to fly with us today. Please return your tray tables and seatbacks to their original positions."

"Well, I certainly appreciate the education. Any last-minute tips?" Diane asked, putting up her tray table.

"Enjoy yourself, and never, ever leave camp without your dust mask and goggles, not even to go to the portable toilets—we call those portos. The dust storms can be intense and sudden. And always bring your cup and ID. A lot of the bars won't serve you without them. If you have any problems, ask for help or find a Ranger. They are Burners like you, and they're there to help.

"If you find yourself near the nine o'clock side, look me up. My camp is Creative Deconstruction."

"OK, I'll do that."

The flight touched down in Reno and pulled to the gate. Diane waved goodbye to Badger and walked to baggage claim.

CHAPTER 3

D iane!" a woman's voice exclaimed.

Diane turned to see her friend Stacy barreling toward her and was swept up into her arms. Both women laughed and fell to the ground as the embrace overbalanced them. Getting up, Diane took in her friend.

Stacy was of middle height, with dark bronze skin. Her large breasts were stuffed into a multicolored corset, and her long, dark hair was an explosion of multicolored braids with colorful cloth strips woven into them. Small, tight cutoff shorts showed off her long legs down to her dusty green leather boots. Intricate and beautiful tattoos covered her shapely arms from shoulders to fingertips.

"Is this Burn chic?" Diane asked, admiring her friend.

"You know it!" Stacy said, taking a spin, ending with her legs crossed, hands on her hips, looking back at Diane over her shoulder. "Especially the braids. The playa dust is alkali, plays hell on your hair. With these, you don't have to wash it."

"There are my bags," Diane said, pointing to a duffel and a roller bag on the conveyor belt.

Stacy leaned down and, without apparent effort, grabbed

the bags, one in each hand, and lifted them off the conveyor. Diane watched as Stacy's shoulder and arm muscles flexed, deeply defined.

"Wow! Yoga paying off?"

"I've been teaching a bit. It's fun," Stacy said, slinging the duffel over her shoulder as Diane extended the handle of the roller bag. Stacy tucked her free arm through Diane's and guided her out the door into the warm sunshine.

"Are we leaving directly?" Diane asked as they walked up to a small pickup truck with two bicycles on a roof rack and black and yellow storage tubs in the bed. A two-wheeled, enclosed box trailer was hitched behind the truck.

"No, we have a room in Fernley a little up the road. We have early work access passes to help build the camp, but they are not good until tomorrow. We have to do some last-minute provisioning and preparation," Stacy said.

The trip from the small airport in Reno to Fernley was quick, and the two women chatted and caught up. The air was warm as they drove through the mocha hills lining the highway. From Reno, the highway rose into rock-covered mountains. A small river was on their right, with grass and green trees and a railroad track running alongside, a slice of life in an otherwise drab brown landscape. A silver passenger train passed by them, heading toward Reno.

"What is that?" Diane asked, looking out the window at a cloud of dust off the highway.

"The train?" Stacy said, glancing. "Holy shit, it's the wild mustangs! I've never seen them before."

Diane watched, fascinated, as the dust cloud revealed brown horses galloping along the river and then over a hill, out of view.

As they drove out of the mountain pass, the land opened up, with plains to the south and dark mountains to the north. Taking the exit for Fernley, they checked into the motel and headed across the street to the superstore.

"So you brought everything I told you, correct?" Stacy asked.

"Yes, clothing and camp gear. It was a little bit late to get other items."

"Well, here is the list of what we have to get. I have a lot, but it's our last chance. You read and I'll grab. I hate having to come to a corporate store for this stuff, but there was no time."

Diane unfolded the list as they walked in, with Stacy pushing a cart. Looking at the long list of items, Diane noted the check marks by some.

"Okay, I'll assume you have the ones that are checked off," she said.

"Yep."

"When did you get so organized?" Diane teased.

"Not bringing something and really needing it a few times overcame my usual disorder. Okay, lotions and potions," Stacy said as she stopped by the drug section.

"Skin lotion, eye drops, cough drops, aspirin, B-12. Antacids you have checked. Sunblock," Diane read. "Body powder and diaper rash cream?"

"Spend a week in booty shorts and you'd be surprised how tender you get," Stacy replied, placing more items into the cart.

"And tampons," Diane continued. "I just finished my period a day ago, though."

"Doesn't matter. You will get it at the Burn."

"For real?"

"Never fails. Besides, it's good to carry one as a gift for other ladies. I usually leave one near the porta-potties in deep playa," Stacy said while walking down the aisle.

"Condoms, lube, wet wipes."

"The wet wipes are how we will keep ourselves clean until the showers are set up. Condoms and lube should be self-explanatory," Stacy said, smiling.

"How about these?" Diane asked, holding up a box of condoms.

"Here's to hoping the playa provides." Stacy grinned as she placed them in the cart.

"Alright. Toilet paper and some food items, along with water," Diane said, consulting the list.

"Water we have in a fifty-five-gallon barrel in the truck, along with two five-gallon emergency drinking water jugs in the trailer. Running out of water sucks. Our camp is having water delivered, but shit happens. My first year, I brought only a few gallons, because the camp leads were supposed to bring in the bulk of the water. Well, they broke down, and we ran out. That was unbelievably miserable and won't happen to me again. Oh, and don't ever put wet wipes in the porta-potties, they clog the pumper trucks. And while there usually is paper in the portos, I like to carry my own."

Walking up and down the aisles, they selected various foods. Diane raised her eyebrows as Stacy placed a massive pack of boxed macaroni and cheese into the cart along with a tray of instant soup.

"I haven't had that stuff since I was in college!"

"Trust me, you need to push calories out there. You will drop weight, no matter what. I prefer using the canned evaporated milk. It's heaven in the mac and cheese, and it won't spoil."

"Eggs, bacon, bread . . ."

"I use the eggs that come premixed in the cardboard boxes," Stacy said, placing them in the cart. "I have three more frozen in my cooler."

"I didn't know they came like that," Diane said.

The women found the rest of the food items on the list and then headed up to the liquor section, where Stacy asked Diane to find another shopping cart. When Diane returned, Stacy began placing multiple bottles of whiskey into the cart, then started loading up cases of cheap beer. Diane's eyes grew wide as Stacy put the eighth 30-pack into the cart.

"Do we need to have a talk about alcohol consumption?" Diane asked. "An intervention on shitty beer?"

Stacy turned to Diane, cocked her head, and counted off on her fingers.

"First off, this 'shitty' beer is delicious cold, and it's one of the only brands that doesn't give me heartburn. Second, when it's hot as balls, you need something cold and delicious. Third, it's not all for us. Running out of beer sucks almost as bad as running out of water. Fluffing our campmates is a lot of fun and really appreciated. Fourth, the cans can be recycled on the playa at the recycling camp, while bottles have to be hauled out. The cardboard boxes can be burned in our burn barrel. You'll see."

"What's fluffing?" Diane asked.

"Fluffing comes from the porn world, where it might be someone's job to fellate the actors to keep them hard. On the playa, it means taking care of your campmates in a way that keeps them working, seeing as how blowing them would probably make them take a nap."

Diane threw her head back to chortle at the description. It felt great to be able to cut loose and laugh so freely. They pushed their loaded carts to the registers.

"Oh, wait," Stacy said and headed off into the store, returning with a large package of tube socks and two gallon jugs of white vinegar.

"Okay, I get the socks since we can't do laundry, but what's with the vinegar?" Diane asked.

"It's for soaking your feet and cleaning playa off stuff. Playa is super alkaline, so the vinegar neutralizes it. What we don't use out there, we can use for cleaning the vehicle. It's the only way to get playa off. The dust eats seals, belts, all the things."

The women completed the rest of their shopping and took their purchases back to the hotel.

"So what should I expect?" Diane asked as they walked into the room.

"Let's unpackage this stuff and talk about it," Stacy said. "What should you expect? Hard to say."

"Is this part of the Leave No Trace thing?" Diane asked, indicating the pile of boxes and wrappings they were creating.

"Yes. We pack out everything we pack in. That's Radical Self-Reliance. You need to take anything you will need or want with you. Food, water, stuff. There is no place to get anything out there," Stacy replied. "So what do you want to happen?"

"I don't know," Diane said. "Something?"

"Well, just experience it. Be open to it . . . and, well, everything. You'll get the idea. Get inspired, say yes to everything you can. You're gonna love it, and then hate it, and then love it. Now let's see what you brought," Stacy said. "I have stuff you can wear, but did you bring any costumes?"

Diane picked up her duffel and placed it on the bed. Pulling clothes out, Stacy looked at the various items.

"I was afraid of that," Stacy said, holding up a feather-fringed leather vest and sequined shorts.

"Afraid of what?"

"This is your Indian princess outfit from college, right?"

"Yeah. It still fits, and . . ."

"Nobody likes a fucking bragger," Stacy said with a deadpan expression.

Diane regarded the serious look on her friend's face. Then the women were reduced to peals of laughter.

"What's the problem with the costume?" Diane asked, wiping her eyes.

"Well, for one, it's fucking tacky and disrespectful to the First Peoples, and that will irritate people. Two, there's the MOOP problem with any feathers and sequins."

"What's MOOP?" Diane asked.

"MOOP is matter out of place, like litter, trash, anything someone is going to have to pick up. And it's expected for you to pick up MOOP when you find it."

"Okay. There's a lot to remember."

"Oh, and have you kicked the smoking yet?" Stacy asked.

"I might have one every now and then. Why?"

"We will pick you up a tin tomorrow. You use it for your ashes and cigarette butts."

"You don't even want ash on the playa?"

Stacy leaned in closer to Diane. "Leave No Trace means leave no trace. Now, where are the clothes you are wearing home?"

"Here," Diane said, taking some items from her duffel and handing them to Stacy.

Stacy produced a large plastic bag and slid the clothes into it. Sealing the top, she pressed the bag so that the air came out of a small valve and then handed it to Diane.

"What's that do?" Diane asked.

"Keeps the dust off. It's incredibly nice to wear clean clothes after you are out and have a shower. Don't open it until then."

Stacy then picked up a plastic package and began to open it.

"And that is?" Diane asked.

"CO detector. For carbon monoxide."

"What do you use that for? Aren't we in a tent?"

"There are cars around, cooking stoves, generators. Say someone turns on a generator at night and points the exhaust into your tent or RV. The carbon monoxide could build up and kill you in your sleep. It's not unheard of at festivals. So we have one in our structure, and we will gift one to someone else."

"There's a lot that goes into this . . . cash, time, effort," Diane said. "I didn't realize how much."

"If you figure that the price varies according to how much you want to spend, it's comparable to a regular person's really nice vacation somewhere. Some people spend more," Stacy replied. "As for time, that depends on the person. Some of the artists work year-round, or for multiple years, to create the art they bring out.

"Now, I don't know about you, but I think a cocktail and an early night are what I'm in the mood for. And probably one last hot shower."

"Sounds good. But aren't there showers at camp?"

"We will have the camp showers set up in a few days, but until then, it's wet wipes."

"Does the camp have a name?"

"Dead Presidents."

"Oh, and do you have a playa name?"

"Yep. Tiger Kite, or TK," Stacy said. "It's 'cause I fly high and am so fierce."

Diane raised an eyebrow at the odd name.

"Admittedly," Stacy said, "the girl who gave me the name was tripping her tits off."

CHAPTER 4

Thursday, August 27, nine days until the Man burns

Diane and Stacy rose early, had breakfast at a nearby diner, and made a quick trip to a truck stop to top up the gasoline and fill a few gas cans. They also popped into an auto parts store for a spare air filter for the truck. Stacy explained that when they left the playa, they would put on the new air filter and get rid of the clogged one. Turning left away from the highway on a two-lane road, they meandered through a well-watered river valley, where signs stated they were entering the Paiute reservation.

Diane took it in eagerly as the radio played soft, trippy, upbeat music, most of which was new to her. Stacy, who was slow in waking up, sipped her coffee while driving. The speed limits through the small towns were very conservative, and Stacy obeyed them all.

The sun was beginning to rise as they drove. Diane noticed other cars and some RVs traveling in the same direction, some with blue tape along their window seams. This intrigued her, but she kept her thoughts to herself to let Stacy wake up.

"Helps with the dust," Stacy said, breaking the comfortable silence.

"What?"

Stacy pointed to the small RV trailer in front of them.

"On the window seams. The exterior painter's tape keeps some of the dust out. You can see, though, they used some interior tape too. It's going to come off pretty soon."

"Why do they do it before getting there?"

"The dust is very fine. As soon as you hit the playa, it's going to be on everything, in everything. Since you need to clean the seams really well to get the tape to stick, you have to do it ahead of time," Stacy replied. "Tape does stick out like a sore thumb for law enforcement, though."

"Is police harassment an issue?"

"Some years are better than others. Since the Black Rock Desert is federal land, like the First Peoples reservations, marijuana isn't legal."

"I haven't done any drugs in years. Is it an issue with our camp?"

"If someone became a problem because of choices they made, they might have to leave, and they probably would not be invited back. The camp is not here to be your babysitter, or your mom, or a cop. We will help you, but you have to help yourself first, you know? Expecting other people to repeatedly manage your life is not a realistic expectation. Being together, working together, and having fun together, that's why people come to our camp."

"Are there ever any issues at the Burn because of people doing drugs?"

"Sometimes things happen," Stacy said briefly, then pointed. "You see that coming up?"

"The metal thing?"

"Yeah. It's a cattle guard. Free-range cows are walking around out here. Keep a close eye out for them. I saw one get hit once. Not a good day.

"Notice the RV is a rental, and the rental name is covered? That's for Decommodification. No advertisement. It's not mandatory, but some people take it seriously."

"You mentioned medical personnel, and earlier you talked about a medical clinic. What's involved in that?" Diane asked.

"There are medical facilities on the playa now. Your ticket fee covers the use. You got the medical flight insurance I sent you?"

"Yes."

"Good. There's an airport. If you do have something serious happen and you have to be flown out, the cost is extremely high. So a little insurance can go a long way."

The two fell silent, taking in the stark natural beauty of the harsh land around them. Brown was the predominant color higher up and green lower down, around a small river. After passing through the little town of Nixon, they drove uphill from the valley, the road winding to the right, hugging a small mountain.

"There's Pyramid Lake," Stacy said. "It's sacred to the Paiutes."

Diane looked up at a beautiful large lake spread out to the west of them. She could see a small island in the distance. The view was breathtaking, as far from the familiar cityscape she lived in as possible.

As the road wound upward, the view of the lake dropped away behind a line of brown mountains. A sparse lowland plain opened before them, with umber mountains close by to the west and another mountain range further to the east, a desolate landscape of scrub brush and white sandy soil in contrast to the river-fed valley behind them. Diane smelled an earthy, acrid, tangy scent in the air.

"That's the first scent of the playa," Stacy said, noting her sniffing. "Pretty soon we have to roll up the windows and keep the AC on max so we don't suck in the dust from the air inside the truck. Keeping the AC on max will recirculate the air inside the car instead of cooling the air outside, though, so no farting."

"Whatever," Diane said, laughing.

The light music was perfect for the dreamy landscape, harsh yet beautiful. The miles rolled under the tires as Stacy and Diane drove in an ethereal silence for the next hour. Diane felt as if she were floating through the landscape, rendezvousing with something unknown in the distance.

"Empire up ahead," Stacy said. "Do you need to use the bathroom?"

"I'm fine for a bit," Diane replied.

"Okay, we will stop in Gerlach. It's only a little farther. It's the last chance until the playa. And the last chance, for the duration, for a clean flush toilet."

Empire, a small village with only a store and gas station near a large gypsum mine, came and went. Diane saw the signs for Gerlach and a widening of the plain to the east. It was a pale landscape, devoid of any growth or adornment, a flat moonscape at best. Small fringes of dry bushes grew near the elevated road that petered out quickly into the whiteness.

"Is that it?" Diane asked. "Is that the playa?"

"That's it," Stacy said in a small voice.

Diane turned to find her friend smiling faintly and looking intently at her. Stacy seemed to be waiting for her reaction.

"It's so . . . so . . . ." Diane searched for words to describe what she was seeing.

"Kinda hard to explain?" Stacy supplied.

Diane took a deep breath as she marveled.

"Yes, I'd say that is accurate," Diane replied.

Stacy guided the car over some railroad tracks and took a left onto the narrow road that led into the small town of Gerlach. A little motel and gas station, followed by buildings from another time, then some small houses, constituted the town. A small casino, a bar, and a coffee shop lined the road. Stacy pulled up to a homey, ramshackle bar. As they got out, Diane noticed a steady traffic of cars passing through the town.

"Just use the bathroom and we will head out," Stacy said, walking to the door. "The portos in the Gate line are horrific, and we don't know how long the Gate line will be."

"An hour or so?" Diane asked.

"We are arriving early to build the camp, so the line should be comparatively easy, which is a gift in itself for us. Today is Wednesday, and the Gate officially opens on Sunday—as in, right at midnight on Saturday night. The Burn goes for another week, until the next Sunday. The next day, the Monday, is called Exodus, because after the Temple burns, everyone leaves. The Gate line in for the general public can be six hours or more, it can back up most of the way to Empire, sometimes beyond. And sometimes the line for the Exodus takes just as long."

"Six hours?" Diane said. "Wow, and we are here for twelve days?"

"If you want the full experience of build, burn, and takedown. I thought it was important. And yeah, it's a gift we get to come in early. Some years, a dust storm has closed the Gate for ten hours. Oh, and when it rains, nobody moves until it's dry. Huge mud problems. That's why we bring extra garbage bags to wrap our feet. You pick up ten pounds in ten steps. Also, if it gets really bad, you might have to use the garbage bags to line the bucket and use it as a toilet."

"Guess I'd better go, then," Diane replied. "You could have told me the other stuff before I came."

"Yeah, but it wouldn't be an adventure then," Stacy said. "I'll grab some sandwiches and drinks. Easy-to-eat food is important in line."

The bar was out of another time. Old furnishings and wooden walls were clean but worn. The two ladies used the facilities and headed back to the truck.

"Here we go," Stacy said, pulling out.

They'd made it about two blocks when Diane spotted what appeared to be a small bazaar set up on the side of the road on the edge of the small town.

"What's that?" Diane asked.

"It's a shop for Burner stuff. Things like costumes, lights, masks."

"Really? Out here?"

"Yeah. Some people make a living off the Burn. I used to have a bit of heartburn over it, but now I think, good for them. Unlike the plug-and-play camps, those still kind of piss me off, but that's my own baggage. Let's shelve that for a while. This is the last stretch, I love coming home, and this is my coming home mix," Stacy said as she pushed a button on her car stereo.

Stacy steered the truck around a curve to the right, hugging a small hill to their left. The small amount of vegetation they had seen in town had dwindled to sparse patches near the road. As they drove, Diane could see other cars, trucks, and RVs slowing in front of them. She felt both a calm and an excitement come over her. The music was a perfect soundtrack, happy beats and rhythms.

An electronic highway sign showed the entrance where Stacy turned in. The truck left the road to drive onto the dusty white earth. Ropes designated multiple lanes, and Stacy picked the farthest one to the right, driving slowly along at the assigned ten miles per hour. The lane was firm but dusty. Tracks from previous vehicles crisscrossed in the dust.

On the edges of the lanes, small signs were posted, with sayings and instructions. White playa stretched out on the sides and in front of them. Everything moved smoothly, but Diane could see the brake lights of cars far ahead.

A light, filmy haze of dust rose from the ground. The tangy scent in the air was much more potent. Diane could see a hazy white cloud of dust in the distance.

"Is that Black Rock City? Is that a dust storm?" Diane asked, looking over at her friend.

Stacy, with a huge smile, leaned over, wrapped an arm around Diane and kissed the crown of her head.

"I'm so happy!" Stacy said. "The look on your face is priceless! When was the last time you felt childlike wonder?"

Diane smiled back, sheepishly.

"Yes, that is the city, part of it, anyway," Stacy said. "But no, that's not a dust storm. It's just like that a lot. It will get worse as more people come and drive on the playa. That's why you need to keep a dust mask and goggles with you all the time, and I mean all the fucking time. Unless you want playa lung."

"Understood," Diane said, soaking in the surreal landscape. "What's playa lung?"

"Kinda like bronchitis with plaster of Paris on top. It's when too much dust gets in your lungs. It sucks. I got it toward the end of my first year"—Stacy leaned close to Diane—"when I didn't take the mask thing seriously enough."

Stacy held Diane in a mock-serious gaze until Diane waggled her eyebrows, and both laughed.

"Okay, okay, you'll be fine," Stacy said. "Here is the Gate."

Diane looked up to see that the vehicles in front of them had stopped. There was a row of multiple wooden shacks ahead. They were obviously intended for traffic, though all but two entrances were blocked. Stacy pulled up behind the line of stopped vehicles.

"Is this where you ring the bell?" Diane asked, having read about the ritual.

"No, that's the Greeters," Stacy replied. "Here they check tickets, vehicle passes, and early entry passes and search vehicles for stowaways."

The line of vehicles moved along, getting checked in. Diane observed them as well as the people around her. The license plates were from all over the country. Music played, and people seemed to be happy, if a little tired.

When they made it to the front of the line, Stacy handed the tickets and early work access passes to the Gate worker. The vehicle pass went onto the inner surface of the windshield, along with multiple passes from previous years. Diane had not noticed those before.

Moving on from the Gate, they slowly approached a row of large tripod structures. Pulling up to a lane between two of them, Stacy stopped the truck and got out, calling back to Diane, "Come on!"

Diane got out of the car and joined Stacy, who was talking to a tall man and a short woman.

"I understand we have a Virgin!" the tall man said loudly and flamboyantly.

"Yes. Yes, I guess I am," Diane said.

"Well, roll in the dust, honey," the woman said.

"Dust! Dust! Dust!" Stacy chanted. "I'll do it with you."

Diane and Stacy lay down on the ground, rolling in the white, fine, powdery soil, which was the consistency and texture of talcum powder.

"Do a dust angel, like this," Stacy said, lying on her back and moving her outstretched arms and legs.

Diane copied her until she sneezed so hard that dust flew from her hair. As she and Stacy got to their feet, she saw that the dust covered their hair, skin, and clothing.

"Now ring the bell, ring the bell!" Stacy said.

"Ring it hard!" the tall man said, handing Diane a piece of pipe.

Diane took the pipe and slammed it against the bell, which was a gas cylinder with its bottom cut off and suspended by a chain. The loud sound was deeply satisfying.

The three watching hooted and clapped.

"Welcome home! Do you hug?" the tall man asked, his bright teeth shining against his dark skin.

"Yes, absolutely," Diane said, stepping into his outstretched arms. She could feel the man's strength as they embraced. It was very comforting.

"Welcome home, you beautiful soul," he said, still holding onto her.

Diane smiled and relaxed into the embrace. This was not a

perfunctory hug. This was something genuinely different. She had expected the man to release her to signal the end of the embrace, even though she still had not released him, but he didn't.

"It's okay. Take all you want," the man said. "Welcome home."

Diane held on to him for another few moments, then stepped back and looked into his handsome face.

"You gonna be okay," he said.

Diane nodded, turned to the woman, and hugged her as well, thinking, *I don't know these people, and they don't know me, but this feels right and good.*

"Welcome home," the woman said, handing Diane and Stacy two bundles of paper and some small books. "Here are your guides. Do you know where you're going?"

"Three-thirty and E," Stacy replied. "Dead Presidents."

"Okay then, have fun," the man said, waving.

The pair got back into the truck and slowly pulled forward.

"So, what now?" Diane asked.

"Now we find our camp. Here it is on the six o'clock road. Follow it to E and—see the map?—then to three-thirty, like the wings of a phoenix. And from now on, while we're here, call me TK or Tiger Kite. I'm home."

TK inched the car along at five miles per hour. The slow pace gave Diane time to take in the strange landscape around her. The vast plain was segregated into squares delineated by blue string and marked by small flags. Dotted across the landscape were vehicles and tents. People were obviously setting up on bare patches of land.

Diane watched wide-eyed as a woman in leather chaps, a

cowboy hat, and nothing else, carrying a parasol, walked down the road. An older man with a gray beard, wearing a green unitard, was riding a unicycle with an oversized tire. Two people, one in a gorilla costume and one in a banana costume, stood on opposite sides of the street making rude gestures at each other. Clearly, she was somewhere different.

"You get to see the city being built," TK said, not even noticing the antics.

"It gets built for seventy thousand people?"

"No, seventy thousand people build it. Here is E, so we take a right and keep on. If we kept going straight on six o'clock, we would come to center camp."

"Coffee and ice?"

"Ice is at Arctica. They are located in various places around the city. Probably not open for another day or so," TK said.

Diane returned to watching the scenery crawl by. People were walking around, riding bikes, and setting up their areas.

"Here it is," TK said, turning off the road and into one of the squares of ground.

CHAPTER 5

H i, I'm Sequoia. You a hugger, Diane?"

Diane nodded and stepped forward into the offered embrace. The man was huge, not just tall but legitimately a massive human being. Thick arms encircled her waist. He was so large and powerful that Diane was a bit frightened he might hurt her.

The worry was baseless. The embrace was gentle—incredibly strong, but gentle. She could barely get her arms around the sides of his barrel of a chest. Huge hands pressed against her spine.

"Nice to meet you. Are you guys hungry, thirsty?" Sequoia asked, looking down on her. His smile was brilliantly white, reflected in his sparkling green eyes. His face was framed by long brown hair and a thick beard.

"My turn," TK said, running toward Sequoia and launching herself up into his arms, wrapping her legs around his waist.

Sequoia's laugh boomed out of him as he easily held TK in his arms and spun around.

"Wheeee!" TK squealed, burrowing her face into Sequoia's shaggy brown beard and long hair.

"I'm Twinkle. Hi. Diane, right?" said a small woman to Diane's left. Diane took in the pretty round face and jet-black hair cut into an attractive bob, topped with a wide-brimmed sunhat. Twinkle's arms were open, and Diane embraced her too.

"Thanks, Twinkle," Diane said.

"Here you go," Twinkle said, handing her a dog tag on a chain.

"What's this?" Diane asked, looking at the piece. Inscribed in the metal was a relief of the four heads of Mount Rushmore, with "Dead Presidents" etched in red.

"Camp swag," Twinkle explained. "I have a couple more you can have to give out to interesting people."

"I don't have anything to give you," Diane said.

Twinkle laughed. "It's a gift, not barter or exchange. You don't have to give me anything. You'll get it."

Diane watched as TK climbed up Sequoia's body like a squirrel to end up sitting on his broad shoulders. Both wore gleeful expressions. Diane slipped the necklace over her head.

"Thank you so much," Diane told Twinkle, giving her another hug.

"You're welcome," Twinkle replied, turning to look at TK and Sequoia frolicking together.

"Ha! Give me a ride, motherfucker!" TK yelled, holding on to Sequoia's forehead.

Sequoia complied and galloped away from the camp, with TK bouncing and laughing.

"Well, they will be busy for a bit. Let me show you around," Twinkle said, taking Diane's arm in her own. "Is it alright to take your arm like this?"

"Yes," Diane said, feeling instantly comfortable.

"You're a Virgin?" Twinkle said.

"Yes."

"Great! If you have any questions or need anything, don't hesitate to ask. I'm the mayor of Dead Presidents this year, so I'm here to help you."

Diane looked around the plot of land. At the center was a large beige shipping container. The doors were open, and a broad array of items was strewn all over the ground. An RV was parked at the side of the camp, and two beige carports had been placed to the side of the shipping container.

"You guys will be here in the carport ghetto," Twinkle said, and then she walked up to an open panel of the carport and stuck her head in. "Anyone home?"

"Hey, what's up?" a male voice came from the interior.

Diane looked inside. The floor had a tarp taped to the heavy-duty vinyl sides of the structure. The tarp was covered by a large area rug. A tent was set up on one side, with a plastic shelving unit and chairs on the other. It was quite homey.

"Jeremy, this is Diane. She just got here with Tiger Kite."

A thin young man emerged from the tent. Diane judged him to be in his early twenties, with short brown hair, a wiry build, and a scruffy yet handsome face.

"Hi, Diane," Jeremy said sheepishly. He didn't maintain eye contact with her, Diane noticed.

"Jeremy is a Virgin too. So you guys can share your experiences," Twinkle said. "Wrapping up your nap, Jeremy?"

"Yeah. I'm still a little tired. The heat, I guess."

"Well, force yourself to drink if you have to, and take it easy. You have to acclimate out here for a bit. Do you have the restorative mix I gave you?"

43

"Yes, ma'am," Jeremy said, risking a smile and a look at Diane. "I can work some more."

"Well, drink it and just relax a bit more. It's a marathon, not a sprint," Twinkle said. "I'll get you for dinner."

"Okay. Nice to meet you, Diane," Jeremy said.

Twinkle walked away from the carport back to TK's truck and trailer. Diane followed.

"It's the heat," Twinkle explained. "Jeremy is a sweet, shy kid. He is my Virgin this year, so I'm in charge of making sure he's okay, like TK is for you. You should take note, you need to acclimate as well. Don't push too hard to start, and wear a hat in the sun. It really helps."

Twinkle glanced at Diane. "Sorry, is that too 'bossy Momma Bear' after just meeting me?"

"No, I think I'll need the help. I appreciate it." Diane looked at the large beige metal shipping container in the middle of the plot of land. "Does that stay here year round? Does every Virgin get a sponsor?"

"No and no," Twinkle laughed. "It's our container, but it is stored with all the others and delivered wherever our camp is placed for the year. It's a big help to have our infrastructure in one place and not have to haul it out every time. And no, not every Virgin gets a sponsor, but it's a real good idea."

"Oh, that makes sense," Diane said.

"So, over there are the porta-potties." Twinkle pointed. "You can find them at night by the blue light."

Diane followed the finger to see a line of porta-potties about a hundred and fifty yards away. Twinkle and Diane turned at the sound of singing to see TK and Sequoia skipping back hand in hand.

"Good, let's get you set up," Twinkle said, climbing into the truck. She pulled it up behind the container so that the trailer doors were even with the last carport in line. TK, Sequoia, and Diane walked to meet her.

"Okay, here we go," TK said, opening the trailer doors.

The trailer was packed from top to bottom with a jumble of items, predominantly stacks of black tubs with yellow lids. Everyone began pulling things from the trailer. Soon, a pile of tubs and sturdy poles lay on the ground.

"These first," TK said, dragging two of the bins over.

"Have you guys drunk water lately?" Sequoia asked. "Setting up can be draining in the heat."

Diane tried to remember. "I could probably use some."

"I'm a bit parched myself," TK said, then went to the truck cab and pulled out two reusable water bottles, one red and one blue, handing them to Sequoia.

"I have my water container set up," Sequoia said, then ducked into his carport.

Diane and TK followed.

Sequoia's carport had an inflatable queen-size mattress on one side and a sitting area on the other. In the middle, in line with the door, a table held a large blue water container. Sequoia filled the bottles from its spout and handed them to Diane and TK.

"Here you go," he said. "Drink up."

Diane drank deeply, chugging the water until the bottle was almost empty, then refilled it.

Back outside, Sequoia and TK quickly arranged the poles in a pattern on the ground, with connecting pieces in between.

"Sequoia and I met my first year," TK said.

"Yeah, playa Virgin buddies," Sequoia said.

Sequoia and TK assembled the pieces into a lattice of poles faster than Diane would have thought possible.

"What can I do?" Diane asked.

"Help me with the top piece," Twinkle said.

Diane followed Twinkle to where she was pulling a large piece of the heavy-duty vinyl from a bin. The piece unfurled in Diane's arms, raising a cloud of dust. Diane let out a ferocious sneeze, the front of her body now covered with the fine white powder.

"Yep, that's playa," Twinkle said.

"We're ready," TK said.

Diane and Twinkle dragged the piece to lay it over the framework. The four of them spread it out and then stepped back.

"Okay, grab a leg," TK said.

"Wait," Sequoia said. "We have to connect the ends first."

TK and Sequoia each grabbed a section of vinyl from a bin and went to the opposite sides of the carport. They quickly used bungees to attach the triangle pieces to the frame.

"Okay," Sequoia said. "Now the poles."

Each of them grabbed one of the legs on the ground and lifted the side of the carport. The baked-dry earth crunched under their feet as they worked. Diane was very aware of the pounding sun. Already she could feel its effects. It had to be at least a hundred degrees.

"Watch your fingers," Sequoia said. He slipped the slightly smaller end of a sturdy metal pole into a hollow pipe in the frame, snapping the leg into place. TK, Diane, and Twinkle copied the motion with their own poles. Four metal poles were now connected to the frame above.

"Once more on this side," Sequoia said.

They repeated the procedure there, Sequoia lifting the structure this time and the women snapping the legs into place. Diane could instantly feel the difference in being under the fabric and out of the sun.

"Everyone on a corner," TK said.

When everyone was in place, they lifted the entire structure and moved it into alignment with the next one.

"Okay, I'll leave you to it," Twinkle said.

"You loop these, and we will anchor the legs," TK said, slipping the bungees over Diane's arm. "Sequoia and I will attach the long pieces to the sides."

Diane slid the bungees through the holes in the vinyl fabric.

"No, wait," TK said. "You have to get them around the pole, then into the top and side holes, like this."

TK demonstrated the technique, and in no time the sides were on, forming a sturdy structure on what had been bare ground moments before. Diane watched as TK and Sequoia used a power tool to drive extremely long screws through the legs of the carport.

"Why do you use screws?" Diane asked as she worked.

"They're lag bolts," Sequoia explained, lining up another with a base plate hole and driving it into the ground. "People used to use rebar, but that's for chumps. Too much work. If you don't anchor the carport somehow, a big dust storm will launch it into the air. I've seen whole carports get blown a hundred feet up."

Diane found it hard to believe such a heavy structure could be moved like that. It had taken four of them to move it.

She continued threading the metal-rimmed holes on the fabric. The work was simple, and she was finding that she enjoyed it. It was so different than being in a sterile boardroom, discussing and deciding.

By the time she had finished, TK and Sequoia had fitted the outer panels and zipped everything up. A center exterior panel flipped up on a frame, making a doorway. Four roll-up windows were in the walls.

Diane stepped out of the carport and eyed the creation. It had gone up quickly. She was glad she hadn't had to figure it out by herself. Sequoia wandered off to let them finish.

"Drink water again," TK said. Diane dutifully complied.

The next hour involved TK and Diane laying down a tarp, taping it to the sides of the vinyl walls, and then setting up their two tents inside, one on each side of the carport, so that each had a sleeping area. It was true, Diane was realizing, that the dust got everywhere, absolutely everywhere. She was covered. Still, the physical labor was welcome, though she was unaccustomed to it, and working with her friend to make their nest was very satisfying.

"Alright, a little decorating," TK said, pulling some large scarves out of a bag.

Diane and TK hung the colorful cloths around the inside of the drab carport, making an attractive and comfortable space. TK hung up a small chandelier in the center of the framing and ran an extension cord outside to a small generator.

"Sequoia is letting us tap into his generator for power," TK explained, threading the extension cord through the bungees and attaching a power strip near the door. "Now give me a hand with the carpet."

The long, rolled-up piece of carpet was heavy and dusty as they took it from the trailer. Diane grunted with the effort of lifting it, but TK seemed unaffected. Once it was unrolled and in place, they set two chairs and a small folding table on it, adding the large cooler as a footstool and table.

Stepping outside and looking in, the two women surveyed their work.

"It'll do," TK said. "What do you think?"

"I think—" Diane began.

"AAAAhhooooooooooo owt, owt ooooooo," came a barking sound from behind them. A noise of flexing metal came from on top of the shipping container.

"Aw, yeah," TK said, smiling and nodding her head. "Come on."

"What's that?"

TK grabbed Diane's hand and pulled her to a folding ladder set up next to the shipping container. Diane could already see people on top of the container. Obviously, the metal flexing sound was from them moving around on top of the large, pale metal box.

"Follow me," TK said, scampering up the ladder.

Diane followed, reaching the top, sticking one leg out onto the edge of the container. As she did so, the ladder started to shift. A primal wave of terror gripped her stomach, and instinctively she shut her eyes, her body frozen, waiting to fall and hit the ground but unable to do anything about it.

Suddenly, two strong hands gripped her shoulders, lifted her, and placed her on top of the container.

"It wasn't fully settled," Diane heard a voice say. "You have to be careful."

Diane opened her eyes to see Jeremy looking into her face. She would not have believed he was strong enough to lift her like that. No one else on the container had noticed the event, because they were watching the sun setting over the mountains.

"Diane, hey, get—" TK began. Then, realizing something was wrong, she came over. "You alright?"

"Yeah. Yes, yes, I am," Diane said, beginning to laugh, the fear gone now. "Problem with the ladder, but Jeremy here made it alright." Diane turned to Jeremy. "Thank you. Can I give you a hug?"

"Sure, anytime," Jeremy said, smiling as he received her embrace.

"Safety third," TK said, pulling on her arm. "Now check it out."

Diane walked with her, the top of the container flexing loudly under her feet. It didn't seem to bother anyone else, so she figured it was safe. She looked out at the sun dipping into the crest of the rocky ridgeline stretching across the horizon. In the camps around them, people were howling and hooting. The group on top of the container had their arms around one another. Each of them was smiling ear to ear. TK put her arm around Diane and, seeing Jeremy standing apart, beckoned him over.

The elevation on top of the container gave a much better view of the landscape around them. Diane could see the roads and grid patterns of other camping areas spreading all around and far into the distance.

"Here, look this way," TK said, turning Diane around and pointing. "There, see that?"

Diane looked where her friend pointed, at a space where the grid pattern ended and openness began. A structure much larger than anything else around was in the center.

"It's the Man," TK said. "You see it, Jeremy?"

"Yeah, I see it."

Diane could see it too, through the haze, this structure from which the gathering took its name. It towered over the landscape, a crude figure, legs apart, with a barrel-like torso and an upside-down triangular head. Diane couldn't tell whether it had arms. It seemed so simple, yet so significant. The hazy plain surrounding it held shapes and figures, the heat making shimmering mirages hiding true forms.

She linked arms and howled along.

CHAPTER 6

Diane and TK spent the next hour completing their nesting. With the help of the chandelier's light, they arranged their living space to be more accessible and comfortable.

Besides their tents and central seating area, a table held their five-gallon drinking water jug for easy access. TK had also brought an extensive array of hooks, hangers, and storage devices that she hung from the sturdy poles of the structure. A plastic shelving unit held their food and other items out of the way.

After they blew up their air mattresses and placed their sleeping bags and other bedding in their tents, TK showed Diane how to hang her daily use equipment on an ingenious rope-and-hook device by the door. Jackets, clothing, and a laundry bag for each of them hung from a sturdy pole of the structure. A long mirror hung by straps in the corner.

"Here are your lights for going out at night. I see you have your headlamp and a very nice belt and leg bag," TK said. "Where did you get that?"

"A friend," Diane replied.

"Nice friend. Let's get you kitted out," TK said, laying items on the table beside the water container. "You have your backpack with a water reservoir. Night goggles, day goggles, sunglasses, couple of snacks, dust mask, shemagh, and a small multi-tool."

"What's a shemagh?" Diane asked, picking up the large, colorful, square scarf. The deep blue fabric was edged with bright yellow tassels and decorated with embroidered designs.

"It's the shit, is what it is," TK replied, taking back the cloth. "You can wrap it around your head to keep the sun off, use it to keep warm, wash your face, dry off, bind a wound. See, it can be wrapped in different ways, like this. If you need something, your shemagh might do it."

TK took the cloth and folded it in half, making the square a triangle.

"Easiest is just to put it on your face and tie it in the back. It will add some protection for your dust mask in a bad storm." TK demonstrated. "Or on top, one end shorter, wrap the long end over your face and around, like so."

TK's head and face were covered securely with the shemagh. She looked very stylish with only her eyes showing.

"You'll get the hang of it," TK said, unwrapping the scarf. "Now, these are your blinky lights. If you go out at night, wear them. People need to be able to see you from the front *and* the back. Otherwise, you're a darkwad. Used to be called a darktard, but that's lost favor for obvious reasons."

TK attached the small LED lights to Diane's belt and handed her a plastic LED necklace. She then snapped a cup with a screw-top lid to the belt.

"Put your ID in one of your pouches, and here is my old

playa coat that should fit. Try it on." TK handed over a white faux-fur jacket.

Diane put the thigh-length coat around her. She could tell it would be warm.

"And the best part is the upgrade," TK said, turning off the chandelier. The carport was instantly dark, with only a small illumination through the vinyl walls. "Reach into your right pocket, feel the controller, and push the switch."

Diane did so. The coat was illuminated from within by flashing and dancing colored lights. Diane turned to look in the mirror. The lights were beautiful. She felt herself begin to tear up. TK's generosity, and her own gratitude, were overwhelming. She turned and embraced her friend.

"Thank you, TK," Diane said through tears. "I can't believe how generous you are. I'm—I'm—"

"You're welcome," TK said. "You have helped me way more than I'll ever be able to repay."

TK took Diane's face in her hands and looked her in the eye.

"Who dropped everything and flew across the country to help with my mom's funeral? Who came to be with me when my father went into a hospice? Who, I might add, gave up her trip to Tahiti and quit her job to be with me when I needed it? I'll never forget that. Not ever. I love you, Diane. You're my sister. I'll always have you right here," TK said fiercely, patting her heart.

Tears came to Diane's eyes as the two women embraced in a long and satisfying hug.

"Hi, guys," Sequoia's voice came from the entrance, followed by his head. "Oh, sorry, didn't mean to interrupt. Nice coat, Diane."

"We're good," TK said, then turned to Diane. "Right? All good."

Diane smiled and wiped her eyes, taking a deep breath. "Yep, I'm great."

"If you guys are ready," Sequoia said, "Twinkle is cooking lasagna on the grill."

"I can eat," TK said.

"How do you cook lasagna on a grill?" Diane asked.

After stowing most of their gear in its hanging spots, they followed Sequoia out to the front of the shipping container. An aluminum pan of lasagna had been placed directly on the grill. The sauce was bubbling and smelled delicious. Lanterns provided just enough light to see. Twinkle had set up a table with a big bowl of salad and paper plates, and the lasagna had a scoop so they could serve themselves. Diane filled her plate and brought chairs out of the carport for herself and TK. Balancing their plates on a cooler, they ate in a circle with their new campmates.

Diane looked around. There were lights in other camps, but not many. Their own was sparsely lighted as well. She was thankful for the headlamp around her neck.

Leaning back, patting her belly, she felt very relaxed as the people around her chatted in the darkness. She sipped a beer until nature began to call.

As she walked to the porto with her headlamp on, she saw dust suspended in the air. A few other headlamps could be seen bobbing down the road or moving around in other camps, and off in the distance Diane could see the headlights of a few slow-moving cars, but it was mostly full darkness. Still, Diane could see a long way in each direction. She noted that the campsites were, for now, relatively sparsely populated.

After using the porto, which was an adventure in itself, Diane adjusted her headlamp and walked back up the road she had come down, noting the blue string on the ground marking the edge of a campsite as well as the edge of the road. Along the string, spaced evenly, were small orange marker flags. Two flags together seemed to denote a corner. While the Dead Presidents plot looked huge, there were some plots with much smaller footprints.

Diane almost missed the camp because its shapes seemed different in the darkness. TK's voice and Sequoia's laughter were reference points to guide her.

"You made it back," TK said from the darkness.

Diane looked toward the voice, illuminating TK with the headlamp.

"Ahh!" TK said, holding up her hands to shield her eyes. "Turn it off!"

Diane looked away and shut off the light.

"Sorry," Diane said. "I think I'm going to turn in."

"See you in the morning," TK said.

"Sleep tight," said someone in the darkness.

Diane could see the solar inflatable box lights hanging on the edge of the carport. She started toward them but then unexpectedly banged her foot on something in the darkness.

"Shit," Diane said, briefly stumbling.

"Watch out for that," TK said. "That's why we can't have nice things."

Diane turned on her headlamp as she entered the carport, thankful they had set up during the last light of day. She found the wet wipes and used them to cleanse her face and body as well as possible. It did make a difference. Searching the toiletry bag, she found her toothbrush and brushed her teeth after taking a swig from her water cup. It hadn't occurred to her where to spit, so she shrugged her shoulders and swallowed.

Diane slipped out of her shorts and shirt, then crawled into the tent and sleeping bag. Lying there in the darkness, listening to the voices murmuring in the camp, she wondered what she had gotten herself into.

CHAPTER 7

Friday, August 28, eight days until the Man burns

Diane awoke to soft light coming through the walls of the tent. Enjoying the warmth of her sleeping bag, she rolled her head, shifting on her air mattress. After a lingering moment, the call of nature pressed her attention.

Unzipping the tent, she crawled out onto the carpet, sat in a chair, and put on her boots. Grabbing her shemagh and goggles from their hook by the door, Diane picked up a roll of TP and walked out into the camp.

The surroundings were still. No one was stirring in the camp in the early morning. Striding to the street, Diane looked around. Vehicles and tents dotted the landscape. As she walked down the dusty road, the space around her felt open, the landscape dotted with the beginnings of . . . something.

A sewage pump truck was working by the porta-potties, pumping out and spraying down. Diane waited until they were done to use a clean one. *This is not terrible*, she thought. *Make a note to be here after the cleaning.*

Wandering back, Diane could see people stirring in other camps. A figure some ways down the road appeared to be jogging in her direction. As it got closer, Diane could see it was a man, nude except for sunglasses and running shoes. He was tall and lean, with close-cropped hair. His fit, cut body was rippling with defined muscles. Each step caused his legs and six-pack stomach muscles to flex under a glistening sheen of sweat. He held a water bottle in his hand. His thick penis bounced along with his gait like a metronome.

Diane continued walking slowly, sneaking looks at him, embarrassed yet transfixed. She couldn't help but marvel as the man passed her with a nod of his head and a smile, just as she reached camp. Diane watched as he passed, enjoying the view despite herself, the spectacle of his muscular back and ass moving down the road riveting her attention until he was out of sight.

"I guess I just had one of those 'in the moment' things," Diane said to herself under her breath, grinning.

A burning blush was in her face as she turned into the camp and walked to the carport. The experience had felt strange, but oddly, not sexual at all. Well, not very, anyway. She hung up her gear and could hear rustling sounds from TK's tent.

"You up?" Diane asked.

"Hmmm, getting there. Is there coffee yet?" TK's voice asked.

"No. I can heat the water, though."

"Great."

Diane lit the small camp stove under the already-prepared coffee percolator. Sitting in the folding chair, she began to brush the tangles from her hair. As the percolator began to burble, she wiped her face, neck, arms, and body with successive wet wipes. The dust seemed to have gotten everywhere, but eventually she did feel cleaner. The pile of used wet wipes went into the brown paper bag by the door that was designated for burnables.

"Is that coffee I smell?" Twinkle asked from outside the door.

"Got a cup?" TK asked, climbing out of her tent.

"Got Irish cream *and* a cup," Twinkle replied, stepping into the carport.

"I usually wait until 8:00 a.m. to start drinking, but it's a vacation, I suppose," Diane said, pouring coffee into three cups. Twinkle put a healthy slug of white liqueur in each. The women savored the sweet white alcohol in the coffee.

"Mmmm," TK said, with her eyes closed. "Perfection."

"We are whipping up a little breakfast. Then we will assemble and get to work," Twinkle said, leaving the carport.

"Taskmaster," TK said in a jesting tone, then turned to Diane. "Did you find everything you need so far?"

Diane tried to suppress a grin. She could again feel a redness creeping up her neck and face.

"Did you get sunburned? Oh my God, are you blushing?" TK said. "You are! What could make you blush this early in the morning?"

Diane shook her head. "I may have seen a handsome naked guy jogging by."

"Well, that's something to get up for," TK said, then thought for a moment. "You think he'll do another lap?"

Diane laughed at TK's reflective look, then added, "I'm hungry. Let's grab some food."

"You go ahead. I got my morning stuff to do after the coffee."

Diane grabbed one of the breakfast burritos stacked in a pile on a table outside of Twinkle's small camper. She saw people on the container and went up to meet them.

"We will put the bar here," Twinkle said, pointing down to the area in between the shipping container and the street. "Sequoia and TK will be lead builders on that job. It will give us both shade and a rest area. The kitchen will be behind the container, same drill. If we can get those up, we will see what the time and heat are doing. Okay, ten minutes and let's start grinding."

Diane wolfed down her burrito and joined the group to start unloading the materials from the shipping container. During the work, she met her new campmates, a motley crew of ages and sexes that were pretty evenly distributed. The jobs were physical but not truly arduous, and Diane found herself enjoying being a part of the process.

The three carports for the bar area went up fairly quickly next to the huge metal box. It was clear the other campers were experienced in the setup. A wooden bar and back bar were removed from the container and assembled in short order to complete the initial setup.

"Union break!" Sequoia shouted to the crowd.

"Okay, take ten," Twinkle said. "If you don't have to pee yet, you're not drinking enough. Hydrate, people. Virgins against lead builders for cornhole."

Diane dutifully walked back to her carport, grabbed her water bottle as well as TK's, and headed to the now-covered bar area. The fabric sides had been left off, and a few camp chairs and barstools had been pulled up. She walked to where TK and Jeremy were sitting and handed TK her water bottle.

"Thanks. You have water, Jeremy?" TK asked, taking a drink from her own bottle.

"I don't feel very thirsty," the young man replied.

"Mistake number one, fucker," Sequoia said, walking up with a couple of beers in his hand. "Here, this will do you good."

Sequoia handed one of the beers to Jeremy, who accepted it.

"Thanks, man," Jeremy said, popping the top.

"Less talking, more swallowing," Sequoia said, draining his own can in a couple of quick gulps.

"Is that what your priest told you?" TK asked snarkily.

Diane and Jeremy snorted in unison at the comment.

"No, I heard it from your mom last time I saw her. She was tired of blowing your dad."

"Couldn't be my mom. She never gets tired of taking her teeth out," TK shot back. "Unless she was taking a break from all the bus station cock from your boyfriends that you couldn't handle."

The whole group laughed at the irreverent and salty banter. Diane mused that any of those statements in her corporate environments would have resulted in an HR nightmare.

"God damn," Jeremy said under his breath, obviously uncomfortable.

"It's okay, Jeremy. This camp is mostly good people who say 'fuck' a lot," TK said.

"Let's do the game," TK said. "Jeremy and Diane against me and Sequoia."

Diane saw the two wooden ramps and pile of bean bags set up in front of the bar. They played a spirited game, trying to toss the bags through the holes. The rest of the camp watched and commented, cheering them on until TK finally made the winning throw and danced around in victory.

"You fuckers about fucking done fucking off?" Twinkle said, walking up behind them.

"Fucking right," Sequoia said. "TK and I will get on the kitchen."

"Jeremy and Diane, I'd like you to work with Steven here to pull the playa tech and bar stuff out of the container."

Diane looked to Steven, who was an older, compact, muscular man dressed in a blue long-sleeved T-shirt, khaki shorts, and desert boots. He had short-cropped gray hair and a long goatee, and he wore thick, black-framed glasses. An air of energy and competence surrounded him.

"Hi, I'm Steven. You hug, bro?" Steven asked, stepping forward to Jeremy.

Jeremy nodded and was embraced.

"Welcome home, brother," Steven said, giving a strong hug. He then stepped back and looked Jeremy in the eye. "You a vet?"

Jeremy nodded. "10th Mountain."

"Navy corpsman, First Marines," Steven said with his hand on his chest. He then turned to Diane.

"I hug," Diane said.

"Cool," Steven said, but he made no move to embrace her.

"How did you know Jeremy was a veteran?" Diane asked, covering her discomfort.

"Like knows like," Steven said. "Okay, we do the playa tech here and here. It's all cut-out plywood that we assemble into furniture. It's cool because it breaks down and can be easily stored. I made some new pieces this year. You paste on the pictures, then lacquer, lacquer, lacquer. It's called decoupage. I did comic book heroines on this one and comic book heroes here."

Diane and Jeremy looked at the pieces Steven had already

assembled. They were barstools fitted together from four separate parts each. Pictures from comic books adorned the pieces, having been lacquered in place. The wooden parts felt both smooth and gritty.

"So first we separate the pieces by theme, and then we assemble in the shade. Got it?"

"Yep," Jeremy said while Diane nodded.

Separating the pieces under Steven's direction, the trio began assembling the various types of furniture.

"These ones are pretty graphic," Jeremy said, indicating a table with vintage pictures of nude women.

"It's up to the artist, whatever they were feeling at the time," Steven said. "It's also pretty inclusive nudity, with both men and women. The bar is pretty well covered with whatever you like to look at."

"You said you did the pieces. Are you an artist?" Jeremy asked as he fiddled with the pieces of a stool.

"I don't know about the description 'artist,' but I put together things and help the real artists with their stuff," Steven replied. "Buddy of mine has an art piece he is assembling out on the playa. After I get done with the camp today, I'm going to help him and his crew."

"That's sweet," Diane said. "What's the piece?"

"Hearts of Fire. It's a fire piece, obviously. You guys want to check it out sometime?"

"Absolutely," Diane said.

"Me too. It sounds rad," Jeremy replied.

"How's it going?" Twinkle asked as she walked up.

"Perfect," Steven said in a loud voice. "Got some good Virgins this year."

"Well, it looks like you are about done. We are cooking up hot dogs for lunch. Who wants some?"

Diane smelled the cooking meat, and her stomach rumbled. She nodded along with Jeremy and Steven in response to Twinkle's pointed finger.

They moved the assembled furniture into position around the bar structure and headed back into the kitchen area. Where there had been an open space, now there were three carports, enclosed on three sides, with tables arranged in the middle and gas grills and stoves on the sides. Tables and chairs formed a communal seating area in the center. More tables and stoves surrounded the perimeter of the area, along with water containers, coolers, plates, and utensils. A tarp made up the floor of the structure.

Diane walked in and once again was amazed at how quickly the structure had gone up. The camp now had a functional communal kitchen and bar, and it was only noon on the first build day.

About twelve people were getting food, talking, and laughing in the kitchen. Diane met the ones she hadn't yet, exchanging hugs and names. It would take a while to remember everyone's names.

Snagging a hot dog and a beer, she sat down beside TK and Sequoia. They had paper plates, while she had grabbed a hard plastic one.

"Next time get a paper plate if you can," TK said, taking a bite of her hot dog.

"We can burn paper," Sequoia explained. "Saves on washing until we have the evap pond set up. In a perfect demonstration of Leave No Trace, we would wash with our melted ice water and not burn paper. Ideally, that is."

"Alright everyone, heads up," Twinkle said loudly to the group.

The conversations stopped, and everyone paid attention to the small woman standing at the head of the table.

"The bar is up. Bring your bottle donations there where we can lock them up. Steven is bar manager this year, along with Gracie," Twinkle said, indicating an attractive blonde woman sitting at the table, "along with Petals, who will be here later tonight. Steven will talk about bar rules, and we will go over them in a bit. First rule here is to have fun. Congratulate yourselves on getting out to the dust."

Applause, hoots, and cheers came from around the table.

"We have two Virgins this year. Stand up, Jeremy and Diane!"

Jeremy and Diane stood up to applause from the other campers.

"We will all look out for them. Our medical leads are Sparkle and Greebo," Twinkle said, indicating the couple at the end of the table.

"If you get hurt or out of sorts and can't fix it yourself, check in with them. I'm the 'drink water' police, so expect that message a lot. This is our camp, and we are responsible for one another, so respect one another and help when you can.

"Now let us talk about consent. It is imperative to get approval for whatever you do with one another, and non-consensual actions will be dealt with swiftly. Those are to be brought to me if they occur, first for education and, if necessary, for other action. If I am not available, speak with some of our veteran campers. If someone from outside the camp causes problems, I will handle it, or we will get the Rangers if necessary. I have an event radio and can call for assistance."

Twinkle took a drink from her cup, then continued.

"Build is going well so far, but we have a couple more days, so pace yourselves. Lead builders are Tiger Kite and Sequoia, if you have any questions, ask them. Upcoming today will be siesta from noon to four. You can relax, explore, whatever, until then because of the heat.

"Getting acclimated and not getting heat exhaustion are crucial right now. We want to get the evap pond setup in place if it's not too windy so we can get showers up tomorrow.

"About the kitchen, our rule is, *you dirty it, you clean it*. As you notice, there are no trash receptacles in here. You bring it, you pack it out. We will have the burn barrel in place tonight, burnable items and food waste can go in there. Anyone wanting to be productive during the siesta can decorate the bar in the shade. I'll ring the bell at quarter to four, and I don't want to go looking for anyone. Everybody good? Great. Steven?"

"Okay, the bar," Steven said, standing up. "No one under twenty-one drinks at the bar, period. The cops will issue us a $1,000 ticket. No one wants that. An ID has to be a physical, state-issued ID or passport. Printouts are not acceptable in this bar. Sorry. Have them come back when they have it. The only exception is if Twinkle or a bar manager approves it, and then the responsibility is on us.

"Any bottle that goes into the bar is bar property. There is no taking of bottles from the bar for personal use, period. The bar will be open from four-ish until midnight through the week. It will be shut down for the burns, both Man and Temple. Shifts are three hours, and they're available with no experience necessary. Talk to a manager about signing up. Clean the bar when done. All liquor must be locked up when there is no bartender present. Bartender's choice of music. Gracie, what did I miss?" Steven asked.

A large-framed woman with dark red hair, booty shorts, and a tiny halter top stood up.

"No religion or politics at the bar. One warning, then 86. No shirt cockers, but nude is fine. Additional rules will be posted. That's it."

"Okay, siesta and we will hit it again," Twinkle said, then walked out of the kitchen.

Diane and TK left the bar and walked back to the carport. The day was already becoming noticeably warmer.

"How are you feeling?" TK asked. "Wanna chill or explore?"

"I'm pretty good," Diane replied. "I wouldn't mind checking out the neighborhood."

"Great. Let's get our stuff and go for a walk."

After gathering their things, the two women walked out the back of the camp and onto the road.

"You guys taking off?" Sequoia asked from behind them.

"Lady time," TK said over her shoulder. "See you when we get back."

Sequoia waved and popped his head back into his carport.

Strolling down the dusty road, Diane took in the surreal landscape. Camps were coming together, the city beginning to take shape.

"What do you think so far?" TK asked.

Diane thought about TK's question. The physical labor and sun had started to affect her.

"It's good. It's so . . . so . . ."

"Different?" TK supplied.

"Yes, I guess that's the word. Different."

Diane watched the ground as she walked, felt the dust soft underfoot. Her feet made small waves in it. Some dust clung and some fell back. Her friend was walking along with her, talking happily. Diane was aware of the chatter but was not really listening. She was reflecting.

Aware of an emotion in her chest—a twinge, a feeling of something rising to the top—Diane stopped and put her hand over her heart as TK walked on. Looking around, Diane could see both modernity, in the people bringing structure to the harsh landscape, and the primal ancientness of the raw land stretching out around them.

The sun was starting to get to her, she thought. That, and not being used to working in a hot, dry climate. While she was in pretty good shape, the physical labor and the cruel environmental conditions were taking a toll.

Diane felt lightheaded. She slowly inhaled, the feeling rising to her throat, to her eyes. She could feel the beginnings of moisture there. She was aware that TK had come back to stand at her elbow.

"Diane, you okay?"

"Yes. It's just—whew—something. I don't know." Diane nodded, wiping her eyes with her shemagh.

TK looked into Diane's eyes, dipping her knees as she lightly touched Diane's chin to bring her head up.

"Diane, it's okay. This is normal out here."

TK embraced her friend, holding her close.

"Let it come. You don't have to hold back. Not with me. You're safe."

Diane could feel the tension in her body as she resisted the emotion and the embrace.

"It's okay," TK said softly as she lightly rocked her friend. "It's okay."

Diane could feel herself relax against her friend as the tears started to flow. It made absolutely no sense to her. She wasn't a crier.

"It's okay. You're okay, you're safe," TK said.

Diane could feel a quiver in her stomach. It rose through her chest and manifested in her throat as a sob.

"It's okay," TK said, gently rocking. "You're safe. Let it go."

Diane finally released any attempt at control. She let the racking sobs come. Soon she was aware of more arms around her. She looked up. Two young women were embracing her and TK. Diane put her face back onto TK's shoulder. She could feel someone's head against her back. She felt safe and comfortable as waves of emotion came out.

As suddenly as it had come, the storm of raw emotion subsided, dwindling quickly. Diane drew a deep breath and slowly looked up into her friend's smiling face.

"Hi," TK said, smiling brightly, her eyes sparkling.

Diane nodded. She felt lighter than she had in a long time.

"Hi," TK said again.

Diane looked at the faces of the two women with them. They both looked into her face, smiling. As suddenly as the tears had come, overwhelming laughter boiled up from Diane's belly. In a split second, all the women were laughing uproariously. Diane sniffled while laughing, and one of the women handed her a tissue. When she blew her nose hard, it sent the group into another fit of giggles. TK had to put her hands on her legs to get her breath.

The laughter gradually subsided. Diane and TK embraced

the other women, who then went on their way. TK took Diane's arm, and they began to walk back to camp.

"Wow, that was just . . ." Diane marveled. She felt light and joyous. A weight she hadn't known she had been carrying had been lifted.

"Yeah, that happens out here," TK said. "Stuff just comes up sometimes. Stuff you didn't know you had."

"Yeah . . . wow," Diane said.

"It also means you probably haven't had enough food and water. When your body is stressed, all of the junk you have been keeping together, burying and suppressing, comes out. We will get you set up with food and drink."

Twinkle was at the bar chatting to a tall, dark-skinned man with dreadlocks and a full beard. He was shirtless, in shorts, with a straw cowboy hat. Rock music was playing, and they had drinks in their hands.

"Pepper!" TK chirped, grabbing the man in a hug as he turned.

"TK!" The man said, sharing a rough hug with the smaller TK.

"Pepper," TK said, coming out of his arms, "this is Diane. Diane, this is Pepper. We go way back."

"Prepper, you hug?" Diane asked.

"Of course," Pepper replied, embracing her. "And it's Pepper, like salt and pepper. Or like the speck of pepper in this sugar bowl. 'Token' seemed pejorative, as well as obvious, and it was already taken anyway."

Diane grinned at that and took the proffered whiskey shot from Twinkle. TK stopped by the carport to drop off their things, grabbed the bottles of whiskey, and headed to the bar, where Steven was putting away other bottles.

"Thanks. Put them there," Steven said, indicating with a nod of his head.

"How's it look this year?" TK asked, sitting down.

"Pretty solid so far," Steven replied. "You guys want a cold one?"

"That sounds pretty good," Jeremy replied.

"Why not?" Diane said. "It's almost noon."

Steve handed cold cans of beer to Diane, Jeremy, and TK. Diane popped the top of hers and took a sip. It was delicious, and the cold liquid going down her throat made her feel better. Diane closed her eyes and savored it.

"Damn, that's good," she said.

"I told you," TK said.

"You guys want a sandwich?" Twinkle asked, walking up to the bar with a plate. "Two left."

The women eagerly accepted. They chatted at the bar while eating. Other campers started to assemble. Laughing at a raunchy nursing story from Twinkle, Diane realized she was having fun.

After the siesta, the group spread out a huge, thick, black tarp, easily twenty by fifty feet, for the evaporation pond. They wrapped long two-by-fours along the edges, and then Diane and TK lay down across the heavy black material and rolled together the whole length, laughing, to get out trapped air.

"How does this work?" Diane asked, looking at the unfamiliar structure.

"The black plastic is anchored down like this," Twinkle said, pointing to the boards on the edges.

Plastic pallets were placed in one corner for the showers. One had poles supporting vinyl walls, and the other had no walls.

But both had long PVC poles with ropes and pulleys like a flagpole.

"Now, when we pour water into it," Twinkle continued, "the water is spread out over a large surface area and not on the playa. The sun heats up the water, and it evaporates without impacting the environment. Spreading the water where it pools speeds up the process. When we are done, we will give it time to dry, then take the plastic away for disposal."

"Fuck yeah," TK said. "Showers tonight!"

TK grabbed a camping solar shower bag, filled it from the drum in the bed of the truck, hooked a large carabiner through the handle, and ran it up the pole.

"Why is one shower wrapped with vinyl and one open?" Diane asked.

"Naked shower and modest shower," Twinkle said. "If you want people to wash dishes, take a naked shower. Or take one just to show off."

"Dishes?" Diane asked, laughing.

Twinkle pointed to where Jeremy and Steven were assembling two playa tech counters with sinks at the opposite end of the evaporation pond. Diane wandered over and watched as the white PVC drain lines were run to the evap pond. A five-gallon blue water container was on one side, with plumbing lines running to the sink faucet. A dish drying rack was on the other. Steven slipped nylon stockings over the ends of the PVC pole drain lines and secured them with tape.

"Is it up higher to help it flow?" Diane asked.

"Yes," Steven replied, stowing his gaffer tape.

"What's with the pantyhose?"

"Catches all the food scraps," Steven replied, then pointed down. "The foot pump here sucks the water down and then into the faucet. It's a manual bilge pump for a boat. Wanna give it a try?"

"Sure," Diane said.

"Make sure the faucet is open and the container has water. Start pumping with your foot," Steven said.

Diane did as she was told. After a few pumps, she was rewarded with a stream of water from the faucet.

"That's great!" Diane said. "Where do we fill the water?"

Steven pointed to a huge black plastic container.

"Five hundred gallons will be dropped off tomorrow," Steven replied. "Back when I started, you had to bring your own. Sometimes camps run out of water, and they are basically fucked. You have to arrange the delivery from the vendor way ahead of time. Now we can do dishes, brush our teeth, and clean up. If you have water, I suggest conserving it unless you have a bunch, maybe by not taking a shower tonight. We need to make sure we get our water. Weird things can happen sometimes, like a cracked container."

"Here are the push brooms," TK said, walking up. "Virgin chores are spreading the water in the evap pond around so it will evaporate, filling shower bags, and filling dishwashing water containers."

"That's a wrap!" Twinkle yelled. "Everybody to the bar. Shots are on Sequoia, but drink water too. Good job, people!"

The sun was edging to the horizon, and after a drink at the bar, Diane joined other people on top of the container. She was tired, sore, dirty, and hungry. It was day two without a shower. Her bed would be an air mattress in a tent. And she was grinning from ear to ear. Surrounded by her campmates and friends, Diane howled at the setting sun.

"Good job," Twinkle said again. "You're on your own time now. Showers are open. First come, first serve. You have to use your own water."

"Fuck yeah," TK said as she walked to the carport.

Moments later, she emerged wrapped in a towel. Sequoia walked behind her with a towel around his waist. The two raced to the showers, laughing.

Diane collected her toiletries, wrapped herself in a towel, and wandered to the showers. Sequoia was lathering up in the immodest shower.

"There's at least half a bag left," TK said, popping out of the vinyl stall. "Once we finish up here and have a bite to eat, we will venture out for a bit."

"Twenty minutes?" Sequoia asked, standing nude under the water.

Diane kept her eyes on the ground, not sure where to look, a bit embarrassed by his nudity and wanting to give him privacy. Sequoia appeared not to care about privacy at all.

"Done," TK said.

Diane stepped into the modest shower. Drawing the vinyl closed, she sprayed her body with the warm water. The sensuous feeling of cleaning herself was almost sexual. After soaping and rinsing quickly, she dried herself and went back to the carport. The feeling of being clean was welcome after the hot days.

Diane looked forward to exploring this strange place.

CHAPTER 8

That's yours, Diane," TK said, pointing to a bicycle.
Diane walked to the cruiser bike. Its faux-fur–
covered frame was threaded with LEDs, winking and blinking.

"The code for the lock is 'SASS.' Don't ever leave your bike
unlocked, not even to walk into the portos," TK said.

"Theft is a problem?" Diane asked, mounting the bike.

"Usually just an altered person grabbing the wrong one, but
it happens," TK said, mounting her own. "The bikes have a tag
with the camp name and location, and you would be surprised
how many find their way back. But no tag, no return. No bike
is considered lost by Rangers until the end of the Burn, so just
lock it up."

"Follow me!" Sequoia roared and started to pedal.

The group began to pedal slowly, taking a right down a
dark street. Diane followed the blinking lights of TK's bike.
Suspended dust particles winked in the light of her headlamp.
The night was cool but not cold. With the setting of the sun,
the only illumination was scarce or from their own lights. Turn
followed turn. The white, dusty soil was not difficult to pedal
in, and the thick tires of the cruiser glided along.

Diane could see Jeremy taking in the sights as well. She admired his dark curly hair, longer on top and short on the sides, and his narrow, handsome face. He saw her looking at him and smiled. She smiled back, enjoying the moment.

"No, take a left. Let's go to the Man!" TK yelled at Sequoia, who was starting to outpace them.

"Ahhh, I'll beat you there, slow-ass!" Sequoia roared and accelerated off into the night.

"Dumbass! We have Virgins!" TK yelled after him, but it was no use.

Diane was glad TK had stayed with them. She was completely turned around now.

"We'll find him there," TK said.

"Wouldn't want to get lost the first night," Jeremy said.

"You got food and water, you'd figure it out," TK said. "Getting lost for a while can be a lot of fun."

TK led them along until the cross streets ended. She pulled forward and stopped. Diane and Jeremy pulled up beside her.

"Okay," TK said, pointing. "We just came down four o'clock, and this"—she swept her hand—"is the Esplanade, where the playa starts. To the right is three o'clock, and then over there is five o'clock." Diane wrinkled her forehead, trying to orient herself. TK watched her in the glow of their headlamps.

"This will help," TK said. "Hold up your left hand in front of your face."

TK pointed to the middle of Diane's palm. Jeremy watched with interest.

"That's where the Man is, in the center." TK moved her finger to just under Diane's index finger and traced a semicircle down her palm to end under her pinkie finger. "This is the city.

It's based on the face of a clock." TK pointed to the bottom of the palm. "This is six o'clock." TK pointed to the right side of Diane's palm. "Three o'clock." She pointed to the left side. "Nine o'clock. Get it?"

Diane gazed upon the sparse, huge expanse of land before her. Even in the gathering darkness, the feeling of openness filled her with a sense of hesitation and fear. She was thankful that she had a guide with her, not knowing if the courage to venture into it would have come.

"Thought we were on three-thirty. Where's that?" Jeremy asked.

"The half streets are in the middle, but you have to go back and turn to get to them. These blocks are full blocks. Get it?"

"Yeah," Diane replied.

"Okay. Now turn around. See the lampposts?"

Tall wooden poles lined the lane in two parallel rows, leading off into the distance.

"They are at three o'clock, six o'clock and nine o'clock," TK said. "Real useful for figuring out where you are, especially if you're caught in a dust storm."

"Where do they go?" Diane asked.

"Funny you should ask," TK said, starting to pedal again. "Six o'clock is the center of the city. It leads directly to the Man. Three and nine do too, but they are east and west. Beyond the Man should be the Temple, and then it's deep playa all the way out to the trash fence."

The three of them meandered along between the poles. Up ahead, Diane could see bright construction lights. After being on the city streets, the openness was a change. She could see figures—not statues really, but, well, the impression of art stuff—all around her. She could make out what seemed to be small structures seemingly being built with scattered lights, construction noises coming from different directions.

Presently, TK stopped at a rope lying on the ground. Diane and Jeremy pulled up next to her. A large structure with a huge wooden figure on top was before them. The strong construction lights turned the night into day. Figures were walking inside the construction site.

"Whoop, whoop! Beat you." Sequoia came zooming out of the darkness.

"Will people work 24/7? Will we be able to visit?" Jeremy asked.

"The crews will usually build 'til they can't, in order to have it ready," Sequoia said. "Once it's finished, then you can get up to it until it burns."

Diane watched the workers moving around while she took a long drink from the tube to her backpack. She had become surprisingly thirsty in a very short time.

"Wanna head off to the Temple?" TK asked.

"Sure," Diane said.

They began pedaling deeper into the playa, the light of the Man's construction behind them. Small spots of light shone out in front of them, guiding them.

"Keep your eyes open for unlit art pieces," Sequoia said. "This early, they may not be fully done. That's one reason the pedal bikes are better than the electric bikes. Some of those things go thirty miles an hour, and that causes plenty of bad injuries."

The ride was a slow ten minutes. The temperature had dropped slightly but was not uncomfortable.

"Ah, shit," TK said.

"What?" Sequoia asked.

"Look back toward the Man."

Diane and Jeremy turned as well. Where it had been a clear view to the construction lights, now it was hazy. As they watched, the view became more and more blurred.

"Okay, put on your goggles and dust mask. Quick," TK said, pulling up her shemagh and pulling down her goggles.

Diane clumsily jostled with her backpack and the bike until she just laid the bike down rather than fumble with it. Pulling the goggles out, she aligned them on her forehead, then slipped them over her eyes. Looking up, she was glad she had gotten them into place, as the cloud of dust immediately surrounded her. She grabbed the shemagh and tied it quickly around her face.

She could see the others and their lights, but nothing much past that. The views of the Temple and the Man were gone from sight. A rising sense of panic began to envelop Diane along with the maelstrom of dust. Cut off from any visual reference points more than a few feet in front of her in the dark, she froze. The wind and dust pulled at her clothes, pulled at her hair. Pressing the cloth of the shemagh closer to her face, she closed her eyes.

Strong arms embraced her, then another set and another. In the center of the embrace by TK, Sequoia, and Jeremy, she tensed further, then relaxed. Nestled in the embrace, she felt warm and safe. The heat from the bodies close to her counteracted the sense of being alone. TK laid her head on Diane's shoulder. Sequoia's beard rested on top of Diane's head.

"Yeah baby! Yeah!" Sequoia bellowed.

Just as suddenly as it had come, the dust cleared. Diane opened her eyes to see TK lower her shemagh and smile at her in the glow of the LED lights. The lower part of TK's face was clean in comparison to her nose and goggles, which were covered by the fine white dust. TK's wide smile was infectious, and Diane laughed.

"Holy shit," Jeremy said. "That was intense."

"Damned right!" Sequoia said, releasing his embrace and stepping back.

"I told you, right?" TK said. "You good?"

"Yes," Diane said, nodding. "So much for the shower."

"Got to appreciate it when you're clean," TK said.

Jeremy stepped back and went to pick up his bike, which had blown over. TK picked hers up and mounted.

Moving off as a group, they headed toward the bright lights of the Temple site. The building was standing alone in the bleak lighting provided by construction lamps mounted on poles. Generators hummed, and workers swarmed the site. Yelling and hammering could be heard from around and within the structure. The air was growing colder.

"How long did this take to build?" Diane asked.

"I heard they started two weeks ago," TK said. "Look over there. Diane, do you see the lady with the pole?"

"Yes," Jeremy said.

"She's a Temple Guardian," TK said. "They keep people away until it's finished, and they watch over the Temple when it's open, twenty-four hours a day. They're volunteers. Volunteers make this whole thing possible."

"Why does it need a Guardian?" Jeremy asked.

"Things happen in the Temple," Sequoia said.

Observing the activity, Diane was impressed at the dedication of the workers, still toiling so late.

"Ready to head back?" TK asked over her shoulder.

"Yes, I am," Diane said, taking a last glance at the half-constructed structure and wondering what it would be when finished.

CHAPTER 9

Saturday, August 29, seven days until the Man burns

Diane opened her eyes to the noise of the wind lightly blowing and surging against the carport. There was light enough to see outside her tent. The camp sounded quiet. Sitting up and stretching, she could feel some tightness in her muscles from the unfamiliar work.

Trying to be quiet, she slid out of her sleeping bag and blinked away the sleep in her eyes. Slipping on her clothing from the day before, she started the single-burner stove on the table. With the flame caressing the bottom of the coffee percolator on low, Diane put on her shoes and gathered her shemagh and goggles.

The shower had been glorious, the quick wash and rinse both invigorating and restorative. The night air had been somewhat chilly, though. She reminded herself to shower before sunset next time. The brief period between being clean and then shortly after coated with the ever-present dust would take some getting used to.

Leaving the carport, Diane could see no one moving yet in camp. As she walked to the porta-potties, she breathed in the morning air. It was cool enough to be comfortable but not too chilly. Finishing her morning ablutions and snagging a cup of the ready coffee, Diane climbed the ladder to the top of the storage container and sat in a chair.

Sipping the coffee, Diane looked out on the lightening sky, the dust haze red in the dawn. She smiled. The morning had long been a time to herself, a time to focus and prepare for whatever the day might present. Some people in other camps, early risers as well, were beginning to stir.

As she sat there, she slipped out her phone and tried to log into her work email. She had not been out of touch with her office for so long in years. She felt guilty logging in now, but she was compelled to at least get a sense of what was going on. Her email was not logging on, though. Each entry resulted in an access-denied message.

Switching to texts, she saw that her team had at first been frantic but had then seemingly calmed. Stella must have told them Diane was fine and to carry on. Diane also saw a text from Stella informing her that her access had been cut off until her return.

"Busted," a voice said, directly behind her.

Diane sat up, startled. Jeremy was standing there looking at her phone.

"I didn't hear anything," Diane said. "How did you do that?"

"I can be quiet sometimes," Jeremy replied, looking at her. "Sorry if I scared you. Checking into the world?"

"Guilty," Diane replied sheepishly.

"It's hard to let go. I'm guilty of it too."

"Hmmm," Diane replied. Then, noticing how he was dressed, she asked, "Headed out?"

"Thought I might before it gets too hot. Want to come?"

"Where to?"

"My brother's camp. He texted me last night, said he'd arrived."

"Let me grab my stuff," Diane replied.

Jeremy went down the ladder, then held it. Ducking into the carport, Diane grabbed the essentials, happy to have staged the equipment in one place. After jotting a brief note to TK on the small whiteboard by the door, she grabbed her bike and joined Jeremy on the road. The street was peaceful, the pace slow and easy.

"Why isn't your brother camping with you?" Diane asked as they rode.

"He is camping with his rugby club, a group from New Zealand," Jeremy replied. "It's a small camp, so I couldn't get a ticket through them. But I could go through Dead Presidents."

"Makes sense," Diane said.

"Street K. Now we turn," Jeremy said. "Is it Saturday already? I'm losing track."

"Yeah, I think so," Diane replied. "TK said the Gate opens tonight at midnight, so the Burn only gets bigger from here."

"I think this is it," Jeremy said, stopping in front of a dusty plot. "There's my brother's truck."

They locked their bikes and looked around the half-built camp.

"Do you think it's too early?" Diane asked.

"No, not for Ollie."

As they wound their way through the equipment and piles of items, a tarp suddenly lifted from the ground and a man erupted, moving fast. Diane froze, surprised. Jeremy smoothly pivoted, grabbed the man's arm, and put him to the ground.

"Diane, meet Ollie," Jeremy said as he held the man's arm straight up with a firm hold on his wrist.

"Ow, leave off!" Ollie said.

Jeremy released his arm and squatted beside him.

"You good?" Jeremy asked.

"Can't bruise steel," Ollie replied, scrambling to his feet. "How have you been?"

"Good," Jeremy replied, shaking Ollie's hand.

Diane could see the resemblance in the men's faces, even though Ollie had four inches and thirty pounds of muscle on Jeremy. Still, Jeremy had controlled Ollie much more easily than Diane would have expected. There was more to him than met the eye.

"You guys eat?" Ollie asked.

"Not yet," Jeremy said.

"Well, come on, then," Ollie replied.

Diane and Jeremy followed him to a large green army tent and then inside. As her eyes adapted to the gloom, Diane saw five large men and two women eating and drinking coffee.

"Tane!" Ollie thundered. "This is my brother Jeremy and . . . Diane, is it?"

"Yes."

A huge and muscular man rose from the table and walked over to Jeremy. His face was covered in black tribal tattoos. His imposing appearance was offset by the kindness in his eyes.

"*Tena koe*, Jeremy, if you are the brother of this one," Tane said. "Welcome. Do you know the *hongi*?"

The man towered over Jeremy, but Diane could see that he was relaxed, for all his fierceness. Diane had never seen anyone like him in her life.

"No, I don't believe I do," Jeremy replied.

"Let me show you, if you consent. It is the traditional Māori greeting."

Jeremy nodded.

"I place my hand on your shoulder," Tane said, doing so, "and then we touch foreheads and noses. We share the breath of life."

Tane leaned down and touched foreheads with Jeremy.

"Welcome home," Tane said, then looked to Diane. "And yourself, Diane?"

"Yes, please."

Diane stepped closer to Tane, who placed his forehead gently against hers, their noses touching briefly. In this manner, she and Jeremy were introduced to the rest of the people. All of them except for Ollie were Māori.

"Our first victims—er, students," a pretty woman named Ahora said. Unlike the men, she had an intricate tattoo only on her chin.

Jeremy looked quizzically at Ollie, who laughed.

"They want to introduce Māori culture in the Burn. One way is by doing the *haka* and teaching it," Ollie said.

"What's a *haka*?" Jeremy inquired.

"Funny you should ask," Tane said, smiling and gesturing them outside.

Diane and Jeremy went out of the tent, then turned to see the people they had just met lined up like bowling pins, facing them.

"Now, don't get scared," Tane said. "The *haka* is a traditional Māori ceremonial dance or challenge. It is also a symbol of community and strength. We bring it here to teach and include others. And now . . . the Ka Mate, written by Te Rauparaha."

Diane watched as Tane began chanting. Others in the group struck fierce poses, their faces twisted, their tongues sticking out.

"*Ka mate, ka mate! Ka ora! Ka ora!*" Tane and the others chanted as they struck poses and slapped their thighs.

The performance was over quickly.

"That was powerful!" Diane said, clapping.

"Would you like to learn it?" Ahora asked.

"Yes, absolutely," Diane replied. "Is it okay if I do it?"

"Yes," Tane said. "If you are interested, come to our classes. We have a lot of history to share. There are even *hakas* that are just for women. We plan on having the classes, then doing a *haka* in the evening. Stop by if you can."

Jeremy and Diane stayed at the camp for a bit, learning more about the *haka*. They both had fun. Ahora showed Diane how to put her face into a fierce scowl until they were all laughing. Other people had started to drift over and be introduced to the ceremony.

"We should probably head back to camp to finish setup," Jeremy said.

"Thank you for coming, my friends," Tane said. "Take a piece of bread. It is our *rēwena* bread, made from potatoes."

Diane and Jeremy exchanged hugs with each camp member, and each took a slice of the offered bread. It was tasty and sweet.

"*Mihi mo inaianei,*" Ahora said. "Goodbye, my friends."

"Come again soon," Ollie said.

"Come to our bar tonight," Jeremy shouted back. "We are right down the road."

"Bet on it," Ollie replied.

Jeremy and Diane headed back to camp on their bicycles.

"Wow," Jeremy said. "That was fun!"

"Best morning ever," Diane said.

In camp, most people were now up and about. After parking her bike and locking it, Diane joined the others under the bar canopy. She found a seat next to TK and sat down.

"Good time?" TK asked.

"Best morning," Diane replied.

"Alright people, here's the plan," Twinkle said. "Get up the yoga tent and light garden, finalize the bar decorations. And then camp chores. All Virgins with Steven to learn the camp chores, the rest with TK and Sequoia."

At that moment, a large RV pulled into the area in front of the bar, blaring its air horn. The sound of air brakes setting was followed by the opening of the door. A small, lean, muscular woman with dark blue hair stepped out. She was wearing knee-high red leather boots with buckles, bright red booty shorts, and a tight baby doll T-shirt with BITCH bedazzled on it, baring a defined six-pack. Large Jackie O sunglasses set off a gorgeous face.

"Who do you have to fuck to get a drink around here?" the woman loudly demanded of the group.

"Sheba!" TK and Sequoia said together and ran to the woman.

Sheba reached up, grabbed Sequoia's hair in one hand, and laid a huge kiss on him. She then stepped into TK and dipped her as she gave her a deep kiss on the mouth. They were all laughing as they walked over to the bar, Sheba stopping to give three people deep kisses and hugs.

"Sheba," TK said, leading the woman over, "this is Diane, my friend and Virgin."

Sheba looked Diane up and down and stepped forward with her arms raised.

"Consent, Diane?" Sheba asked.

"Sure," Diane said.

Sheba leaned in, taking Diane into her arms, and laid a deep kiss on her mouth. Diane was surprised, and her eyes widened. She could feel the kiss from the bottom of her toes to the top of her head.

"Mwah," Sheba said, pulling away. "Good kisser. Which team do you play for? Or are you a switch-hitter?"

"Wh-what?" Diane could feel herself blushing to the roots of her hair.

"Just trying to plan my week," Sheba said, looking over to Jeremy. "Who is that?"

"That's Jeremy, Twinkle's Virgin," Sequoia said.

"He spoken for?" Sheba asked.

"Not that I've heard," TK said.

"Excuse me, then. Momma's got a need," Sheba said, then strode over to Jeremy.

Diane watched Sheba's stride. She was poetry in leather boots, confidence personified. Sheba struck a pose with her hand on her hip as she talked to Jeremy. Diane watched as she leaned in and kissed the young man, and then the two of them walked to Sheba's RV and through the door. A young man and woman came out of the RV, then the door closed.

"Holy hell," Diane said in wonder at the scene, adding, "I didn't expect *that* when I gave consent."

TK and Sequoia laughed at her.

"Yeah, it's best to clarify sometimes," TK said. "Sheba is Sheba."

Diane watched as Sheba's RV started slowly rocking.

"Wait," Diane said. "Is that what I . . ."

"That's Sheba," TK said. "Living in the moment."

"I wouldn't bother knocking on the door," Sequoia said.

Diane smiled despite herself. She walked over to where Steven was standing at the bar.

"I guess I'm with you," Diane said.

"We will give Jeremy a bit," Steven replied. "Have a seat."

Diane finished her cup of coffee. In time, the door to the RV opened and Jeremy and Sheba emerged. Sheba grabbed Jeremy's head and kissed him, then pointed to the RV and then toward camp. Jeremy climbed back into the RV and closed the door, firing it up. Sheba strode purposefully toward the bar.

"Steven," Sheba said, pulling out a long black holder and putting a cigarette in the end. Steven placed a glass in front of Sheba on the bar, splashed some whiskey into it, then held a lighter for her. Sheba downed the whiskey and leaned into the proffered fire.

"You're a peach," Sheba said to Steven, then strode away.

Diane watched her approach the area for the yoga tent and start barking orders. Jeremy walked into the bar with a silly grin on his face.

"Ready to work?" Steven asked. "Or do you need a rest?"

"I guess I'm ready."

"Well, let's get after it," Steven said.

Diane watched Jeremy, bemused. The quiet young man seemed somewhat lighter in energy.

"Fun morning?" Diane asked teasingly.

"It's shaping up well," Jeremy replied, smiling.

"And it's not over yet," Steven said. "Let's grab these shower bags and fill them."

The three got to work. Steven showed them how to fill shower bags, fuel up and start the generators, and spread the water around with the brushes in the evap pond so it would dissipate quickly. The three then did a MOOP sweep through the camp, collecting small bits of trash and debris. Walking slowly through camp, Diane picked up splinters of wood, sequins, and a cigarette butt.

They moved the burn barrel, a fifty-five-gallon steel drum with artistic figures and designs cut into its sides, to a spot near the front of the camp. By the time they were done, the rest of the campers had gotten the large tent structure for yoga up.

Directed by Steven, Diane and Jeremy moved on to driving thick, long steel rebar stakes into the ground, leaving about two feet of each sticking up. They then slipped long PVC pipes over the rebar, with tall, colorful flags that slid over the full length of the pipes. These marked the edges of their plot of land. The bold colors of the flags brightened up the drab landscape. The wind was increasing as they finished, enough to start to bend the PVC poles.

Diane got her goggles and mask and continued moving from job to job, lending a hand where needed. Her body was tired, her hands aching from the unfamiliar manual labor, but she ignored it and pressed on. The city was rising around her. Despite the physical strain, she felt a part of something greater than herself, a group working toward a goal.

A large, metal-barred geodesic dome went up in a complicated manner after a couple of tries. People were on ladders as well as standing in place supporting the various bars. TK was on Sequoia's shoulders, tightening bolts and swearing and laughing until the whole thing was accomplished. The light was starting to fade in the sky, and the strong wind had died off again.

"Ice, who needs ice?" Twinkle said to the group. "Arctica is open for a short window. Get your money and talk to TK."

"Diane," TK said, coming over to her, "you want to go on an ice run?"

"Sure," Diane replied. "What do we need to do?"

"Get a list of orders and money, I'll get the ice bike. Grab your stuff and meet me in the bar," TK said, then handed her a small, zippered bag. "Put the money in here."

Diane got her equipment and a pad of paper from the carport. People were waiting in the bar when she got back. She wrote down orders for bags and blocks of ice and put the money in the zippered bag as directed. TK pulled up on a cruiser bike covered in fur, with a small cart attached behind.

"Let's go," TK said, pulling off on the bike.

Diane scrambled, putting the money and notebook into her bag, then unlocked her bike and set off. TK was meandering slowly, waiting for her, and she had no trouble catching up.

"It's a little way, no need to rush," said TK, waving at people in a camp they were passing.

"So, Sheba," Diane began. "What's that about?"

"Jealous?" TK teased.

"I've never seen anyone just grab someone and go off like that," Diane replied.

"Don't be judgy," TK said. "You have your eye on Jeremy?"

"I—I—" Diane stammered.

"You don't have to be embarrassed. He's cute and seems nice."

"What about Sheba?"

"Sheba won't sleep with him again. That's her MO. She just lives in the moment," TK said. "More than anyone I have met."

"I see," Diane replied.

"Probably not, but you might. Sheba is great people and very, very moral. Hers are just different morals than most other people live by. There's no gray area with Sheba, it is all radical honesty."

"Eleventh principle?"

"No, that's entitlement," TK replied.

"I thought it was consent," Diane said. "There was one thing I was curious about."

"Yeah?" TK replied.

"It's nothing, but it made me feel awkward. Didn't know if I had done something wrong."

"I'm sure you didn't," TK said.

"I met Steven with Jeremy," Diane said. "He greeted Jeremy and hugged him. I expected a hug and told him I hug too, but he just said 'Cool' and didn't hug me. God, I feel stupid just saying it. Is that entitlement? Did I feel entitled to a hug?"

TK laughed. "No. Just about everyone hugs here, it's a Burner thing. Steven wasn't being rude. He is a Mormon, and he was married for a long time, then his wife died. His belief structure is that he is married to her forever, in this life and the next. He is very cautious about connections to women he doesn't know. We talked about it a long time at the bar one night."

"That makes sense now," Diane said. "I thought Mormons didn't drink."

"He doesn't, just bartends," TK replied. "Here we are."

Diane followed her, pulling up near a tall dome covered in

heavy tan material. Parking their bikes and locking them, they walked to the end of the long line.

"This is not bad. Later in the day and into the week, it can be hours," TK said.

They watched and chatted with the other people in line. Moving along at a moderate pace, they neared the entrance.

"Diane, over there," TK said, pointing. "You see those two people in khaki? With the radios and hats? Those are Rangers."

"Kinda look official, like cops or something," Diane said.

"No, they are Dirt Rangers. They are just Burners like us," TK said. "See the deputy sheriff and Bureau of Land Management trucks with lights? Those are cops. The Rangers are who you go to first if you have conflicts or problems. That way the cops don't have to deal with it and do cop stuff."

"Oh," Diane said. "Am I a Burner now?"

"You always were, you just didn't know it," TK said. "Whoot, whoot! Thank you, Rangers!"

The Rangers waved back. Suddenly the whole line was calling out, "Thank you, Rangers! Thank you, Rangers!"

The Rangers laughed and waved and continued on their way. TK and Diane went into Arctica for their turn and purchased their ice order. Loading into the bike cart was accomplished, and they headed back. The heat had certainly increased. Diane was very aware of the sun.

"Man," Diane said as she pedaled. "I should have brought my sun hat."

"Yeah, you start to notice the heat this time of day," TK replied. "Look there, that's cool."

"What?" Diane asked.

"Look at the dust devil. Behind the girl in front of us."

Diane looked ahead. There was what looked like a tiny tornado, about six feet tall, slowly moving behind a girl on a bicycle, perfectly matching her pace. Diane continued to watch as the girl took a right at the next street. The dust devil turned as well and followed behind her.

TK and Diane both stopped and gaped, then looked around to see if someone else had witnessed this. A man standing by the road turned and met their gazes.

"Did you guys see that too?" he asked.

"Yeah," TK said. "Kinda trippy."

"Playa magic," he said. He tossed them a casual wave, then turned back into his camp.

Continuing on, the women were back at their camp in no time. Diane helped unload the ice, enjoying the cold of it against her body after the hot ride in the sun.

"You still feeling the heat?" TK asked.

"Yeah, I guess I still have to acclimate a little," Diane admitted.

"I got this. Give me a hand with the ice and I'll teach you something," TK said, hoisting two bags.

Diane lifted the remaining bags and followed her friend. When she entered the carport, TK had set out two of the plastic buckets on the floor.

"Grab the other handle of the cooler," TK said. "Lift the whole thing onto the one bucket in the center, with the spout over the other."

Diane did as she was asked and watched as TK opened the spout of the cooler. The water splashed and filled the bucket until there was only a trickle. TK closed the spout, and they lifted the cooler back into place. After filling the cooler with fresh ice, TK pulled out a jug of vinegar and poured a measure into the water. She then grabbed a couple of beers and took the bucket by the handle.

"Follow me," TK said, walking out and into the bar and finding a seat there. Curious, Diane followed her and pulled up a seat next to her.

"Now take off your shoes and socks and slide your feet in there," TK said.

Diane did as instructed. She flinched. The water was icy cold. But she could feel her body temp cooling off as she put first one foot, then the other, into the water.

TK handed her a beer. Diane cracked it and took a sip.

"Ahhh, that's nice," Diane said, relaxing into her chair.

"It's a good way to cool off. And the vinegar will help your skin," TK replied.

They spent the rest of the afternoon siesta there in the shade of the bar. Diane met and chatted with other campers, found out about their past Burns and experiences. The afternoon was too hot for exploring, the wind was gusty, and the camp was all but built, so there was plenty of time for friendly conversation, and the laughter was a welcome respite. Diane drifted off after a few beers and whiskeys. She awoke to the sound of music playing. People were sitting at the bar.

"Hi, sleepyhead," Twinkle said. "You have a good nap?"

"I guess I did," Diane said, sitting up. The sun had dropped, and the temperature seemed cooler. She took her feet out of the bucket. Her toes had wrinkled. "I didn't mean to fall asleep. I wanted to help."

"Don't worry about it. We have enough people finishing up now. Since you're a Virgin, I wanted to make sure you didn't overwork. I would have let you sleep, but I thought you might want a shower with warmer water before the dusk hits. It can get a little chilly when the sun goes down."

"What do I do with this vinegar water?" Diane asked. "Pour it in the evap pond?"

"No," TK said. "That just adds more water to evaporate. Pour it into the flower watering can over there and spread it on the road. Keeps the dust down."

Diane did so.

"Shower now?" TK asked.

"A shower sounds fantastic," Diane replied.

"Well, grab a bag and take your turn."

Diane could see a camper finishing up their shower and went to gather her own things. Standing on the plastic pallet, letting the water moisten her, then soaping up, felt spectacular. The water was warm enough to be comfortable. Diane took her time scrubbing and lathering, wanting to get as clean as possible.

As she walked back to the carport, the wind felt glorious on her clean skin. The gossamer fabric of the wrap she wore caressed her in the light breeze. She could see the light fading as sunset approached. Hurriedly, she stowed her toiletries, threw on some clothing, and scrambled to the top of the container to watch the sunset. Her steps on the ladder were more confident now. TK, already there, slipped an arm around her waist and hugged her close.

"I can't believe it's only been three days," Diane said as she looked out at the camps being built. The spaces were filling up.

"It just gets bigger and bigger from here," TK replied. "You feeling up to going out after this?"

"Yeah. What do you have in mind?" Diane replied.

"Steven is headed out to his friend's art installation after we eat," TK said.

"Sounds great."

They saw the sun touching the mountains, heard the howling, and joined in.

CHAPTER 10

The man's back and shoulders were straining. Dust was in the creases of his muscles, accenting them. Long hair, dark, curly, and tied with a cord, fell almost to his waist. A dusty black kilt held up with a wide leather belt rode low on his narrow hips. His torso was a V shape, climbing to his broad shoulders. Thick, muscular calves disappeared into worn black leather boots.

All of this Diane took in as she rode up to the towering art piece illuminated by construction lights. The man turned and looked at Steven, then at Diane. His stern, serious face, intimidating, tanned and rugged, lit up, the thick black beard split by white teeth. His eyes, smoldering green, shone with pleasure. They landed on Diane and held her gaze, and she was lost in them.

"Malcolm," Steven said. "How are you, my friend?"

The two men hugged, loudly clapping each other on the back. TK stopped beside Diane with Sequoia. Diane was trying to tear her eyes from the dusty god in front of her. Sequoia was off his bike, leaning back to take in the massive structure of pipes and shapes. TK reached out and touched Diane's chin, gently closing her mouth.

"I wonder what this is gonna look like working," Sequoia said.

"I wonder what his thighs taste like, hmmm, Diane?" TK said softly so that only Diane could hear. Diane blushed furiously and took a drink of her water instead of speaking. She was grateful for the shadows, confident that her face was scarlet.

Steven brought Malcolm and his team over to the group and introduced them. Hugs were given all around. Hugging Malcolm, Diane inhaled his scent of masculinity and physical effort and was intoxicated.

"What are you building?" Jeremy asked.

"Hearts of Fire," Malcolm replied. "Two eighteen-foot metal sculptures, a woman and a man experiencing passion. Flames come out from their chests so that they launch fire at each other, igniting the rose of love between them."

"Here, you guys, I brought you food," Steven said, pulling covered trays and water from his bike cart.

"Thanks, buddy," Malcolm said. "I'm famished."

"How long have you been building this?" TK asked as the team started eating.

"Four days straight so far," Malcolm said after swallowing. "We sleep where we drop. The sculptures are in place, we are doing final checks on our connections, the inspection is in a bit. We look like we are going to make our deadline for our art grant."

"This is a grant project for the Burning Man Organization?" Sequoia asked.

"Yeah," Malcolm replied. "They have a deadline. If you don't make it, then you don't get the grant."

Diane stepped back, taking in the structure. There were a

couple of bright construction lights on the site. The figures made sense, a man and a woman facing each other. Crudely human yet sensuous shapes, made of twisted steel, towering above the crowd. Stainless steel ovals were centered in their chests.

She had never seen anything like it.

"We were about to test it," Malcolm said. "Want to watch?"

"Hell, yeah," TK said.

"Alright. Dougie, we good to go?" Malcolm asked a dusty man by the control console.

A thumbs-up from the man and Malcolm nodded.

"Alright, with you guys here we have enough for a safety cordon," Malcolm said. "Spread out in a circle and keep people away."

The group spread out. Diane watched as some last-minute checks were made. Twenty feet from the structure, she was in the dark of night, focused on the steel pieces.

"Here we go," Malcolm yelled. The construction lights went out, the darkness fell.

As Diane watched, she could hear a slight hissing sound. Small flames, equally spaced along the figures, popped into being. Where crude steel once was, graceful silhouettes now glowed.

"Phase 2," Malcolm's voice carried out from the darkness.

More flames, flowing within the figures, shunted through various pipes and orifices, gave them movement. Small metal reflectors and crystals, cunningly placed, turned the fire and light.

"Ohhh. Ooooh." Sounds came from Diane's lips and from the darkness around her.

"Phase 3."

Within the chests of the sculptures, glowing fires started to build. A hissing, whirring sound built to a roar until they both erupted, spewing fire toward each other. A metal piece between their chests—a single metal rose—started to glow.

Wow, Diane thought. *Just wow.*

The rose hung in the air as the fires all started to shut down. Diane could hear cheers and cries from the other people around the structure. She joined them.

"Man, that was awesome!" Jeremy said.

"Congratulations, Malcolm," Steven said. "Three years to get that together?"

"Yeah, about," Malcolm said. He turned to face Diane as she walked up. "What do you think?"

"It was extraordinary and beautiful," Diane said. "Stunning, just stunning."

Malcolm hugged her.

"I'm glad you were here," Malcolm said, then turned back to the group. "A few more adjustments and then we should be good. Will I see you at the party tomorrow, Steven?"

"You bet," Steven replied. "Dead Presidents blowout tomorrow night."

"We will keep watch over the piece all night tonight in shifts, then through the day. Should be able to slip away by then," Malcolm said.

The groups waved their goodbyes. The Dead Presidents mounted their bikes and headed off on the dark playa, back toward the lights of the city. Diane kept the blinking lights of Steven in front of her, to not get lost.

"Hey, you," TK said, pedaling beside her. She was grinning.

"Hey," Diane replied, smiling herself.

"Like the art?"

"Well, yes," Diane said. "It was amazing."

"You're humming and smiling."

"Am I?" Diane replied. "Race you to the Esplanade."

Diane stood on her pedals and began furiously pumping, speeding into the night, passing Steven, heading for the light. Her crew—that's how she thought of them now—were shouting and cheering behind her. Diane took a bearing on the nearest lamppost, speeding toward where the first camps were being built. She slammed on her brakes, panting and laughing, as TK and Sequoia stopped beside her.

"God, I have to pee," Sequoia said.

"Me too," Diane replied.

"Follow the blue lights, should be two streets up. This is five o'clock," TK said, then pedaled up the road.

Diane noticed that the spaces around them, which had been empty plots on her previous night's ride, were filling up or already full. The group passed shapes, towers, and what appeared to be buildings taking shape. People moved in the glow of work lights, lanterns, and headlamps bobbing through camps. Voices, music, and laughter came from the darkness.

"Oh, thank God!" Sequoia said, pulling up to a row of portos.

"I'll watch your bike," TK said. "Go ahead."

Sequoia jumped off his bike and scurried to the porto. He returned soon, and TK and Diane walked to other portos.

"Be sure you check the seat and floor before you sit," TK said before disappearing.

Diane went into her porto and fumbled with her headlamp.

"Shit," she said, trying to figure out all the straps she would need to undo just to pee.

"What's up?" Sequoia's voice came from outside.

"Woman stuff. I need light . . ."

"Here," Sequoia said.

Diane could hear something on the top of the porto. The interior was suddenly illuminated enough so she could see. Sequoia must be pressing his flashlight against the roof.

"Thanks!" Diane said, looking around. The space was pretty clean, it even had a roll of paper. Undoing enough of her stuff to do her business, she was done in a flash. She buckled up enough to move and came out.

"Sanitizer at the end," TK said.

Diane walked over, got a squirt on her hands, and headed to the bikes. Mounting up, she followed TK's and Sequoia's lights. The streets were very dark, and she was a bit confused as to where she was.

"Where's Jeremy? Did we lose him?" Diane asked.

"It happens," Sequoia said. "It happens a lot when more people are here. That's why you have to carry all your own stuff. What's the camp location, Diane?"

"Three-thirty and E," Diane replied.

"Right. Don't forget. It's on your tags on your stuff, right?"

"Like the bike?"

"Anything you might lose and would want to see again, such as bike, coat, bags, belt, water bottles."

"People will bring that stuff back?"

"Yeah, or to the Lost and Found," TK said, pedaling. "But no name or camp, no return."

"Here we are," Sequoia said, gliding into the camp.

The bar was lit up, people were milling about, music was playing. Diane dropped off her bike and stuff, then went over to take a seat at the bar.

"What can I get you?" Twinkle asked with a smile from behind the bar.

"Whiskey, I guess," Diane said. "What's good?"

"Try this. See if you like it," Twinkle said, pouring a trickle into Diane's cup.

Diane tasted the liquid. It was smoky and sweet. She nodded. Twinkle added a healthy slug to her cup, then moved off.

"Enjoy your day, dear?"

Diane turned and saw Sheba standing behind her. Her hair was swept up onto the top of her head. She was wearing a dark silk dress that flowed and clung at the same time. The glow of the chandeliers and lamps in the bar cast a subdued glow over her.

"Got a light?" Sheba asked, indicating her cigarette.

"Got another?" Diane asked, pulling out a lighter.

Sheba took the proffered light, cupping Diane's wrist to steady it, and inhaled. She then pulled a pack from the top of her boot and offered Diane a cigarette. Diane took the cigarette and lit it. Sheba sat down beside her.

"I understand I may have taken you aback today with my forwardness. I apologize if I made you feel in any way uncomfortable."

Diane shook her head, surprised.

"Don't answer, darling, I can see it in your face," Sheba said, touching her arm. "Was your cap set toward Jeremy? Did I intrude on your plans?"

Diane was taken off guard by the direct question.

"I . . ." Diane began.

"Again," Sheba said, "I can see it in your face. Do not worry. *Nous avons eu une bonne baise*, nothing more. He is very gentle, that one."

"You did what?" Diane asked, not understanding the French phrase.

"It matters not. We shall now be good friends. What do you think so far of"—Sheba gestured with the cigarette—"of all this?"

"It's a lot," Diane replied. "A lot to take in."

Sheba laughed, tapped her ash into an ashtray.

"Tell me more," Sheba said, leaning close.

"I saw artwork tonight like nothing I've ever seen. Fire and steel . . . and . . ."

"And what?" Sheba leaned closer, searching Diane's face. "Hmmm, something else?"

"Well," Diane said, dropping her eyes. "There was—"

"A man?" Sheba asked, her blue eyes sparkling. "A woman? Which? I demand you tell me now."

"An artist."

"Oh, delicious," Sheba said, chuckling. "A wispy-limbed Adonis, painting gauze on ripe breasts?"

Diane laughed. After only a few minutes, she felt completely comfortable with this unusual woman.

"No," Diane said definitively. "He is definitely masculine, working in fire and steel."

"Hmmm," Sheba said, taking a drink from her cup. "And you want this man? Sexually?"

"I—I—" Diane stammered.

"Wait," Sheba said. "We are dry."

With this, Sheba bounced down from her barstool, turned, and clambered up onto her knees, reaching over the bar and filling two cups. Diane was surprised to see that when Sheba's dress rose up, her ass was revealed, with no underwear in sight. A wolf whistle sounded from the darkness. Sheba turned, waved to the darkness, and sat back down.

"Now, you want this man, yes?" Sheba asked, handing Diane the almost-full cup. "Tell me, and more importantly, tell yourself truly."

Diane took a drink from the cup and considered, then shared a deeper thought than she normally would have dared.

"Yes, more than anything right now," Diane said. "I can't explain it."

"Yes," Sheba said. "Now the truth comes out. You must go to him. Take him."

"I . . ." Diane started. "It's kind of late. What time . . ."

Sheba grabbed Diane by her neck, looked deep into her eyes.

"The time is now. Your time is now!" Sheba said intensely.

"What if he is gone? What—"

"No think, only do. Now drink with me, my friend, and live."

Sheba drank, raising Diane's cup with her other hand and pressing it to Diane's lips. Diane gulped, choking down the whiskey, finishing the cup, breathing heavily.

"Okay," Diane said, gasping. "I got this."

"Good," Sheba said, taking Diane by the shoulders, pulling her to her feet, and turning her around. "Remember, a kiss is not a contract, and tonight is not tomorrow. Live *now*."

With that, Sheba smacked Diane on the ass, propelling her forward, and walked with her to her carport.

"Gather your things," Sheba said.

TK wandered up to them.

"Where are you going?" TK asked.

"She goes to live," Sheba said, "to taste life, to experience passion and truth."

"A dinner party?" TK asked.

"An artist," Sheba said, reaching into a pouch at her belt and handing something to Diane.

"Condoms?" Diane asked, staring at the packages.

"Of course," Sheba said. "We live as adults, not children. You have enough now, your goggles, your mask, shemagh. Water." Sheba reached into the cooler on the ground. "Here are some beers. Now go. You have all you need. You have the most important thing."

"Her vagina?" TK asked.

Sheba turned to TK.

"Her soul," Sheba said dramatically, then turned to look Diane in the eyes. "Her soul."

"Make me proud," TK said.

CHAPTER 11

Diane mounted the bike and turned on the blinking lights. Her head was swimming. Sheba's speech had been exhilarating, like something from a king on the eve of battle. Diane rode forth to meet her quest.

As she steered the bike along the dark street, more cars, trucks, and RVs were passing than she would have expected. Noise from motors, music, and laughter was in the air. The vehicles crept slowly, dust suspended in multiple headlights as they slowly drove to their destinations.

"That's right, the Gate opened tonight," Diane said to the darkness.

Navigating down myriad streets, Diane finally arrived at the Esplanade, the final road before the playa. She steered between the lampposts, trying to remember where the art piece was. She felt slightly confused about the direction, but she knew it was beyond the Man, beyond the Temple. In deep playa.

As she pedaled into the darkness, the wind blowing past her and ruffling her hair, her thoughts turned to self-doubt.

"What the fuck am I doing?" Diane said to the night as she pushed the bike on, wanting to turn back but wanting to move forward. A vision of masculine energy was driving her on. She passed the lights of the Man, each downstroke of her foot producing a slight squeak from the chain. There was barely any moon. The lights from her bicycle were a glowing aura pushing away the dark under the endless sky. The beam from her headlamp reached out before her over the dusty gray of the playa.

Diane moved forward for what seemed like an eternity. The Temple site came and went. She stopped at the edge of light beyond the perimeter and scanned the daunting darkness before her, taking a gulp of water from the bottle, the alkaline taste from the dust in her mouth clearing from the warm liquid.

With the Temple to her back, pointing her bike to the left, she pressed forward.

I probably won't even find it, Diane thought. *God, it's got to be two in the morning, and I'm bumping around in the middle of nowhere.*

Excitement and resolution both gripped her. Her stomach was fluttering, her mouth dry, sweat beading on her brow, disappearing in the dryness of the cool night. A ripple of red flashing lights looked familiar far in the distance, and she steered toward it. Her legs were beginning to burn, each press of the pedal making them shake from exertion.

What the fuck am I doing? Diane thought again. *I know nothing about this guy.*

Stopping again in the quiet darkness, she felt alone but not afraid. She straddled her bike and drank from the water bottle until it was empty. Turning back for a moment, she could see the city, lights, and movement from vehicles far behind. The night was silence around her. She began moving forward again, her breath and pounding heartbeat physical touchstones in the aura of light.

Diane stowed the water bottle into its rack as the wind began to pick up. She straightened her goggles and wrapped the shemagh around her head, then across her face over the dust mask. Then, looking up, she realized she had reached the art piece. The flashing red blinkers had guided her here across the silent, dusty plain.

The site was dark and quiet. Parking the bike, she stood for a moment, the art piece towering above her. She switched off her bike lights and headlamp and took a few deep, centering breaths, waiting for her night vision to return. Taking the cans of beer from her saddlebag, she slowly walked around the perimeter, heading for the control console. The minimal light from the stars and the subdued flash from the perimeter lights were all she had to see by.

She breathed shallowly, sipping from the fresh night air. Her stomach was fluttering with anxiety and excitement. Diane tried to think what she might say, but nothing came to mind. Stepping carefully, she could just about make out the control console. Thinking of strong shoulders and big hands, she steeled herself to walk forward.

"Can I help you?" A woman's voice came directly from the gloom at Diane's feet.

Diane jumped, startled, and let out a yelp.

"Are you okay?" asked the woman.

"Well, uh . . ." Diane stammered. This was not what she had been expecting.

"Did you come looking for Malcolm?" the voice asked, sounding amused.

Diane blushed deeply, surprised that the glow from her face didn't add to the light.

"Yes, I met him earlier tonight. And I . . ."

". . . wanted to talk about art?"

Diane thought she could detect an undertone of teasing.

"Well, yes, I guess," Diane replied. "Well, I . . . guess I . . ."

"Is that a beer in your hand?" the voice asked. "My name is Susan, by the way."

"Diane. You want one?"

"Sure. Have a seat."

Diane took a spot on the ground, the rough, dry playa crunching under her, and handed Susan a beer. They popped the tops, and each took a sip.

"Ahhh, that's good," Susan said. "I have the watch until dawn. Have to protect the art piece."

The two women sat in silence. Diane felt she was being somewhat sized up.

"So did you really head out here to talk to Malcolm about art?" Susan added, her tone light. "Or something else?"

Diane smiled in the darkness. She could just make out the figure of Susan.

"Something else, maybe," Diane admitted. "Is it that obvious?"

Susan laughed. "Honey, you're the second one tonight."

There was a beat of silence as Diane realized what Susan had said. Then both of the women began to giggle.

"Oh, that's priceless," Diane said. "I can't believe I rolled out here in the middle of the night."

"Well," Susan said, laughing, "at least you didn't volunteer on an art project for a year."

There was another beat, then the women started laughing in waves.

"You volunteered because you wanted to be with Malcolm?" Diane asked. "Did it work?"

"No, he's fucking clueless," Susan said. "Brilliant, gorgeous, and completely focused on his work. I was getting to the point of considering giving him a roofie—not that I'd ever do it—but then something else happened."

"What's that?" Diane asked.

"The work," Susan said, gesturing at the sculpture. "I fell in love with the work. When I started, I couldn't weld, didn't understand electricity, metalworking, propane fire stuff, nothing. The woman I was before wouldn't have spent the night protecting a piece of art in a desert in a sleeping bag. But it changed . . . I changed. And now the piece is here, and I helped, really helped. My work as a part of a team made this happen. And now that I know how to do it, I'm planning my own piece."

The two women sat in the dark. Diane finished her beer.

"If it's any consolation, he has a micropenis," Susan said as Diane got to her feet.

"What?" Diane said. "How would you know if you haven't been together?"

"He wears a kilt," Susan said. "I hold ladders."

"Does he really have a micropenis?" Diane asked, laughing.

"No, not really. It's a baby elephant trunk," Susan said, shaking her head. "What a waste. I've known him for a year and don't know anyone he has even dated."

"Okay," Diane said. "I guess I should go, then. It was great meeting you."

"You too," Susan said.

Diane walked to her bike. She mounted up, turned on her lights, and headed off.

"Nothing ventured, nothing gained," she mused aloud.

Pressing forward into the night, Diane noticed that the going was easier. She wondered if the deceptively flat plain was actually sloped a bit, with a gradual decline as she headed back to the city. The lights in the distance twinkled. Watching them, Diane realized that they were becoming dimmer, not brighter. Suddenly she realized what was happening.

Slipping the neoprene dust mask into place, she bound the shemagh tighter. Just as she had adjusted her goggles, the dust storm hit. Visibility instantly dropped to zero. Between the dust and the darkness of the night, Diane was close to blind. Controlling her breathing, Diane strove to calm herself. The mask and shemagh allowed her to breathe, albeit with effort. Without them, the dust would have been too much. She was grateful to have been warned so many times to be equipped.

Dismounting her bike, Diane began to walk slowly in the direction she believed would take her to the city, or at least the Temple or Man, to orient herself.

How long could it last? Diane thought as she walked.

The direction felt correct, and Diane was confident the city couldn't be very far. She was very tired—the trip out had taken a lot of strength—but she was smiling to herself. The whole thing was rather ridiculous. Diane kept walking forward, slowly pushing the bike, yawning under her mask. She wiped the dust film from her goggles.

It must be dying down, Diane thought. She could see slightly better.

Her legs were starting to ache, her feet were beginning to

hurt. Then she was able to make out a faint yellow glow ahead, a globe of some kind, small in the darkness. Changing direction, she made for the light.

Soon Diane could see that the light said TAXI in black letters. Walking closer, she could see it was on top of a vintage yellow taxicab. Her mind had trouble processing that there was a vintage cab in the middle of a dust storm in the desert. Walking around to the driver's door, she could make out a sign on the door reading "Black Rock City Taxi." Another sign, on the passenger window, said "Video in Use."

"Need a ride?" a voice said from the now-cracked driver's window.

"Um," Diane said, her voice muffled by the mask, "yes, I guess so. I'm a little lost."

"Put your bike on the back and get in," the driver said before rolling up the window.

Diane lifted her bike onto the rack attached to the rear bumper of the car. She opened the passenger door and slid onto the huge back seat. The dust was minimal inside, and the car was quiet. Small lights illuminated the back seat. She couldn't see much of the driver.

"Rules of the ride," the driver said. "You're talking or you're walking. This is a video archive of Burning Man experiences, video and audio. Do whatever you want, but you have to tell a story. Agreed? You give consent?"

"Sure," Diane replied. "I consent."

"Where are you headed?"

"Why are you out here?" Diane asked.

"Waiting for you, of course," the driver replied. "Now, where to?"

"My camp, I guess," Diane said. "Three-thirty and E, Dead Presidents."

"Okay," the driver said. "What's your story?"

The cab began to move forward slowly. The driver hit a switch, and yellow LEDs on the outside of the car began to flash. Diane began to speak about her adventure that night. She had dropped the mask but kept her goggles on, and in this disguise, she felt safe discussing the night's events on video.

The driver was mostly quiet. Now Diane could see that he was a bit older than she. He wore a collared shirt and a hat. His voice was soothing, drawing more of her story out of her. He prodded her for more detail at a few points and laughed at others.

The ride went smoothly, and almost too quickly, the car stopped.

"Three-thirty and E," the driver said. "Your stop."

"Thank you," Diane said, then opened the door.

The storm had passed, and she was in front of Dead Presidents. Everything was dark and quiet, and there was already a lightening of the sky. She removed her bike from the back of the taxi and tapped the side. The cab slipped away, its yellow lights flashing, illuminating the street. Diane looked down at the bike to turn off its lights. When she looked up, the taxi was gone.

Man, what a weird night, Diane said to herself, and then she walked into the camp and went to bed.

CHAPTER 12

Sunday, August 30, six days until the Man burns

Diane awoke to the sound of her tent zipper opening. Cracking an eyelid, she saw TK smiling at her.

"Ten more minutes," Diane mumbled.

"Nope," TK said as she crawled into the tent and on top of Diane, burrowing her face into Diane's neck, making snuffling sounds.

Diane turned her head back and forth and, despite her drowsiness, started to laugh with her friend.

"How'd it go?" TK asked, waggling her eyebrows in Diane's face.

"Hmmph," Diane said. "I'll never tell."

"Coffee?" TK asked. "It's the first day of the rest of your life. I will not let you sleep through Burning Man. We still have to finish build."

"Coffee," Diane agreed.

TK moved out of the tent. Diane could hear her rummaging around while humming to herself. Blinking her eyes, Diane sat up. Despite the lack of sleep, she felt pretty good.

TK knelt by her tent flap and handed her a mug of coffee.

Diane sipped it, waking up. She could taste the Irish cream. It would be easy to get used to that.

Smiling at her friend's enthusiasm, Diane roused herself and took care of her morning necessities, then wandered over to the evap pond sink. Peeking into the empty shower structure, she saw a half-full shower bag hanging in place. Slipping back to the carport, she grabbed toiletries and a towel. The water was cold but exhilarating, and the quick rinse brought her fully awake and ready to meet the day. The weather was clear, and the morning sun felt good on her skin.

Diane dressed quickly and headed to the bar. TK was standing by the burn barrel, talking to a man who had obviously just arrived. Diane had noticed that the new arrivals were easy to pick out. They were clean. Anyone on the playa for more than a day had a general dustiness about them.

"Diane," TK said, "meet Billy."

"Hi, Billy," Diane said.

"Hi, Diane," Billy said. He raised his arms and she stepped into them willingly. His thin, strong arms embraced her. He was at least a head shorter than she.

"He was in the Gate line for eight hours," TK said.

"Wow," Diane said.

"Dust storm last night shut the Gate down," Billy said, leaning against his truck. "There was some impromptu partying in the line, but I just racked out."

"What's on the trailer?" Diane asked.

"It's the Starfish!" TK exclaimed.

Diane cocked her head in puzzlement.

"The Starfish art car!" TK said. "An undersea enchantment ride!"

Billy laughed.

"I'll get it together today sometime," Billy said. "First, I'll find Twinkle and see where to set up. Then I'll get the Starfish up and going. The registration starts today."

"We have to go to the DMV," TK said. "Department of mutant vehicles. You get to see all the art cars!"

"Sounds good," Billy said. "Nice to meet you, Diane. Talk to you later, TK."

"What about the camp chores?" Diane asked TK as Billy walked away.

"I did them for you," TK said. "Gassed the generators, sorted the burn materials, filled the shower bags, and did a bar cleanup. We can do the MOOP patrol while you drink your coffee. Then we complete the build."

Wandering the camp in a grid, overlapping lines, the two women scoured the ground. Diane was surprised that TK picked up the smallest items, including glitter, splinters from boards, sequins, and other small detritus. Nothing was too insignificant to be picked up. Diane was also surprised by how much was already on the ground.

"Circle up," Twinkle announced from the bar.

The camp assembled. Diane was surprised to see so many new faces. The plot of land the camp occupied was filling up. The camps around them were filling up as well, as more people arrived. The city was taking form.

"Today is the last push before the party tonight," Twinkle said to the assembled group. "We need to put the floor in the yoga tent, finish the lights on the bar, and then pick up our areas. Let's get to it."

Diane went with the group to do the floor of the yoga tent.

They heaved heavy, dusty vinyl sheeting rolls onto the heavy-duty utility wagon, then laid them out underneath the structure and staked them to the ground. The job was made harder by the wind that built up in surges, but finally it was done.

After a short break, Diane helped to string more lights in the bar. LED ropes and chandeliers were connected to power cords, each of which needed to be covered so no one would trip over it. Diane worked with Jeremy, digging a trench in the dirt. Just as they completed this task, the wind started to build, the dust moving in waves down the road in front of the camp. Diane could feel the dry air sucking the moisture from her body.

"Take a break," Twinkle said, through her dust mask, to Diane and Jeremy. "Wait out the storm. The container is not a bad place for that. Grab a chair."

They found camp chairs and headed to the shipping container. Most of their camp was already there. The box was dim inside but gave shelter from the harsh wind and dust. Sipping water, Diane took a swig when a bottle of whiskey was passed around. Listening to the conversations of people she hardly knew, she could feel the comradery inherent in doing a difficult task together. It pulled people together quickly to face adversity, got them out of their regular routines.

After an hour, gradually, the wind died down. The sound of the dust scouring the steel sides of the container diminished.

"Let's MOOP it and start packing all the stuff we don't need," Twinkle said at the door.

The wind had moved a lot of loose items, and some were completely spread out around the plot. Walking the camp area, Diane was surprised at how fast it had filled up with campers arriving. RVs lined the perimeters to cut down on the wind.

Tents, shade structures, vehicles, and a reflective hexagonal structure with hard sides held together by gaffer's tape made a jumble of pathways through the already full plot of land.

With all the campers working, the land was set to rights within an hour. Finally, lighting touches around the camp and bar were finished. A flagpole was erected, and a Dead Presidents flag was strung.

With TK and Jeremy, Diane finished putting a mailbox attached to a piece of rebar on the side of the road.

"What's this for?" Jeremy asked.

"We get mail," TK replied. "There is a Burning Man post office, and you can send messages from there to any camp if you know its name and location. There is also a newspaper, *Piss Clear*. Volunteers deliver it."

"Does it get read?" Diane asked.

"More than you might think," TK replied.

They moved on to mounting two signs saying "Keep Out, Private Area."

"People wander through here?"

"Yeah," TK said. "It's considered rude to wander through other people's private camping areas. All the camps are supposed to have some open interactive areas to them, though, like our bar and yoga tent."

It was midafternoon when the work was completed to TK's and Sequoia's satisfaction. Most of the camp was relaxing in the bar and dome areas, rehydrating and enjoying cocktails. Diane, exhausted from the unfamiliar physical work, sun, and dust, took a shot of whiskey and lay down in the stifling tent.

The sound of music pulled Diane from her nap. It had been a good one despite the heat. Wiping the drool and sweat off her face, she blinked awake, stretched her arms and sat up. It was still light outside.

Diane fumbled with her water bottle and took a deep satisfying drink until the entire quart was drained. Slipping out of the tent, she stretched and twisted again, limbering up. Diane noticed as she did so that there was a thick covering of dust over everything in the carport, every single thing. TK's insistence on putting her going-home clothes in a plastic bag made much more sense now. Diane filled her bottle from the five-gallon container on the table, then sat down, sipping it.

When was that? When did I get here? Diane thought. *Only five days? Has it only been five days so far?*

So much of the experience had been living on another level, condensing the amount you could experience in day-to-day life into a new and higher gear. It was exciting when you were doing it, overwhelming if you tried to take it all in. Diane understood now why you couldn't really explain this to anyone who wasn't here. You had to immerse yourself in it.

Closing her eyes, she let her mind wander. Voices, laughter, and music could be heard around the camp. The heat had diminished but was still oppressive. Diane could feel that she was becoming acclimated but was still probably dehydrated. She realized she had not peed during the afternoon. Finishing her second quart of water, she realized that, most likely, dehydration was why the shot of whiskey after lunch had hit her so hard. Refilling her water bottle, she resolved to drink water until she had to use the bathroom.

How does this all work so well? Diane thought as she sipped. *How can so many people come to such a desolate and hostile area and thrive?*

"Good, you're awake," TK said, coming into the carport.

"I'm up," Diane said, opening her eyes.

"We're on salad squad for dinner," TK said. "I suggest you take a shower and meet me in the kitchen. Tonight is traditional spaghetti night. Good carb base for the alcohol."

"You're planning to get drunk," Diane said, scooting her feet out and sitting on the edge of the air mattress. She could see TK had already showered, because she was standing there wrapped in a towel.

"I know I'll probably get drunk tonight," TK said. "But the spaghetti will slow the booze, and the water I'll be pounding will help me not spend tomorrow with a hangover."

"Sure, I can see that," Diane said, getting up.

Diane gathered her things and used the porto, then went to the shower. She had to wait for another camper, then rig a full shower bag. As before, the sun-warmed water felt glorious. She'd been dusted by the tornado and crusted with sweat and sunblock, and the simple soap and water restored her. As she soaped herself, she noticed the skin on her legs and arms was becoming tanned.

Back in the carport, she applied lotion, then put on a simple, clingy cotton dress and fresh socks and shoes and went to the kitchen. TK pointed with a knife at a pile of vegetables. The kitchen was bustling, with pots of sauce and noodles simmering on the gas grills. People were chatting and drinking at the center tables. The feel of a big family dinner was in the air.

Diane happily pitched in, chopping cucumbers, tomatoes, squash, and other vegetables. Someone offered her some iced sangria, and she accepted. Before she knew it, the vegetable prep was done. People started filling their plates, finding places to sit, and tucking into the piles of food.

"So what do we need to do for the party?" Diane asked.

"Dishes, trash, get the burn barrel going, generally straighten up," TK said. "Then we get pretty and have fun."

Diane, TK, and Jeremy finished their cleanup chores quickly. TK and Diane retreated to their space and applied makeup while having more sangria. The bar was already attracting people, and the music was loud. Walking back into the bar, Diane spotted Tane, Ahora, and Ollie talking to Jeremy.

"Hello, my friend," Ahora said, sharing the *hongi* with Diane, followed by a hug.

"Hello, Ahora." Diane shared the *hongi* with Tane and Ollie. "What a fantastic outfit."

Diane was admiring the cloak around Ahora's shoulders. It was multicolored, with many textures and fabrics. The men were wearing similar cloths around their waists.

"What can I get you?" Diane asked.

"Always like beer," Ollie said.

"I'll get you a cold one," Diane said. "Tane? Ahora?"

"No alcohol, thank you. Water or juice will be fine," Tane said.

"Same," Ahora said.

The bar only served whiskey, so Diane searched her cooler, noticing that TK had topped up the ice. She found a cold beer and two coconut waters.

"Will these work?" Diane asked.

Ollie took his beer eagerly, opening it and taking a sip.

"Is this a joke?" Tane said in a powerful, serious tone, looking at the coconut water. His face, covered with tattoos, looked ominous in the firelight from the burn barrel. "Do you think because we are native islanders and brown-skinned people we want coconut water? Is that how you think of us?"

Diane's eyes grew wide. Tane loomed over her as he stepped close, glaring into her eyes. Jeremy went to step forward, his face serious, but Ollie grabbed his arm.

"Oh, your face!" Tane said, his face splitting into a smile. He wrapped a big arm around Diane's shoulders. "That was priceless."

Tane was laughing, holding Diane.

"You big dickhead," Ahora said, pushing Tane away roughly. "You scared her."

Ahora wrapped her arms around Diane, giving her a hug.

"You good?" Ahora asked, peering into Diane's face.

"Yes," Diane said. "I'm good."

Ahora turned to berate Tane some more. Jeremy came to stand in front of Diane.

"Are you okay?" he asked.

"Yes. Why do you guys keep asking me?" Diane asked.

"Because it looked like you were about to pee your pants," TK said, walking up.

Tane came over to Diane, his head hanging down, and got down on one knee. Tane reached to her with his big hands. Diane hesitated, then placed her hands in his enormous ones. Tane looked up, his face serious.

"Diane," Tane said, looking at her earnestly, "I apologize if I scared you. I forget myself sometimes. Do you forgive me? Can we still be friends?"

"Yes," Diane said, smiling.

Tane stood up and took a sweeping bow.

"Then I will have a drink with you to celebrate our friendship." Tane took her hand and put it in the crook of his elbow as he walked her into the bar.

Laughing and sitting at the bar, Diane chatted with many people. Finishing her drink, sitting between Tane and Ahora, she watched Sheba walk into the bar, dressed to the nines in a blue velvet dress cut plunging low and held together in a clasp below her breasts. Below the clasp, the dress fell open to display Sheba's six-pack abs. Blue velvet short shorts and blue velvet thigh-high boots completed the outfit. Sheba's hair was in intricate curls festooned with a crown of black sticks. Her face was made up perfectly, with dark eyeliner and bright red lipstick.

Sheba strolled to the bar like a panther and stood directly in front of Tane. The man was easily three times her size, but she leaned forward fearlessly toward him. Tane stared back, taking her in.

"You're in my seat, love," Sheba said.

Tane raised his eyebrows and vacated the chair.

"Thank you," Sheba said. She sat down, slid her cup onto the bar, and turned her attention to Ahora, ignoring Tane standing awkwardly next to them.

"That is lovely," Sheba said, looking at Ahora's facial tattoo. "Is it traditional?"

Diane wasn't sure how Sheba had done it, but within seconds, Sheba and Ahora were chatting like long-lost friends. Tane wandered away to stand by the group of people next to the burn barrel.

"Oh, my," Ahora said, raising her glass to cover her speaking. "Who is that?"

Diane looked over. Malcolm had entered the bar with Susan and Steven. Wearing worn leather pants, a white tank top, and a long-tailed black coat, he smiled as he walked up.

"Diane," Malcolm said, giving her a hug. "How are you?"

His hug smelled like heaven. Diane blushed despite herself. She looked over his shoulder at Sheba, who was raising one quizzical eyebrow.

"Who is this?" Malcolm asked.

"Malcolm, this is Sheba and Ahora," Diane said.

Malcolm gave them each a hug. As he went to pull away from Sheba, she pulled him back in for a moment. Malcolm laughed, got drinks from Sequoia, and rejoined Susan and Steven a few feet away.

"Is that the artist?" Sheba asked.

"Yes," Diane said. "Unfortunately, he is apparently clueless about his attractiveness. He just cares about art."

"What a waste," Ahora said, taking one last look.

"Well, you know what this means, then," Sheba said.

"What's that?" Diane asked.

"We three will have to hold him down and fuck the art out of him," Sheba replied.

"I think I would help you," Sequoia said behind them.

The three women, soon joined by Sequoia, erupted into peals of laughter. Malcolm looked around quizzically.

TK appeared at Diane's elbow with a drink in her hand.

"Having fun?" she asked.

"I feel I have been neglecting you," Diane said. "What are we doing tonight?"

"I'm enjoying watching you enjoy yourself," TK said. "But I thought we would explore the art on the playa after some city stuff. A friend of mine has an art car and agreed to take us out."

CHAPTER 13

That sounds fantastic," Diane said, taking another drag of her cigarette.

"Would you guys like to come?" TK asked Ahora and Sheba.

"I have plans," Sheba said, "so, regretfully, no."

"Afraid it's a no for me as well," Ahora said. "Another night, though."

Diane lit another cigarette and freshened her drink. As she sipped, a small wooden boat pulled up on the road in front of the bar. An honest-to-goodness boat had driven up. It was strung with lights along the rails and from the bow to the mast.

"TK!" a man shouted from the boat.

"Garrett!" TK shouted back, then turned to Diane. "You're gonna love this guy."

TK walked to the road. Diane followed, depositing her cigarette in the burn barrel, which had cutouts of figures and the words Dead Presidents. The words and figures were illuminated by the dancing fire within. Diane walked to where TK was chatting with the man. He had long hair underneath a top hat set at a jaunty angle. His attractive face was framed by a goatee and split by a white-toothed smile. He had the appearance of a cheerful satyr.

"Diane," TK said, with her arm around the man, "this is Garrett."

"Hi, Garrett," Diane said, doing the now-customary hug.

"You're a Virgin?" Garrett asked. "You're coming for a ride?"

"Yes and yes," Diane said.

"Well," Garrett said, "gather your things. We will have a drink while you get ready."

"Great," TK said.

TK and Diane walked back to gather their items. Garrett and the others from the boat went to the bar.

"You okay?" TK asked as they donned coats, lights, and backpacks.

"Why?" Diane replied. "Do I not seem okay?"

"No, you seem great. I just wanted to check in," TK replied. "Don't forget to bring a headlamp. And turn on your coat."

Diane put her hand into her pocket and activated the switch. Multicolored lights came alive in the fabric and lit up the interior of the carport. Diane looked at herself in the mirror. TK started for the door.

"TK," Diane said.

TK turned to look at her.

"Thank you," Diane said, looking into her friend's eyes. "I won't ever be able to thank you enough. What you've given me here is more than I could have imagined. I love you."

TK grabbed her in a hug.

"You're gonna make me cry," TK replied. "You're so welcome. It's such a gift to be able to see this place through your eyes, your experience."

"No words," Diane said, shaking her head.

"Wait until tonight," TK said. "You haven't even seen a smidge of this place."

Arm in arm, the two friends joined the others on the art boat.

"Everybody settled?" Garrett said, looking around. "Then we are off."

The boat rocked as TK and Diane boarded, and they quickly sat on the deck, legs dangling, still arm in arm. Garrett explained that the boat was mounted on a two-person electric golf cart with air springs. Garrett sat at the steering wheel and turned on the cart. The boat rocked along as if it were really on the water.

Weaving down the dusty lane, Garrett turned on the music. The boat crept along past camps that were dark and some that were lit up. People drifted by themselves, in pairs, or in large groups, some on foot but more on lighted bicycles. Most people wore some sort of Burner attire or costumes. Some were wearing truly fantastic outfits. The ages of the people were across the spectrum. Just about all of them were smiling.

Looking down the road, Diane saw a man stop and look at what appeared to be a glow stick. As he bent down to grasp it, the glow stick moved just out of his grasp. The situation repeated itself time and again, and the man moved farther and farther across the road. As the boat passed, Diane saw a laughing man with a fishing pole, hidden in the shadows, slowly reeling the glow stick in.

"Hippie fishing," Garrett explained, leaning over. "No license required."

They turned down a busy street, where more people were heading toward the playa. The number of bicycles and the amount of overall traffic increased. Multilevel bars were pumping out music. Other bars were large tents with subdued lighting and no one there. Fire pits and flamework were dotted around. Traffic circles held art and benches to sit on. Fantastical camp names like "Mac IN Cheese," "Kitten Crush," and "Spicy Balls" were posted.

It was so much to take in—not just the visuals but the noise and the dust—that Diane had to close her eyes for a moment to focus and sort it out. She felt TK hand her a flask, and she took a deep drink. The whiskey was warm in her mouth and warm going down her throat. It made her feel better instantly. The burning sensation connected her to her inner physicality, giving her a reference point for the storm of sight and sound around her.

Diane realized after a bit that she had stopped talking to TK. She was just taking in the madness around her. A giant rabbit ran past, chased by a carrot. One camp had people dancing in huge cages and jumping on trampolines to a DJ beat. Flames shot into the air from a man operating a pole device attached to a propane tank.

"That's Mass Carnal Knowledge," TK said, pointing to a large cluster of square blue tents.

"What's that?" Diane asked.

"What does it sound like?"

"An orgy, I guess?" Diane replied, and then teased her friend. "You ever been?"

"Go into it?" TK said. "I'm afraid of getting pink eye just walking past it."

"Judgy?" Diane said, laughing.

"Don't be ridiculous," TK replied. "I'm kidding. The people who run it are some of the nicest I've met."

They came to the Esplanade, the last street before the playa. The traffic was heavy. Multiple art cars went by, lit up with neon lights. Diane saw a flying carpet with neon trim and a giant two-story house filled with people. There were floats and even a contrivance made out of what appeared to be a double-decker bus. Everywhere were people, people, people.

"Have you seen the Man yet?" Garrett asked.

"I took her," TK said. "It wasn't open yet."

"It's completed now," Garrett said. "Let's go."

Crossing the Esplanade, Garrett steered the boat into the playa. With the lights of the city growing dimmer behind them, Diane watched lights all over the dark expanse of the playa, stretching out in all directions. There were neon fireflies and fairies, bikes with neon-outlined tires, blinking lighted whips waving on the backs of bikes. People were walking in the dark, their lights showing their locations.

Artwork was spaced out on the dark plain, red warning lights marking the location of each piece. They passed a colossal metal sculpture, lit up on four sides, twenty feet tall, the welded metal figure of a skeletal dragon in flight.

"Garrett," TK said, "I wanna look."

Garrett nodded, pulled closer to the art, and stopped the car. Getting off the car, Diane and TK walked around the piece. Diane walked closer and touched the figure. The metal appeared to be individually welded bolts, blackened with some sort of coating. The wings loomed menacingly as she walked under them. Everything about the art was intimidating, but beautiful. Walking to the head, Diane marveled at the time and effort it must have taken to make such a thing, let alone drag it out to the desert.

A man was climbing on the back of the beast. He looked unsteadily drunk. She walked to where Garrett leaned against his boat.

"Is that allowed, or safe?" Diane asked him, pointing to the man.

"There aren't any signs saying not to," Garrett replied. "Safe? Well, that's debatable."

As they watched, the man tumbled as he tried to dismount, landing flat on his back in a puff of dust.

"Oh, no," Diane said.

"Safety third," Garrett said.

Garrett wandered over and talked to the man, who waved a hand weakly. He helped the man up and walked back to the boat.

"He's fine," Garrett said. Then, to the art piece in general, he shouted, "Load up."

Diane mounted back up with TK as the boat pulled out and changed direction. The Man figure towered in the air, his triangular head and stick legs and arms outlined in neon. The arms were pointed down at the figure's side.

As they drew closer, Diane could see that the figure was mounted on a large platform with people walking and milling underneath. A coordinated dance performance was happening as they pulled up. Graceful dancers spun and leapt, twirling sticks with ribbons. Diane could see they were very skillful. This was not an amateur show. Live music was playing, with big drums, flutes, and horns. The music was building to a crescendo. More people were coming around to watch, standing in a large ring. The dancers spun faster and faster.

A sudden crash of sound, and the dancers stopped in their

poses, breathing hard and smiling. The crowd surrounding them applauded.

As the crowd dispersed, Diane walked around and under the Man platform, gazing up at the wooden figure on the roof at the apex from underneath. She wandered, looking at paintings and murals arranged on the legs and walls of the base structure. She was fascinated, again, by all of the efforts it must have taken to put this together.

Walking back over to the boat, she could see the group had assembled and was ready to leave.

"I see Billy," TK said, pointing out to the playa.

Diane looked and could see a car decorated like a starfish, with a roof of some sort, lit up by undulating lights. It was with other lighted art cars, off in the distance.

"He must be at the DMV for a night license. We can meet him there," Garrett said.

"You need a license for an art car?" Diane asked, taking her seat.

"Yes," Garrett said, firing up the boat. "You get a day license and a night license to drive. Unless you're differently abled, then you can drive as needed. Have you been on an art car before?"

"No, but I rode in a taxi," Diane replied.

Garrett cocked his head at her.

"She got picked up by the Black Rock City taxi in deep playa, lost in a dust storm in the wee hours," TK said.

"I've heard of that taxi," Garrett said. "That's a legendary ride. Who was driving?"

"Didn't catch his name. Nice guy," Diane said. "Older, distinguished. Distinctive voice and friendly. Dressed nicer than I would have thought. He was wearing a collared shirt, khakis.

Gorgeous pale Stetson. The hat was rounder than others I've seen."

Garrett slowed the car to a stop. Both he and TK looked at her, then at each other.

"Couldn't be," Garrett said.

"What?" Diane asked, confused by their stares. "Did I say something wrong?"

"No," Garrett said.

"You just described someone very particular," TK said.

"Who?" Diane asked.

"Doesn't matter," Garrett said as he moved the car forward.

"I'll tell you later," TK whispered to Diane.

The boat pulled up to a line of other art cars in a row at least forty cars long. There were designs of every sort, and all the cars were lit up. Parties were happening on some, people dancing and drinking. A huge wooden sailing ship, easily fifty feet long, towered above them in the line as they passed it. The women and men aboard it were gyrating furiously to a dance number.

"I like yours better," TK said teasingly to Garrett, craning her neck to look up at the clipper ship.

"It's not the size of your boat, it's how you drive it," he replied.

The vehicles were varied, from a small, simple two-person car to a large, postapocalyptic, hellish race beast with steel pipes going everywhere. A delicate butterfly car with illuminated gossamer wings was in front of the death car. Its wings flapped slowly.

"There he is," TK said.

Garrett pulled up alongside the Starfish.

"Billy!" Garrett said. "Been here long?"

"Garrett," Billy said, getting off his car and embracing the other man. "Few hours. After the line in the sun today, I'm about beat."

"You want us to keep you company?" TK asked him. "We have food, beer, and water."

"That sounds great," Billy said. "I barely ate today. I'm starving."

"We will stay here," TK said, walking over to hug Garrett.

"Okay," Garrett said. "It was great meeting you."

Diane hugged the man. Looking into his smiling face, she felt as if she had known him for years. Garrett returned her gaze.

"I think you fit here," Garrett said, his eyes twinkling. "Here, take this."

Garrett reached into his pocket and pulled out a medallion. Diane looked at it in the glow of the art car lights. It was substantial and felt good in her hand. It had the words Cool Rain inscribed around the edge.

"Cool Rain is my camp," Garrett explained. "Come by when you want to cool off. TK will show you."

Diane fastened the chain around her neck.

"Do you have one from Dead Presidents?" she asked, reaching for the clasp of that medallion around her neck.

Garrett held up his hand. "Twinkle took care of me, see?" He leaned forward, opening his shirt, and showed the tag matching her own.

"Thank you," Diane said sincerely, hugging Garrett. "Thank you so much."

"You guys have fun," Garrett said, mounting his boat. "I'll see you later."

Diane watched the boat motor off into the night, then had a sudden, jarring thought. *Oh, shit! All my stuff is on there.*

"Diane!" TK's voice made her turn and look.

TK indicated the pile where she had already transferred all of their things to the Starfish.

The car in front of them, a giant reclining Buddha, pulled away. Billy pulled the art car forward to the place indicated by a man with a clipboard. TK and Diane stood to the side as the man and Billy walked around the car inspecting various things. As TK and Diane watched, Billy and the man began gesturing and arguing about something. The man with the clipboard walked off, and Billy threw his hands up in exasperation. TK and Diane walked over to him.

"What's up?" TK asked.

"Guy is being a dick," Billy replied, his eyes drooping. "Says I don't have enough lights."

Diane looked at the car. It seemed to her that it had as many as or even more lights than others she had seen riding around.

"It's not a big deal," Billy said. "I didn't put all of them on. I'll take care of it tomorrow. I'm beat for today. Would you mind driving?"

"Hell, yeah, I'll drive," TK said.

"Okay," Billy said, stretching out on the back of the cushioned art car. "Take us back to camp."

TK and Diane got into the submerged front seat, with TK behind the wheel. Diane watched the maniacal glee on her friend's face as she turned the key and slipped the automatic lever into gear.

Slowly they pulled forward, surrounded by lights glowing and pulsing.

"You know how to drive this?" Diane asked.

"Let's find out," TK said, steering the car slowly into the darkness.

CHAPTER 14

Monday, August 31, five days until the Man burns

Diane blinked at the soft light of morning filtering into the tent. Nature was calling, so she slipped out of her sleeping bag and crawled out of the tent. Grabbing her shemagh and goggles, she put on her shoes and walked out toward the portos. Billy was stretched out, deeply sleeping, on the Starfish, where they had parked it in front of the bar on the previous night.

It was early morning, the sun just coming up, and as usual, no one was up and about in the camp. People outside the camp could be seen meandering on the road, though, some weaving a bit. Music could be heard from somewhere in the city. People were still celebrating.

After finishing in the porto, Diane walked over to get a shot of hand sanitizer. At a camp near the road, a man wearing only a shirt and flip-flops was working on a rental RV generator. Diane could hear it was running rough, the man fiddling with something.

So that's a shirt cocker, Diane thought as she passed by.

The man lifted his head. "Do you know anything about generators?" he asked unselfconsciously.

"No," Diane said, trying not to look at his lack of pants. It was a bit difficult.

"Me neither," the man said, picking up a screwdriver. "It worked when I picked it up. Now it's not cooperating. Wife is going to be pissed if I can't keep the AC on."

"Good luck," Diane said, then continued back to camp.

It was odd, Diane reflected as she walked. She had seen many people, men and women, in various stages of nudity since she had been here. But there was something about the shirt cocking that seemed . . . off. The man was not unattractive, and she certainly did not feel threatened by him. It just didn't feel, well, right.

Diane returned to camp, started the water for coffee, and dutifully sat down to drink another quart of water. Slipping her hand into a bag hanging on the wall, she withdrew her phone. She could see a message from Stella and opened it.

"Put away your phone, everything is fine, fuck your Burn," the message read.

Diane grinned wryly and powered off the device. Stella knew her too well. Had she had experiences like Diane's? The intensity of living here was overwhelming, on a completely different level.

Is it like this for everyone? Diane wondered. *Is there a commonality to the Burn experience?*

With the percolator burbling, she poured herself a cup of coffee. It interested her that just having one cup seemed to fulfill a bunch of needs—coffee, whiskey, water—when at home she would use a new one each time. Diane pulled out the guidebook and looked through the events for that day, making some notes. Topping up her cup, she walked out into the camp, heading for the shower. After a few more sips of coffee, she gathered the empty shower bags and filled them, then walked to the camp generators, checked them for gas levels, and topped them off.

Swinging by the kitchen, she collected the burnable trash and deposited it in the burn barrel. Stopping back by the evap pond, she spent some time spreading out the water with the push broom to help it evaporate more quickly. Then she went to the sink to scrub the few pots and pans that had been left soaking overnight. The manual chores felt surprisingly good and straightforward.

Diane looked up and saw Sheba striding toward the large tent structure they had erected the day before. Dressed in metallic booty shorts with a matching barely-there skintight halter top, Sheba stepped into the tent and unrolled a yoga mat on the vinyl sheeting laid on the ground. Diane could see a group of about fifteen people already in the tent, most of them not from Dead Presidents.

"Oh, great," TK said. "Death yoga. Sheba is the best."

"Death yoga?" Diane asked.

"Yep," TK said. "I'll grab the mats and meet you over there."

Diane put her empty cup on the bar and headed over to the class. TK arrived with the mats and laid them out side by side. Diane slipped off her shoes and directed her attention to Sheba, who was standing in front of the class.

"Alright," Sheba began in a powerful voice. "*Namaste*, moth-erfuckers! We begin!"

Diane had taken many yoga classes in her time, and she was familiar with most of the poses. This class was something she had never experienced, a mixture of traditional yoga poses with a martial and challenging direction. Sheba began slowly, both berating and encouraging the participants, raising the intensity. Her harsh, drill sergeant direction pushed them through the challenging routine.

"Get those asses pointed to the sky!" Sheba exclaimed. "Push through the pain. It is weakness leaving your body!"

In the downward dog position, poised on her hands and feet, Diane could feel her arms shake, sweat dripping from her body. Sheba was suddenly in her face, inches away, staring into her eyes.

"You have the strength!" Sheba said. "Hold for three, two, one. And down."

There was a collective sigh from the class participants as they sank to their respective mats.

"As you lie in corpse pose, recover your center. Recover your essence back from where you have left it!" Sheba said, striding around the space. "What have you learned, my friends?"

"That yoga can be tough," a man murmured.

The class tittered, and Sheba took two fast strides and knelt by the man's face. There was a collective pause in the group, like that of children caught in mischief.

"No," Sheba began. "You found out you can be tough. Consent?"

Sheba placed her hand on the man's chest, over his heart.

"Did you die, *mon ami*?" Sheba asked.

The man shook his head.

"Then you are now stronger than you were before," Sheba said as she placed her fingers on the man's forehead.

"All things are possible through faith and discipline," Sheba said, directing her voice to the class. "On your feet."

Sheba walked to the front of the class.

"Thank you for being here and sharing this moment with me. *Namaste*, motherfuckers," Sheba said.

The class replied with their *namastes* as well. Sheba strode to the bar. Diane and TK rolled up their mats and headed over as well. Sheba poured three shots of whiskey and lit a cigarette in a black holder.

"Join me, my friends," Sheba said, handing them each a glass.

Diane blinked at the breakfast whiskey and then took it. Sheba raised her shot.

"May all of the people we love, know that we love them," Sheba said. "May they know that they are worthy of that love. And may love find them all of their days."

Sheba tapped her glass on the bar and downed it. Diane and TK followed suit.

"I'm off. Ta, ladies," Sheba said after she gathered the shot glasses and walked away.

"She is a force of nature," Diane said, watching Sheba stalk through the camp.

"That she is," TK said. "Now grab your book. Let's make a plan that completely won't work out."

Diane picked up the guidebook given to her at the Gate arrival, which felt like an age ago. The book was small and colorful, containing descriptions of activities along with dates, times, and the locations of the camps that were hosting the activities. In her small amount of break time, Diane had been perusing the entries, marking pages for items she found of interest.

"So what's the plan today?" Diane asked.

"Wandering. Did you have anything in mind?" TK said. "There's a pub I want to find as well."

"I got the chores done," Diane said. "I thought we could drop by the Māori camp for the *haka*."

"*Haka*?" TK asked.

"New Zealand Māori dance," Diane said.

"Okay, let's do it," TK said. "And Yester Jester has a show tonight."

"Breakfast burritos?" Twinkle said, walking up to them.

Both women took a proffered tortilla wrap.

"Thank you," Diane said after taking a bite.

Twinkle moved on with her tray.

"There's breakfast solved," TK said, gathering her things. "Take off in ten?"

After filling up her water bottle, Diane stowed some snacks in her bike saddlebags.

"Ready?" TK asked, mounting her bike.

"Let's go," Diane said, pedaling forward.

In only a few minutes of riding, they arrived at the Māori camp. A surprising number of people were milling about in front. Diane and TK parked their bikes and entered the camp, where Diane waved at Tane and Ahora.

"Diane, you've returned," Tane said, leaning forward to greet her with the *hongi*.

Diane greeted Ahora the same way.

"This is my friend TK," Diane said. "I told her about the *haka*."

"Hello, TK," Tane said. "Did Diane tell you about the *hongi* too?"

"Is that what you just did?" TK asked.

"Yes," Tane said. "Do you consent? We share the breath of life. A traditional Māori greeting."

"Yeah," TK said enthusiastically.

Interesting, Diane thought, watching the huge Tane touch foreheads with the comparatively tiny TK. *There is nowhere else in the world I would see something like this.*

TK did the *hongi* with Ahora as well.

"So the cultural exchange is working?" Diane asked Tane.

"It is becoming popular," Tane said. "We had some Rangers stop by and suggest that we move the class, if it gets any bigger, to the Esplanade. So we did it on the Esplanade last night, and now we have twice the number of people learning. It is very gratifying."

"What a beautiful necklace," TK said, peering at Ahora's neck.

Diane looked and saw that Ahora was wearing an intricately carved small green stone around her neck on a leather thong.

"It is a *hei-tiki*," Ahora said. "It has been in my family for six generations."

"Is that jade?" Diane asked, looking at the intricately carved medallion.

"Greenstone," Ahora replied.

"We are ready to begin," Tane said. "Take your places."

Walking to the road, Diane and TK took their places and listened to Tane go through the explanation of the *haka*. There had to be at least two hundred people assembled in the camp and on the road.

With that many people, the noise from the shouted chants was overwhelming. Ahora and Tane, along with their campmates, were spread out, teaching new people. Diane could feel the power of the people together in this experience. It was humbling.

"Thank you, my friends," Tane said at the end of the chant. "From now on, we will be two blocks down, on the Esplanade, at the same times, once in the morning and once at night. Please join us to start your day or your night. *E pai ana!* All is good!"

"Now, where?" TK asked Diane as the group broke up.

Diane pulled out her book and consulted it.

"Well, it's Monday, always a good day to rest after the build," TK said. "I heard of a pub I would like to find."

"Like a bar?"

"Like an honest-to-goodness Irish pub built in a shipping container," TK said. "Sipping a stout beer in the dark AC sounds like a great day."

Diane had to admit that it did sound good.

"I'd like to get going before it gets too hot," Diane said.

"It's supposed to be a scorcher today," TK said, getting up. "We will plan on going by Garrett's too."

The sun was relentless. Diane was glad she had brought a brimmed sun hat, it really made a difference. The city was in full running gear. They passed a raging dance party in full swing. The loud music and blazing sun didn't interest either of them.

TK rolled to a stop at a sprawling building with a road going around it on both sides. Bike racks stretched out on each side, encircling the open-sided structure.

"Center camp," TK explained, putting her bike in a rack and locking it. "Let's get some coffee and shade."

The camp was hectic, with people everywhere lounging on benches, in line for coffee, listening to speakers. A troupe of what appeared to be acrobats were balancing and lifting one another in the center as people watched. As Diane received her coffee and suddenly realized she didn't have any cash on her, TK pulled some out and paid. They found a bench and relaxed, people-watching.

In the various voices around her, Diane could hear different languages being spoken, a lot of them. It reminded her of a bar scene in a sci-fi movie. The shade was welcome after the heat of the sun. They finished their coffees and walked out.

"That's the Information booth over there," TK pointed out.

"What's there?" Diane asked.

"Not completely sure. Never been," TK said. "Maps, general stuff."

"Do you know where the pub is?" Diane asked.

"Not exactly," TK said.

"Want to try Information?"

"Why not?"

Waiting as TK walked up to the Information desk in the open-fronted wooden building, Diane leaned against the wall, watching the flow of traffic.

"Shit!" someone yelled above her. "Look out!"

Diane flinched and looked around. Five feet in front of her, a man dropped to the ground in a parachute, stumbling upon the landing. He quickly caught himself, turned, and promptly gathered his parachute up into a bundle in his arms. He looked directly into Diane's eyes.

"You saw nothing," the man said before sprinting down an alley and out of sight.

TK came out of the building.

"I found it," TK said to Diane, who was looking down the dusty alley. "What's up?"

"Nothing," Diane said. "I saw nothing."

CHAPTER 15

TK and Diane wound their way through the city to the address. A small, dusty shamrock sign by the road read "O'Donnelle Public House." It was located far in the back of the city. The heat was becoming oppressive, and Diane was glad to be off the bike.

There was no sign of a bar. Some empty tents and a shipping container were the only things around. The sign had a small arrow pointing down the narrow space between the shipping container and the back of a large tent.

"I guess down there," TK said.

They walked single file through the small space. The hum of a generator and some machinery whirring could be heard. Reaching the end of the shipping container and turning the corner, they saw a pair of men talking to a speaker mounted on the shipping container. There was only a small space to stand in, with another shipping container opposite them.

"Why won't you let us in?" one of the men asked angrily.

"Because you didn't answer the riddle correctly. Now off with ye, or I'll set the dogs on you," a voice from the speaker growled in an Irish accent.

Grumbling, the two men walked past TK and Diane. TK looked at Diane and shrugged her shoulders, then walked to the speaker box and pushed the button.

"Aye, lasses, hello," the lilting male voice said. "How may I be of service?"

"I heard you serve the coldest stout in town," TK said.

"It is true, if it is true you can convince me."

"I'm game," TK said. "Shoot."

"Shoot, she says. How American," the voice said. "Name a famous Irish poet."

TK cocked her head, then looked at Diane.

"Yeats," Diane said.

"Oh, look who's the smart one," the voice said. "Name a famous Irish hero."

"Cú Chulainn," Diane said.

"Oh, my word, I've not heard that answer in a long time," the voice said.

"How do you know that?" TK asked Diane.

"Some of us studied," Diane replied.

TK stuck her tongue out at her friend.

"What do Irish speakers call Ireland?"

"Éire," TK said, shaking her head at Diane. "I dated an Irish guy."

The sound of a bolt being shot back was heard behind them on the other shipping container. A cleverly hidden door opened a crack.

"Come in before the cool gets out," a voice said.

Diane followed TK through the door into the dark coolness inside. The door closed behind them as their eyes adjusted to the dim light.

This can't be real, Diane thought, looking around.

The room should have been the steel walls of a shipping container. But it was a pub, a tiny pub with dark wooden walls and floor. A gleaming wooden bar with four stools was against one wall, with a couple of small tables and chairs in front of it. Diane looked behind her. The door they had just walked through was wood-paneled on the interior and cleverly made so that the door blended with the paneled walls.

The pub was cold. Dim lighting came from small lamps on the walls and hidden lights behind the bar. A grizzled man sat at the end of the bar, dressed cleanly in slacks and a shirt, a pint glass of dark beer in front of him. The bartender was a smiling man in his sixties, white shirt, black tie, long white apron. Soft Irish music played from hidden speakers. Both men were looking amused as TK and Diane goggled around them.

"What will you be having, then?" the barman asked.

"Two pints, please," TK said, sitting down at the bar.

Diane took a stool beside her. Her brain was still trying to process the pub. It wasn't having a lot of luck. The barman filled two pints two-thirds full and let them rest.

"*Mar, sin cò às a tha thu*," the man sitting at the bar said.

Diane looked at him quizzically.

"He asked where you are from," the barman supplied.

Diane told him.

"Is that Erse? I mean, Irish Gaelic?" TK asked.

"Oh, she's a bright one," the barman said, topping the pints full.

"*Tha fàilte an-còmhnaidh air boireannaich breagha*," The man at the end of the bar said.

"Here you go," the barman said, placing the pints before them on coasters that said "O'Donnelle's Pub" around a shamrock.

"Thank you," TK said, then took a sip. "Oh, that's glorious. I'm TK, and she is Diane."

"Pleasure to meet you, TK, Diane," the barman said. "I am Seamus, and this is Finn."

"Cheers," Diane said, raising her glass.

"*Slàinte*," Finn said, raising his glass.

TK and Diane spent a wonderful afternoon talking and joking with Seamus and Finn. No other patrons were let in, and after a couple of buzzes and no one answering the questions correctly, Finn turned off the buzzer. When the beer rental time was done, Seamus showed them a small door to an actual toilet they could use.

Seamus sang Irish songs, Finn danced with Diane and TK. They did a slow dance, then Finn showed them how to jig. Diane thought she could stay there forever. Time didn't seem to have any meaning in this magic pub. Pint after pint, the four laughed and sang and danced. The world outside the pub had disappeared.

"Well, gentlemen," TK said, slurring, "You've been wonderful hosts. But I think we must be going."

Diane weaved in her seat.

"So soon?" Seamus said.

TK laughed and dug into her backpack. She took out two Dead Presidents medallions, handing one to Seamus and walking to Finn to give him his. TK and Diane hugged Finn and Seamus goodbye, thanking them profusely.

Seamus opened the door by a hidden latch. TK and Diane staggered out of the pub. They made their way, laughing and weaving, back to their bikes. The sun had already set.

"Well, that was a new one," Diane said, unlocking her bike.

TK mounted her own bike and promptly fell over. She lay on the ground laughing, apparently unhurt. Diane walked around, took the bike lock off TK's tire, and helped her up.

"We should probably walk for a bit," Diane said, brushing dust off her friend.

"Let's stay in the back of the city," TK said. "I haven't seen a lot of it this year."

Walking with their bicycles, TK and Diane staggered down the road.

The city was more subdued farther from the playa. RVs, shade structures, and tents were dotted in sparsely filled lots.

"A lot of this is open camping," TK said.

"What does that mean?" Diane asked.

"You get a ticket but aren't with a camp. The Placers put you back here, or you just claim a spot."

"Hi! Want to join us?" A voice came from the shade structure to their left.

TK looked at Diane.

"Why not?" Diane said.

CHAPTER 16

A lantern hung in the structure, revealing a man in his sixties sitting on a camp chair. A woman who had to be in her eighties, with skin so thin it appeared translucent, was sitting in an electric wheelchair. Another elderly woman, wearing a housecoat, her plump, sepia, burnished face reflecting in the lantern light, was sitting in a rocking chair beside her, knitting. A few small tents could be seen close around, but no one appeared to be in them.

"Hello, hello. Sit down, sit down," the woman said excitedly in a strong Southern accent. "Oh, wait, do you hug? I'm supposed to ask that."

TK laughed and bent to give the woman a hug. Diane did as well.

"Easy now, easy now," the woman said, returning the embrace. She felt frail in Diane's arms—her bones were like a bird's—but her hug was strong. "I like that, the hugging. This is Rayleen." She indicated the woman knitting beside her.

Rayleen rocked in her chair, her eyes down, knitting.

"Sit down there," the woman directed. "Paul is not one for hugging."

Diane and TK took a seat.

"You girls hungry?" the woman asked. Then, not waiting for a reply, "Paul, get them a plate, dear, the crawfish étouffée and rice. So many of these skinny girls out here, Rayleen. We got to feed them up."

"Mhmm," Rayleen said, rocking in her chair.

"What's your name?" TK asked the woman as Paul went into the RV.

"Dust Granny," the woman said, laughing. "But I answer to Maybelle."

Paul returned with two heaping paper plates of a brown, steaming mixture over rice. He handed Diane and TK forks and napkins as well. They each took a bite and then looked at each other with wide eyes. It was heavenly.

"You like?" Dust Granny asked, leaning forward with eager eyes.

"Oh my goodness," Diane said, swallowing. "What's in this?"

"Crawfish and goodness," Dust Granny said, leaning back in her chair. "The secret is the roux. Get them a beer, Paul."

"Where are you from?" TK asked, taking another bite, then accepting the beer from Paul. Paul sat back down in silence, watching Maybelle, a bemused expression on his face.

"Thibodaux, Louisiana," Dust Granny said. "Have you all been to Burning Man before?"

"I have," TK said, steadily eating.

"It's my first time," Diane replied.

"Then you're like me," Dust Granny said, clapping her hands. "A Virgin. Lord, I haven't been one of them in a long time."

TK choked on her food, laughing.

"Mhmm," Rayleen said, rocking in her chair.

"What brought you out here, Dust Granny?" Diane asked.

"Call me Maybelle, I like it better. Two boys we met suggested Dust Granny. Takes some getting used to."

"Maybelle."

"I saw an interview on the TV about this place around fifteen years ago. I thought, well, that looks like fun, but I never got around to it. Then one day I was in church, and they had a guest preacher come in, and he started talking about it, getting all worked up, he did. He started saying that it was a pit of sin, with homosexuals and lesbians, drug people, dirty people doing things, terrible things. Shaking his head and tearing up."

"That's why you made the trip?" TK asked, chasing the last of her food around her plate.

"Yes. Well, yes it is," Maybelle said. "He was just so hateful. I didn't buy his tears or his words. Not for one minute. When those preachers get crying, you know the collection plate is coming."

"Mhmm," Rayleen said, continuing her rocking.

Maybelle continued. "So I was there with my friend Rayleen, and I decided I didn't care for that preacher talking hatefully at people he never met. I told him, 'You don't know those people. You been out there?' He didn't like that, me speaking up. His whole manner didn't suit me none."

"Mhmm," Rayleen said, rocking in her chair.

"I know his type. I have seen him looking when he doesn't think nobody else is, thinking everyone is stupid except him, like he's getting away with something. So he just smiled at me with a look like butter wouldn't melt in his mouth. And you know what he said?"

"What?" Diane asked, entranced.

"He said, 'You don't know what you're talking about, Mother Maybelle.' He had information from official sources that bad people doing bad things come out here. And no, he hadn't been, but then again, neither had I. So you know what I said to him?"

"What?" TK asked, leaning forward.

"I said, 'I'm going to go out there and see for myself. I will go out there and find those people. I will feed them and talk to them and tell them about Jesus Christ, my Savior, if they want, and I'll see what there is to see.' Ain't that right, Rayleen?"

"Mhmm," Rayleen said, rocking in her chair.

"And do you know what I found?" Maybelle asked.

"What?" Diane asked.

"People," Maybelle said, taking a sip from her glass. "People, just like at home."

"Mhmm," Rayleen said, rocking in her chair.

"I met me a Chinese man, and a man from Africa, and a couple of young boys from Sweden who helped Paul set up," Maybelle said. "Nice boys, though they smelled like the devil's lettuce, they was just as sweet as they could be. I talked to some Rangers and the Placers and the DPW folks, Department of Public Works. They build the place, you know. I talked to the men driving the water truck, the men in the honey wagon, and two nice women who were in love and getting married. I met a couple of men who had been together for ten years, with three foster kids they adopted. And I fed them, and I talked to them, and all I found was people.

"A man came by," she went on, "and he was upset. He was covered in tattoos, just covered. He looked fierce, didn't he, Rayleen?"

"Mhmm," Rayleen said, rocking in her chair.

"I asked him what was wrong, and he said no one loved him. I told him Jesus loves him and I love him. He sat in that chair with a plate of food and cried like you never seen. I hugged him, and he cried in my arms like no one had ever told him they loved him. I told him to put his tent right there and bring his friends. I told a bunch of them that, and do you know what? They came, and they are about as nice a people as you ever met. We are building ourselves a little village right here. You girls want to camp here?"

"We already have a camp that depends on us, but thank you," TK said.

"Well, if you change your mind or something changes, you come right here. About them people I met, now, some of them are going to have some interesting sunburns, I can tell you that. But they talked to an old woman, and they were kind to me. Two boys who talked to me said they were making the art cars wheelchair accessible for the disabled. Now, why would bad people do that? They are coming by tomorrow evening if it isn't too dusty, to take Rayleen and me for a ride. Isn't that exciting?"

"Mhmm," Rayleen said, rocking in her chair.

Maybelle sat back in her own chair and breathed deeply.

"Whew! I feel a little tired, I think I'll turn in. Thank you, ladies, for stopping by and talking with an old biddy," Maybelle said. "Paul, get them one of those jars of green beans."

"That's not necessary," Diane said. Maybelle waved at her dismissively. Paul gathered their plates and disappeared into the RV. When he returned, he had a Mason jar in his hand. He handed it to TK.

"Now, these are from my garden," Maybelle said. "You take

163

them and think of me when you share them with your friends. Would you pray with me before you go?"

"Sure," Diane said.

Maybelle reached out her hand to Rayleen, who took Paul's, who took TK's, who took Diane's, who completed the circle with Maybelle. They bowed their heads.

"Lord, thank you for letting me meet with these young girls and sharing this precious time. May you watch over them and help them in their adventure here and to find what they are looking for. Amen."

"Mhmm," Rayleen said, sitting back and picking up her knitting.

"Bye," Diane said, leaning down to hug Maybelle.

"You be good, honey, but not too good," Maybelle said in her ear.

TK hugged Maybelle, and they walked to their bikes. They waved as they parted.

"Did that really happen?" Diane said, after they were farther down the road.

"Yep," TK said.

CHAPTER 17

Tuesday, September 1, four days until the Man burns

Diane awoke and fell into her now usual morning routine of coffee, porto, and chores. She was just finishing up taking items to the burn barrel when TK joined her. Then the two of them attended the yoga class.

After wrapping up the class, Diane and TK stowed their things. TK handed her a purple tutu, then slipped on a green one over her own shorts.

"What's this?" Diane asked.

"Tutu Tuesday," TK replied. "Meet you at the bar?"

"Sure." Diane put on her leather hip bag as well as her shemagh, face mask, and goggles, then slipped on the tutu. The assembling of her gear felt so familiar now. Diane grabbed her book and walked to the bar.

"You should throw that out right now," Sequoia said, walking up with Jeremy.

"Why do people keep saying that?" Jeremy asked.

Diane wondered the same thing.

"Well, it's like this," TK explained. "No matter your intentions, there are too many distractions, too many things to do. If you can make even one thing per day that you want to attend, you are doing good. You'll see."

"How about Big Top camp?" Diane asked, looking up from her book. "It's not far, and it starts in an hour."

"I'm down for that," TK said. "You guys want to come?"

"I promised Ollie I would hang with him today," Jeremy said. "Another day, I would, though."

"I'll check it out," Sequoia said. "I have a bar shift tonight, though, so no multiday adventures."

"Untwist your panties, princess," TK said, wryly. "I'll have you back for the ball. Let's get our stuff and meet up in five."

As the group broke up, Diane couldn't help but notice Jeremy looking a bit down. He seemed lost in a moment, all to himself. Approaching him, she touched his arm.

"Everything alright?" Diane asked.

Jeremy smiled but still had an air of sadness.

"Yeah," he said, shrugging his shoulders. "Ollie and I are heading to the Temple for this thing we are going to do. I was having so much fun, it kind of hit me when he reminded me about it last night."

Diane looked into his eyes. She could see something there, something deep down. For a young man, he had gravity and worldliness she wouldn't have expected.

"How about a hug?" Diane asked.

"I'm okay," Jeremy replied.

"It's for me, silly," Diane said, raising her arms.

Jeremy stepped forward, wrapping his arms around her, holding on in a deep embrace.

"Thank you," he said, releasing her and stepping back, smiling again.

"Okay," Diane said. "I'll see you later."

Jeremy nodded his agreement. Diane walked back, gathered her things, and met TK and Sequoia by the bicycles. Mounting up, she glanced back to watch Jeremy walk back to his carport.

"Ready?" TK asked.

Diane followed them into the street.

The number of people out and about was astounding. Moving up and down the dusty lane were bikes, people on foot, and some vehicles.

"Whoop," Sequoia said. "Water truck."

Diane looked up and saw a large truck with a tank on the back. It was slowly driving toward them, spraying water on the road. The spray went a few feet in each direction. The group pulled out of the way to the side.

While they were watching, three women and two men came running after the slow-moving truck, fully nude and laughing. Running into the water spray, they soaped up. They danced as they did, and their movable shower seemed to bring them joy. After thirty yards, they were rinsed off and walked back the way they had come, supposedly cleaner.

"What the hell was that?" Diane asked.

"Not every camp has a shower setup," TK said. "Sometimes you need to get clean. But the water in the tank is supposedly non-potable, so you have to try not to get too much in your mouth."

Diane shook her head at the new absurdity.

They continued down the street. Camps were full of activity. People were on the street, beckoning them in, offering treats, offering spritzes of water to cool off. Diane followed Sequoia's and TK's leads on where to stop and where to pass. They hadn't even gone four blocks yet.

Diane was soaking in all of the new sights around her. She'd been mostly building camp for the past few days, and the city had come fully alive without her being aware of it. Music, laughter, and celebration abounded everywhere. Dusty buildings, dusty tents, dusty façades were all around them. Towers made of scaffolding with platforms spaced at intervals were high above them in different locations. Signs, either hand-painted or professionally printed, abounded in camps about their offerings and activities.

Bars were dispersed around the different camps. They passed a mountain bike obstacle course made of wood. Sequoia swerved in and traversed it. Bike repair shops, tall and billowing tents, RVs and shipping containers, colored cloth, flags, artwork, and sculptures were all around them. Diane noticed that the sightline around her was greatly reduced. Where days before, the ground had been open and multiple streets could be seen, the space had now filled in with people and structures.

TK pulled over to a camp with pop-up shade structures housing multiple clothing racks. Parking and locking her bike, she walked inside. Diane copied her as Sequoia chatted to a guy on the street who was wearing a loincloth and a cowboy hat.

Browsing the clothing, Diane found a cute party skirt and leather halter she thought were her size, along with an elegant fur belt. She saw a small changing room and twitched the curtain aside. Slipping into the items, she walked out and looked into the full-length mirror.

"Nice find," TK said. "Those look good on you."

"They do," Diane said. "I'll have to go back to camp to get my wallet."

"No need," TK said. "These are gifts."

"What do you mean, 'gifts'?" Diane asked.

"Silly," TK said. "You see anyone here? This is a Burner boutique."

Diane looked around. There was no one else in the space.

"You mean take them?" Diane asked. "Isn't that stealing?"

TK laughed. "No, these are gifts from whoever put them out, for anyone to take. There's no stealing when it's free. Trust me."

Diane struggled a little bit with this concept that seemed so foreign.

"But there are good shoes and quality clothing," she said. "Some of these things are really nice."

"Gift, gift, gift," TK said, pointing to various items.

"Oh, wow," Diane said, looking around at the multiple racks of clothing, realizing that someone had hauled all of this, the clothing and equipment, out to the desert just to give it away.

"Get it?" TK said. "Look over here."

Diane followed her friend to the end of the shade structure. A many-armed wire structure decorated with small trinkets stood outside by the road. Cigarettes, condoms, antacids, candy, pendants, and other small items dangled from hooks, clamps, and strings.

"This is a giving tree," TK said. "If you want or need something, then take it. If you have something to gift, then leave it."

"So you need to leave something, like an exchange?" Diane asked.

"No," TK said. "If there are expectations, it's not a gift. This is not a barter system. You'll get it."

"You girls ready after your shopping fix?" Sequoia asked.

"Explaining Gifting," TK said.

"Anything good on the tree?" Sequoia asked.

"Depends on what you need."

"There's a watch," Diane said. "It actually looks nice. Maybe some clothing?"

Sequoia peered at the watch.

"Naw, I'm on playa time," he replied. "And nothing is going to fit me in here."

Diane looked at him. He was around six foot five and at least 250 pounds. She figured he was right. Anyway, she thought he looked very dashing already in his brown kilt and black beret and with various accouterments on his belt.

"Who was the guy?" TK asked as she walked to her bike.

"I got a date for later. He will swing by the bar," Sequoia said.

"Somebody's bear hunting," TK teased.

Diane gathered her clothes and stowed them in her bike's saddlebag. Unlocking the bike and following her bantering friends, she glanced over her shoulder, half expecting some irate shopkeeper to chase them down.

So that's Gifting, Diane mused.

ell, that's a real big top tent," Diane said, locking up her bike in front of the colossal structure.

The trio walked into the giant tent to see people milling around inside. Trapezes and swinging rings dominated the middle area. A nude man was effortlessly swinging from handhold to handhold. The crowd was appreciative and cheered him on. Diane was still getting used to seeing nudity, both male and female. It was less shocking than she would have expected. On the ride over, multiple women had walked and biked by topless, and it had all seemed very accepted and uneventful. She reflected that women must feel very safe and comfortable here to be able to do so.

"Wanna learn how to crack a whip?" a man asked her. He was dressed in a full cowboy outfit, with a cowboy hat, chaps, boots, and jeans, the whole setup. He carried a coiled whip in his hand.

"You bet I do," Diane said.

TK and Diane followed the man to an adjacent area. Sequoia had disappeared into the tent.

The cowboy handed them each a whip and began to demonstrate the technique.

"Let it hang behind you," he said. "Then move your arm forward, allowing the whip to roll out."

Diane watched as the plaited leather rolled out into the air. The thin popper on the end of the braided leather strands straightened at the end of the throw with a small cracking sound.

"Once you have that down," the man said, "you will build to a crack like this."

Flipping the whip behind him, he moved his arm and produced a satisfying crack of the whip.

Diane and TK began to practice as the man moved on to teach another student.

"This is cool," Diane said, practicing with her whip.

TK drew her arm back and rolled the whip out with force. The whip did not crack.

"I think this one is defective," TK said.

"Let's see," the man said, coming back to them. He took the whip from TK and rolled it out, making a loud crack.

Diane moved her arm quickly, copying the man's technique. A satisfying crack sounded. She was smiling as she did it one time after another.

"Looks like you're a natural," the man said, observing her.

"Show-off," TK said, teasing her friend. "I'm gonna find Sequoia. You wanna stay here?"

"Yeah," Diane said. "I'd like to do some more."

TK wandered off into the tent. Diane continued to practice her technique. When TK and Sequoia returned, she was able to crack the whip three times in front of them.

"You ready for the zip line?" Sequoia asked.

"Zip line?" Diane replied, handing the man back his whip and thanking him.

"Yeah," TK said. "Heard it is up, on the Esplanade not far from here."

The three mounted their bikes and threaded their way through the congested street. More and more people were out and about, doing activities, having a drink, or just people-watching. Costumes abounded along with rough-and-dirty Burner outfits.

Bicycles were everywhere, as well as more interesting conveyances. A couple seated in a leather recliner were motoring down the street. Diane could see the woman was driving with a joystick mounted into the arm of the recliner. There was a large beach umbrella mounted on the back, providing shade. They appeared to be having a lot of fun.

Turning onto the Esplanade, Diane was shocked to see the activity out on the broad, dusty expanse. After spending so much time in building the camp, only really going out at night, she found the mass of humanity milling hither and yon to be terrific.

Set against a beautiful sky, the playa spread out as far as the eye could see. A blank, beige, and dusty landscape, swarming with people, sculptures, and other artwork, stretched in every direction. There were fantastical creations of realistic appearance, some of outlandish size. There were huge metal words, easily standing ten feet tall, with people swarming on them. Dance music blared from camps around her.

Turning her view back to the city, Diane saw an honest-to-goodness wooden sailing ship, with masts and rigging, driving down the street. Diane watched as it slowly turned onto the Esplanade and then onto the playa. Other cars, or rather contraptions, were driving down the dusty road as well. It was almost too much to take in. Diane shook her head to clear it.

"It's a lot, huh?" TK said, pulling up beside her.

"Ummm," Diane said. "Yeah, I can't put it into words."

"Wait until tonight," Sequoia said beside her.

"Ready to zip?" TK said. "We will go slow."

"Why don't we park and walk?" Sequoia said. "Then she can take it in a little better."

"Okay," TK said. "Sound good to you, Diane?"

"Sure," Diane replied, stepping off her bike.

"Let's lock them together over there," Sequoia said, indicating an art piece off the road.

"Lock them to the art?" Diane asked, looking at the metal sculpture.

"Absolutely not," Sequoia replied. "Locking them to each other near the art will give us a visual reminder." The three moved their bikes together and looped a lock through each.

Gathering their necessary items, they struck out, paralleling the road. Off the roadway to the left was the city. To the right was the playa. People moved past them, some on bikes, zooming toward their destinations. The earth crunched under their feet until they neared the Esplanade, where it was mostly ground to dust.

"This place is fully underwater in the spring," TK said. "People kayak on it."

Diane found that hard to believe.

The camps on the edge of the playa were an eclectic mix of various offerings. One was obviously a lounge area, sumptuously furnished with couches and carpets. People lounged and chatted under a tent shade structure. Diane noticed a woman walking with a child who could not have been more than four or five years old. The child and mother were both carrying umbrellas as shade against the sun.

"There are kids here?" Diane asked TK.

"Is that a statement or a question?" TK replied.

"Both, I guess."

"Yes," TK said. "People bring their kids. They have a whole section, Kidsville, where the families camp together. It is cordoned off, only families are allowed. They have games and activities, and the kids are watched over. It struck me as odd when I first saw it, but I've never heard of anything bad happening to a kid here."

"I just wouldn't have expected it," Diane said.

"If you look at it," TK said, "the kids get to see the art and spectacle. And we are all put into a childlike state when we are here, of exploring, of having fun without the responsibilities."

The next plot they passed held a large building façade, three stories tall with window cutouts. A large stage dominated the exterior frontage. Nothing was really happening there now.

"They have shows at night there," TK said. Then, pointing ahead, she added, "There's the zip line."

Diane looked to where TK had pointed. It was a tower five stories tall in the distance, with a wire coming down to a smaller platform. The structure was next to a giant skating ramp. To Diane's eyes, it all looked professionally done. Skaters were dropping down the long wooden wall and doing tricks.

"Is it safe?" Diane asked, looking up as they walked closer to the structure.

"Compared to what?" Sequoia replied.

The three stopped at the back of a short line at the base of the tower.

"You guys zipping?" a shirtless man in harem pants and a top hat asked.

"Yep," TK replied.

"Okay." The man pointed to some baskets. "Put your stuff over there and head up."

Placing their items in the designated spot, the trio began to climb steps within the tower, which looked to be made of heavy-duty scaffolding with streamers of fabric. As she climbed, Diane felt trepidation in her stomach. The structure felt secure enough, but she didn't think it had been here even the day before.

Diane looked out at what only days before, when they arrived, had been a sparse landscape. The view was incredible. The streets were well-defined, the city taking shape. The camp spaces were filled with tents, shade structures, and RVs. There were even some other towers dotted about the city. Looking toward the north edge, she could see where the curved crescent of the city ended and the playa began. Rocky, black mountains ringed the desert. To the west, on the edge of the Esplanade, a massive structure was being erected, with five individual towers in front of giant white tents.

To the east, on the playa, Diane could clearly see the Man structure, with the lampposts emanating out from three, six and nine o'clock. Farther out into the white expanse, she saw the Temple. She could make out the dragon sculpture and some other artwork she'd seen. The people below her were tiny figures, fading out to become only specks on the white canvas. The airport was visible far off to the right.

"You ready?" TK asked. "You're after me."

Diane looked up. Sequoia had been harnessed and was being hooked to the zip line by a young woman dressed in fatigues, tank top, and goggles.

"Isn't there a safety brief or something?" Diane asked.

"Don't let go," the woman said to Sequoia, giving him a push.

Sequoia hollered bloody murder as he slipped into the open air, dangling by his harness and his hands as he slid down the thick wire. Diane watched with concern until he slid to the end of the wire and was caught by a crew at the bottom. She could see he was safe and dancing around with his hands in the air.

"Guess it's safe," TK said.

Diane turned to see her friend already harnessed and attached to the wire.

"Slip into the harness," another man said to Diane. She hadn't even realized he was there on the platform with them. A sharp twinge of panic stabbed her stomach, but she stepped into the black, webbed harness. As she did, she heard a shout and looked up. TK had stepped off and slid down the wire, maniacally laughing with joy.

Diane could feel the man buckling and tightening the various straps tightly around her body. She felt a lump in her throat, and her mouth was dry and gummy. Her heart was pounding in her chest, and blood was roaring in her ears.

"Are you ready?" the man asked, snapping her out of her anxious reverie.

Diane took a breath and calmed herself as she blew it out.

"Yes," she said, letting the man guide her to the wire.

The woman hooked her securely to the wire, then placed her hands on the bar. Diane could see TK and Sequoia, safe on the ground, looking up at her. Diane mastered herself and her fear at the moment, but she was still frozen with her hands attached to the handle.

"You sure?" the woman asked her after a moment. "You want this?"

"Yes," Diane said. "I'm sure."

"Don't let go," the woman said, then smacked Diane on the ass.

Diane, jolted from the grip of fear, squeezed the bar tightly as she stepped off into the air. The wind blew by her as she slid, gathering speed, her focus on the lower platform.

It was over before she could register any more fear. Diane was grabbed by the man and woman stationed on the platform. In a moment, they had stripped her from her harness. Shaking with adrenaline, she was quickly surrounded by Sequoia and TK, laughing as they hugged her.

"Well," Sequoia asked, "what do you think?"

"Holy shit, that was fun!" Diane said. "What's next?"

"Guy just said the Temple is opening soon," Sequoia said.

CHAPTER 19

Biking across the playa was hot and dry. Diane's mouth was parched as they pulled up to the Temple and parked and locked their bikes at the low wooden perimeter fence surrounding the site.

The Temple was an ambitious architectural design. Diane didn't know much about architecture, but she knew she hadn't ever seen anything like this. A tall and airy structure, it allowed access at multiple points, and the group entered easily. The Temple looked as if it had just opened and not many people had gotten the word yet. Still, a good number were wandering though the hallways. Multiple nooks led off from the main walkway. The building held a quietness of its own, very different from the rest of the Burn.

Diane touched clean wooden lines, admired the lattice-work above her and appreciated the work it must have taken to build this structure of multiple large circular chambers lining a central hall.

"They're going to burn this?" Diane asked, having trouble believing so much effort would be put into building something to then just destroy it.

"Yeah, on Sunday," Sequoia said in a quiet voice.

Diane could see people bringing items into the building. Pictures, posters, suitcases, and a myriad of other items were arranged or deposited. Many people signed the wooden beams, some apparently writing long passages. TK noticed her gaze and came to stand by her.

"They're bringing their memories," TK said. "Things to remember, people to let go of."

The halls and chambers were mostly empty as they walked through, but Diane did see people in some of the chambers. Some were meditating, some just lying down with their eyes closed.

Diane wandered outside, taking a seat on the wooden fence by the bikes. She watched the people going into and out of the Temple. There was something there she couldn't quite put her finger on.

Reaching into her hip bag, she withdrew a cigarette and the tin for the ashes. She lit up and smoked, trying to wrap her head around what she was seeing. TK and Sequoia walked out of the Temple, spotted her, and joined her.

"Different," Diane said finally, stubbing out her cigarette and closing the top of the tin.

"It takes a couple of times," TK said.

A bellowing shout made them turn their heads. TK and Sequoia looked around for a minute, then wandered over to the source. Diane followed. At one of the entrances to the Temple, a burly man in shorts was lying on the ground, shouting hysterically.

"What's going on?" Diane asked.

"Don't know," Sequoia said, concerned. "Might be having an issue."

"I did it, I did it!" the man shouted, shaking in the dust.

Two Rangers, both petite women, walked over to the man. One stopped to bend over and talk with him, the other kept her distance. To Diane, the man appeared unstable, possibly dangerous. A small crowd had gathered.

"Sequoia," Diane asked, concerned about the Ranger who had approached the man, "is she safe?"

Sequoia said nothing as he observed the scene. Diane didn't know what to think. The two Rangers talked, and one of them used her radio. Diane thought it must be to call the police. She did not think this would turn out well.

The man continued to shout. It appeared to Diane that he was having some sort of mental health crisis. Another young woman Ranger came from the Temple, took a look, assessing the situation, then pulled a water bottle and some sort of snack from her bag. She walked over to the man, and Diane could hear her talking softly to him. The man seemed to calm down. The Ranger gave him the water and food, then sat down next to him, still talking to him. Diane continued to watch as the man finished the water and snack and lay down on the playa. The Ranger put her hand on his shoulder, still talking to him. The whole energy of the scene had deescalated, changing in moments.

"And that," TK said softly, "is a Green Dot in action."

"Green Dot?" Diane asked.

"A Green Dot Ranger," Sequoia said. "They are specially trained to help in situations like this."

"I was sure the police would have to be called," Diane said as she watched the Rangers help the man up and walk him over to some shade, "and that it would be an arrest thing. The man looked unstable."

"That's why we have Rangers," TK said. "So we don't have to use the police. Man, I love this place. It's magic."

"How so?" Diane asked, placing the tin back into her leg bag.

"You'll see. Remember that part about drinking water? This is something that can happen. Too much partying, not enough water or rest, throw in a little stress or mental instability . . . people can lose it," Sequoia said, adding, "Look at that!"

Diane glanced behind them. A huge, swirling tornado of dust was slowly winding its way across the playa. People were shouting and rushing toward it on their bikes.

"Let's go," Sequoia shouted, running to the bikes.

"Go where?" Diane asked.

"There," Sequoia said, taking the lock off the bikes, his face excited.

Diane looked at TK, confused.

"It's kind of one of his things," TK said. "If he doesn't get to chase them, he pouts. If we let him go alone, we will lose him for the rest of the day."

Diane shrugged, pulling on her dust mask and then tightly wrapping her shemagh, keeping an eye on Sequoia as she adjusted her goggles. Jumping onto her bike, she gave chase.

TK and Diane closed the distance, catching up to Sequoia. He went directly at the funnel cloud, which loomed bigger as they approached it. Diane thought it must be two hundred feet high at least, and thirty feet across at the base.

Multiple people on bikes were in front of them, streaming

around them, racing to get to the dust tower. Then Diane saw people disappearing into the swirling mass. Sequoia followed them. Diane and TK drew nearer. They had to swerve to avoid a woman hurtling toward them from the cloud, covered in fine white dust.

Excitement and fear gripped Diane as she first went through the light dust on the edge of the swirling funnel. Then she was enveloped. Her range of sight instantly dropped, and she slowed, suddenly braking when she saw flashing lights almost in front of her. Sequoia was standing, straddling his bike, his blinking lights on, arms outstretched, head back, hair flailing in the wind. TK was nowhere to be seen.

Diane felt a pulse of exhilaration. The dust-driven wind swirled about her, pulling at her clothes, suddenly plucking the shemagh up and away. A grab of her hand missed the cloth as it flew away. Her hair whipped around her head. Diane put her hand over her mask, breathing slowly and shallowly.

Bright light flooded in. The funnel was lifting, disappearing. It had passed them by. Dust covered her goggles. She used her finger to wipe each lens clear. Sequoia was in front of her, arms still outstretched, goggles and face mask on, and completely covered from head to toe in white dust.

Lifting her goggles, Diane could see a few bikes lying on the ground with people in their seats. Apparently there had been a collision.

TK was about ten feet away, holding up her hand in a halting motion. Then Diane noticed TK was holding a camera in her other hand. TK walked toward Diane and Sequoia and then around them, snapping pictures. Sequoia put his arms around Diane's shoulders and pulled her close. Slipping up her goggles, then pulling down her mask, Diane could feel dust falling from her eyebrows and hair.

"Fuck yeah!" Sequoia shouted, running around with his arms in the air. Diane looked at the picture on TK's digital camera. As she'd expected, they were all completely covered in dust.

"That was better than I thought," Diane said.

"Right?" Sequoia said, coming over to crush her in a hug.

"I think I need a drink after that," TK said, washing her mouth out from her water bottle.

"Head back to camp?" Sequoia asked.

"I could use some lunch and shade," Diane said, spotting her shemagh and running over to grab it from the ground.

As they headed back to camp, Diane was astounded at the amount of dust covering their bodies. The hair on her arms was completely frosted with dust. Each hair stood out in stark white contrast against her brown skin.

More surprisingly, she didn't care.

CHAPTER 20

Diane relaxed under the shade of the bar, her feet in a bucket of ice water, a beer in her hand. The camp was so comfortable to be in, she could see why it would be tempting to stay there a lot. The conversation was interesting and free-flowing, laughter coming without effort.

After her shower and the sunset howl, Diane helped prepare dinner. Pepper brought out steaks and grilled them. TK and Sequoia busied themselves with potatoes and green beans. Diane helped Jeremy chop salad vegetables.

"Did you get your thing done?" Diane asked Jeremy.

"Was going to the Temple," Jeremy replied. "We didn't make it."

After polishing off the meal, Diane sat back, sated.

"And tonight?" Diane asked.

Sequoia and TK looked at each other.

"Walking tour," TK said.

"Definitely," Sequoia agreed. "On an art car, you'll find some of the trouble. More on a bike. Walking? You will find *all* of the trouble."

"I'm thinking some dancing," Pepper said, "after the Yester Jester show."

"Oh, right," TK said. "That's a plan, then."

The group dispersed to get ready, Diane choosing leggings, boots, and a frilly top which came to her thighs. Her hip bag and gear in place, she went to the bar to wait.

"Sipping a whiskey," a man beside her said. "Looking so pretty."

Diane regarded the man. He was middle-aged, rail-thin, wearing a sleeveless button-down shirt, rumpled jean shorts, and cowboy boots. A rough face, framed by dusty whiskers and large wooden hoops in his ears, regarded her. He seemed to be a bit drunk, and his eyes didn't look right.

"Are you camping here?" Diane asked.

"No, just passing by," the man said. "Nice to find a place with whiskey and women. Good music too. Devon's the name."

"How many Burns have you been to?" Diane asked.

"Second," Devon replied. "Would you like something that sparkles?"

Diane didn't know what the man was talking about. Something about him did not feel right, and she decided she didn't care for the feeling.

"Nice to meet you, Devon," Diane said. "I think I'll head to the kitchen."

Devon reached out and put his hand on Diane's knee.

"What's your hurry?" Devon asked.

Diane was shocked as the hand gripped more tightly. She was suddenly aware that her back was to the bar and that there was no one else around.

"I don't consent to that," Diane said. "Move your hand, please."

Instead of releasing her, Devon increased the pressure, leaning closer.

"Well, I think . . ." Devon began.

Diane grabbed his thumb and pulled it sharply back.

"Owww," Devon whined, twisting away from her. "Hey, now . . ."

As if by some magic, Diane was surrounded by Pepper, TK, Jeremy, and Sequoia. They were all crowding Devon back from Diane. TK walked right up to Devon and flicked him in one wooden ear loop.

"Think it's time for you to beat feet, pal," Sequoia said. "You ever hear about consent?"

"What are you talking about?" Devon asked, cradling his thumb. "We was just talking."

"Consent, asshole," TK said. Her face was red. "Permission."

Diane could see that Sequoia was fuming, his face set like stone. Sequoia took his index finger and poked Devon in the chest, hard. Diane could hear it thump.

"See, that was me touching you without consent," Sequoia said. "Get it? Or would you like me to squeeze your balls off without consent?"

Devon had had enough. He turned and fast-walked out of the camp and down the road, cradling his hand. Sequoia and TK walked to the edge of the road and then followed him.

Pepper turned to Diane. "You okay?"

"Yeah," Diane said, taking a drink of her whiskey and then setting the cup on the bar. "He's a creep. I've dealt with them before."

"Maybe in the real world," Pepper said, looking at her in concern. "It's not acceptable there, and it's not tolerated here."

Twinkle walked into the bar and up to the group.

"What's up?" Twinkle asked.

Pepper explained what had happened. Twinkle's face changed from concern to seriousness.

"That's not acceptable," Twinkle said. "Sequoia shouldn't have touched him, but I don't blame him. I'm going to call the Rangers. The guy might try that stuff somewhere else."

Twinkle found a black walkie-talkie, and the Rangers were there in ten minutes. They took a description of Devon and wrote it in their notebooks. After radioing in the description, they got a response that Sequoia and TK had followed the man until they'd found other Rangers.

"Will they do something?" Jeremy asked.

"Maybe," Twinkle said. "They will now be on the lookout for the guy, and they will talk to him. If there are complaints, they will probably get law enforcement and either arrest or eject him. It's taken very seriously. You sure you're good?"

"I can handle a creep," Diane replied, nodding.

"That's obvious," Pepper said.

Sequoia and TK returned, walking into the bar.

"The Rangers are taking care of it," TK said, walking up and hugging Diane.

"Alright everybody," Diane said. "I'm good. Let's not let one asshole spoil our night."

The mood lightened as everyone had a drink and relaxed. The group relived the event with every new camper that came to the bar. Everyone was overwhelmingly supportive of Diane.

The incident behind them, Diane, TK, Sequoia, Jeremy, and Pepper set out as a group. All of them walked along for the ten minutes it took to arrive at Yester Jester.

The giant red-and-blue-striped tent had a lighted marquee in front, advertising showtimes. They were thirty minutes early but went in. Finding a seat on one of three five-tiered bleachers, they chatted, waiting for the show.

The bleachers surrounded a seating area on the ground and a three-sided stage. Diane was impressed by the professionalism of the setup. This was not some amateur production, it could have been a traveling Broadway show. The area in the tent was standing room only, with people spilling out the doors. As the lights dimmed and the music started, a woman dressed resplendently in a fantastic white costume came out from the wings.

"Welcome to Yester Jester!" the woman said to a cheering crowd.

The show had a burlesque fantasy theme. First was a juggler tossing flaming bowling pins, followed by a stunning burlesque dancer and a Broadway-style musical dance routine. The finale was a troupe of acrobatic aerialists, women and men climbing and falling on ribbons of silk. The music, lighting, and performances were superb. Diane rose with the rest of the crowd for the standing ovation. The whole theater was rocking with cheers and shouts. The performers came out for multiple bows.

"Thank you, my good people," the emcee announced to the crowd. "Please stay and enjoy dancing and libations."

Diane and TK left their things on the bleachers and filed down to the open area for dancing. The music was unlike anything Diane had heard before. The DJ seemed to be creating beats and loops in the moment. Laughing with delight, dancing with Pepper and TK, she waved at Jeremy to join them. He and Sequoia seemed to be satisfied to sip their drinks and watch. Panting and out of breath, Diane finally had to bow out, breathless, when the fast-paced, funky song stopped. The lights came up.

"Thank you for enjoying our moment," the DJ said over the sound system. "Next show is in thirty minutes, so fuck your Burn! Clear out."

Gathering their things, they streamed out the exit doors and into the chilly night air. They found a bar down the street and shared a drink, discussing the show with the bar proprietors. A lovely couple, serving martinis, the proprietors described the artwork tastefully placed around the tent-enclosed bar.

Moving on, the group found a hot dog cart on a street corner and took their turns in line. Diane was still wrapping her mind around everything being free. Flashing lights beckoned on an otherwise dark street, and the group had a round of Moscow mules in a lounge area illuminated only by neon. The night was alive and pulsing.

Filling their cups again, they walked past a movie screen set up on the edge of a camp, with frumpy couches in the front. No one was around. A black-and-white jazz concert film from what appeared to be the fifties was being projected onto the screen. They flopped on the couches until they were tired of it, then moved on. Their travels had taken them deep into the city.

Sequoia whooped and walked toward a wooden door, the entrance to a giant tent. Walking in, Diane saw a carpeted floor and a sumptuous wooden bar easily forty feet long, complete with a mirrored wooden wall behind it. In front of the bar were club chairs and tables. Down a hallway was a formal dining table.

Men were dressed in finery from another time, women were in gowns last in style a hundred years ago. A man in the scarlet uniform of a British officer was standing and speaking to the seated diners.

Sequoia, TK, and Pepper were already at the bar, talking to the white-uniformed bartender, but Diane hung back. Her brain was vapor locked. This looked like a gentleman's club transported through time. She just couldn't wrap her head around it. Jeremy was at her shoulder, and she could see him gawking as well. It was just too much to take in. Diane turned and walked out of the room through the wooden door to the street, and Jeremy followed.

An art car shaped like a snail rolled by, illuminated from within.

"That was a lot," Jeremy said.

Diane nodded her agreement.

"I think I want to stand here for a bit," Diane said.

"I could do that," Jeremy replied.

"You doing okay so far?" Diane asked.

"It's a big switch," Jeremy said, "from being in control of your environment to not."

"Is that why you came to the Burn?"

"Ollie got me to come here," Jeremy said. "He was tired of me being around the house all the time."

"You didn't go out much?"

"Try not at all," Jeremy replied. "I got out of the army eight months ago, after my last deployment. My injuries and other stuff wrapped it up for me. I have medical disability, so work really isn't a problem right now."

Eventually, TK, Pepper, and Sequoia came out, all smiles.

"A little much?" Pepper asked.

"Unexpected," Jeremy said.

"The looks on your faces were priceless," Sequoia said, laughing.

Smelling food, they found a camp giving away midnight tacos. The food was delicious, and they devoured it walking. Diane figured they were pretty far on the nine o'clock side of the city. At the end of the block, the city ended at the playa, but not at the Esplanade Diane was used to. It was quieter, with fewer lights. Turning to the right, Diane could see a vast structure at least four stories tall. Lights were pulsing out of it, along with a driving bass beat.

"Guess we should go see what the billionaires brought," Pepper said.

They wandered along the edge of the city toward the lights. Diane noticed the camps were getting nicer. At least, they appeared more expensive. Large new RVs were lined end to end, creating a wall. Thick, sturdy tents stretched to the edge of the property line. Diane could not see any way into the camp.

As they walked up to the structure, they saw hundreds of people dancing under a multi-towered structure. Lights hung a hundred feet in the air. A DJ booth was suspended from the ceiling, about fifty feet in the air. People dressed in incredibly elaborate costumes danced amongst dusty people in earth tones and shorts. Controlled flames crawled along the ceiling and walls.

The music was good, Diane had to admit, and loud. Just watching the interplay of humanity was overwhelming. People were shouting and bounding around, losing themselves to the beat, to the moment. Pepper disappeared into the crowd along with Sequoia. TK stood with Jeremy and Diane.

"Unbelievable," Jeremy said, looking with wide eyes.

Multiple booming musical sounds came from the speakers. Diane could see Jeremy tense, his eyes going from wide to focused, searching. Diane reached out and took his hand in hers. The staccato sounds went off again, and Jeremy flinched, his head swiveling.

"Hey, let's go," Diane said, putting her arms around him. "It's okay."

Turning to TK, who was bouncing on her toes, Diane called out, "I'm going to head back."

TK waved at her and danced into the crowd. Diane walked, leading Jeremy away from the noise and lights. As they left the immediate vicinity, the sound dropped. Jeremy's breathing slowed, but he still held her hand. Diane walked with him quietly, not wanting to question him. They turned down a dark street, their lights creating a halo around them in the shadows.

"Thanks," Jeremy said. "I'm good."

Diane did not reply, just kept holding his hand as they walked.

"You can go back if you want," Jeremy said. "Thank you."

"I'm where I want to be," Diane said. "It's a lot to take in."

They walked along in comfortable silence. The night was cool, but they were comfortable in their coats. Diane realized she recognized the lighting around her. They had walked to their own neighborhood. They stopped at the corner of the block. She could see the bar lit up a hundred paces away. Jeremy turned and faced her, dropping her hand.

"Thanks for walking with me."

"My pleasure," Diane said. "I hope you feel better."

"I think I want to walk a bit by myself," Jeremy said.

"Whatever you need," Diane said. "Hug?"

"Yes, please," Jeremy said.

It felt good, holding Jeremy through both their coats.

"Thanks again," Jeremy said, then turned and walked away into the night.

Diane watched him go toward the Esplanade until his lights melded with the city. She felt a little confused and upset that Jeremy wanted to be on his own. Standing in the street, she felt very alone all of a sudden. Even with the whole Burn going on around her, she stood in a little pocket of quiet. It was disconcerting.

She had taken about twenty steps when a telephone rang near her. She looked around. There was a rotary dial telephone on the ground, illuminated by a solar light.

Why not? Diane thought and picked up the receiver.

"Hello?"

"Playa Pies," the voice in the receiver said. "What do you want on it?"

"On what?" Diane asked.

"On your pizza."

"Sausage and pepperoni," Diane replied.

"Got it," the voice said and then was gone.

Diane shrugged, replaced the receiver, and walked until she reached the Dead Presidents bar. Steven was bartending, with one person on a barstool. They were talking and laughing. Diane shrugged off her gear and slipped onto a barstool with her cup out.

"Diane!" Steven said. "Meet my friend Samantha. Samantha, meet our Virgin, Diane."

Diane turned to face the bar and the figure beside her. Samantha was at least six foot four, maybe 240 pounds, broad-shouldered, with masculine features softened by hair in ringlets, a sparkling tiara, and tastefully applied makeup.

She wore a black lace blouse, cut daringly low over prominent breasts on a broad chest. A black leather skirt, flared with slashes of red silk, opened on knee-high black patent leather boots with thick soles. Samantha stood up, and up and up, towering over Diane, brilliant gray eyes smiling at her.

"Hello, Diane," Samantha purred. Her feminine voice was honey poured over thunder. "Do you hug?"

Diane blinked for a moment—while she knew about transgender people, she'd never met one in person—but then she recovered her composure.

"Of course," Diane said, smiling, standing to embrace.

Samantha wrapped long arms around Diane, pulling her close firmly but with grace and gentleness. Diane could smell a heavenly perfume. After a moment, she went to pull back.

"It's okay, honey," Samantha said. "You need more than that."

Diane could feel her shoulders tense involuntarily, then relax. Samantha put her large hand gently on the back of Diane's head. Diane nestled her head against Samantha's ample bosom, resting as she was held securely. It was simply the most amazing hug she had ever experienced in her life. Samantha stroked her hair softly while holding her close. A powerful, almost maternal energy surrounded Diane.

"There you go," Samantha said, her voice rumbling in her chest. "You're okay."

For no reason she could understand, Diane felt emotions rising in her chest, tears coming to her eyes. There was something extremely special about this person. Diane shuddered involuntarily and quietly began to weep. Samantha continued to hold her, stroking her hair while softly humming, the tune rumbling in her chest.

Diane breathed deeply, recovering herself, the emotions passing. Samantha released her, placing her hands on her shoulders, peering into Diane's face with a smile.

"Hi, beautiful," Samantha said, her eyes mesmerizing in their kindness.

Diane smiled back and laughed. Samantha pulled a black lace handkerchief from her bodice and gently wiped Diane's face.

"There we go," Samantha said, tucking the bit of lace back into her dress.

"Thank you," Diane said.

"My work here is done," Samantha said, picking up and draining her cup. "Steven, same time next year?"

Steven came from around the bar and gave Samantha a long hug.

"You know it," Steven said.

"And you," Samantha said, turning and giving Diane a hug. "You have fun. You're only a Virgin once. Find your joy in the moment."

With that, Samantha turned and strolled away, sashaying down the road, lights coming on and twinkling on her coat. Steven and Diane watched until she disappeared into the night. Diane looked at Steven, who smiled back, an amused expression on his face.

"Wow," Diane exclaimed. "What just happened?"

Steven laughed. "A magic moment with one of the most truly incredible persons I have ever met. Can I get you a drink?"

"Yes, please," Diane replied, taking her seat as Steven went behind the bar and poured a measure into her cup. Diane sipped at the smoky whiskey. It was delicious on her tongue, warming as it went down, all smooth and silky with a multitude of undertones and flavors.

"My," Diane said, looking into her cup. "That's something special."

"Private stock," Steven said, placing the bottle into the bar.

"I understand you don't drink," Diane asked. "But you have a private stock of whiskey?"

"I am Mormon," Steven said. "I have never tasted alcohol, smoked a cigarette, or had a cup of coffee."

"Interesting," Diane said. "How did you come to meet Samantha? You guys meet up every year?"

"Yes," Steven said. "How we met is a bit of a story."

"I got whiskey and time," Diane replied, taking another sip of the heavenly liquor.

"Well," Steven said, "I guess we should start at the beginning. I was raised in Utah, in a devout Mormon family. When I was fifteen, I lied about my age and joined the army to go to Vietnam."

Diane raised an eyebrow. "Vietnam? But that would mean you're . . . what?"

Steven laughed. "Older than you think."

Diane pulled out a cigarette. Steven lit it from the lighter hanging from a string over the bar. Diane noticed that Steven's tone and demeanor had changed.

"So I joined up and made it through basic, advanced infantry, and airborne training, and then I was on a plane headed for the jungle with the 101st Airborne. I was eager to do my bit for my country and have an adventure. I got a lot more than I bargained for."

"I guess so," Diane said, taking a drag, then blowing out smoke. "Sixteen is a baby."

"You grow up fast when you have to. I had my seventeenth birthday standing on top of Hamburger Hill," Steven said. "Do you know about that?"

Diane nodded. "I saw a movie and read some articles. Pretty bad."

"Worse than you could imagine," Steven said. "But in all that pain and chaos, I found that I had talents and could keep my head. It opened some doors I wouldn't have expected. So I began a long military career."

Diane finished her whiskey, letting the drops hit her tongue. Steven poured her another measure.

"And Burning Man?" Diane asked.

"Along the way," Steven continued, "I became attached to military intelligence. Participated in very covert things, things that happen all over the world. I was very good at what I did.

"One day I got called into an office with some serious gentlemen who wanted some answers. Precisely, they wanted answers about what a bunch of hippie Satanists were doing out in the desert in Nevada. So they sent me.

"When I arrived, I didn't know what to think. All I could see was a bunch of lunatics running around courting death by inches every day. More enthusiasm than competence. I started doing what I do, gathering information. I had never met anyone in my life like I did at that Burn. I thought I was surrounded by a bunch of unsupervised morons, but I was wrong. Not that there weren't lunatics—they were here too— but what I started to figure out was that we need a place in this country for our 'differents,' our artists and thinkers, to go so they can find the edge and blast over it. And there isn't a better place than the middle of a godforsaken desert in the middle of nowhere. It's out on the edge where you find the truth. We need artists and dreamers and lunatics. Our society cannot be truly free unless we find the edge, and here is the right place for that to happen."

"So what about Samantha?" Diane asked.

"Well, yes," Steven said, sitting on his stool. "Samantha changed me. Changed a lot. One day out here, a dust storm started. Biblical. Couldn't see anything. I was trying to find my tent, and a car came flying out of the dust and clipped me. Threw me a ways. I don't even know if the driver knew they hit anyone.

"So I was lying on the ground, dazed as can be, wondering if after three decades of combat operations I was going to die in the desert, taken out by a deranged driver. And then someone walked up to me. All I could see was two boots standing by my head. Strong hands lifted me up—I was helplessly dazed—and carried me into an RV like a baby.

"That was Samantha. She put me in her bed and took care of me. The dust storm turned into rain, and we were effectively trapped. While we were there, we learned all about each other. I had never met anyone like her, had a whole set of misconceptions and, sorry to say, ignorance about trans people. What I learned in that trailer changed a lot for me."

"Like what?" Diane asked.

"Well, first," Steven said, "people are people. Samantha let herself relax. She let me see her humanity with her kindness. When labels are applied—hippie, gay, conservative—it's separation. Making the person an object, separating a society. In the intelligence field, it's done in other countries as a way of maintaining control of a populace. You create a ruling class by separating people into groups, then separating them further and further, until the country is splintered and control is ensured.

"Samantha made me see the Burn and what it could accomplish by allowing the freedom for exploration. I had judgments about the pierced ones with tattoos all over, about the ones who took drugs. In being forced by injury and rain to stay with someone whom I would not have talked to otherwise, I learned that all of the people out here are just people.

"Samantha is courageous, just getting up every day. For her to live her truth, the courage it must take is incredible. I have been in terrifying situations, seen bravery. Courage is courage. When you see courage and poise and kindness demonstrated to you, in ways you would not expect, it makes you think, can change your mind."

"That's quite a story," Diane replied.

Out on the street, a form emerged from the gloom. The shape became a young man, carrying a box. He walked up to Diane.

"Sausage and pepperoni?" he asked.

"Um . . . yes?"

"Here you go," the man said, handing her the box and walking off into the night.

Diane placed the warm box on the bar and opened it to see a piping hot sausage and pepperoni pizza. She took a slice and bit into the delicious goodness.

This place is weird, Diane thought, taking another bite. *Weird, but good.*

"Hey . . . pizza!" Steven said. "Can I have a slice?"

Diane nodded. Steven grabbed a slice and chewed hungrily.

"How is Hearts of Fire doing?" Diane asked.

"Really well," Steven said, reaching for another slice. "Malcolm has the overnight shift. I took him dinner before I came to bartend. I'll wrap up here around three. I don't mind the late-night shift. I love the random people and conversations that wander out of the night."

Diane finished her slice, drinking from her water bottle, thinking to herself.

"Do you think Malcolm would like some pizza?" Diane asked.

Steven looked at her, raising an eyebrow.

"I don't think he would mind at all," Steven said.

Diane got up and gathered her equipment from around her feet. She filled her water bottle and collected some beers from the cooler. When she returned to the bar, Steven had wrapped a couple of pizza slices in some brown paper. Diane stowed them in the saddlebag of her bike.

The street was dark as she pedaled, turning left to approach the edge of the city instead of the front. People, bikes, and art cars were interspersed randomly. On main arteries leading to the Esplanade, the streets were teeming. She had to be careful to get across. Some blocks were dark and deserted. A few beckoning bars and empty camps with neon sculptures and designs on walls and the ground didn't stop her. Diane pedaled through the dust, amused by how comfortable she felt in this place of sensory overload.

Reaching the edge of the city, she turned on all the lights on both her person and her bike. Pushing off into the darkness, she left the lights of the city behind her. The sound of the music faded.

Deep playa.

As she pedaled into the darkness, the wind ruffling her hair, Diane's thoughts turned to self-doubt.

"What the fuck am I doing . . ." she asked as she pushed the bike on, adding, ". . . again?"

The last time she had ventured out to see Malcolm, she'd been nervous. This time she was calm, devoid of expectations. Now she was just taking a piece of pizza to a hungry artist.

Yeah, right, TK's voice said in her head.

Diane took a gulp of water from her bottle. The dry air certainly sucked the moisture out of the body. The alkaline taste of the dust in her mouth cleared from the warm liquid. Lights and shapes were out in the playa. The Temple was on her left in the distance. Fixing her sight on blinking red lights, she continued. Her tires whispered and crunched on the playa. Her bike chain crunched, too, on each revolution. The dust wasn't bad, though there was a slight breeze.

Diane didn't seem to be getting any closer to the lights. Then she felt her bike slow abruptly, the handlebars feeling mushy, the tires dragging. As she came up off her seat to deliver a powerful push with her foot, something in the bike let loose with a screech and she was unceremoniously dumped onto the ground.

Lying on her side, the wind knocked out of her, Diane struggled to regain her bearings. After a moment, she untangled herself from the bicycle. She did not seem to have any injuries, she was more shaken than hurt. The playa was thick and rough here, deeper than what she had been riding on.

Picking up the bike, she looked out at the red lights she had been aiming toward. They appeared to be moving. Blinking her eyes, she realized it was an art car she had been following, not a fixed point.

Putting down the kickstand, she looked at the chain on the bike's sprocket. It had jumped off and become jammed. Cursing, she fiddled with the chain, which was greasy and encrusted with playa dust. It seemed to be hopelessly jammed, and try as she might, it wouldn't come loose. There was nothing around her. Very far in the distance, she could see the lights of the city.

"Shit," Diane said under her breath, turning her attention back to the chain.

"Problem?" A man's voice, next to her.

Diane jumped, startled. A young man in dark clothing, wearing a glowing necklace, was observing her calmly. The blue glow lit his eyes.

"Chain jumped," Diane said, recovering her composure. "It's stuck."

"Try lifting the seat and working the pedal back and forth," the man said.

Diane did as directed. The chain popped loose and was free.

"It worked," Diane said.

"Now line up the chain on the big gear and roll it slowly forward."

Noting idly that the man's accent seemed Australian, Diane lined up the chain and rolled the bike forward. The chain lined up on the gear correctly.

"Back in business," the man said. "Anything else?"

"I'm a little lost," Diane said.

"Where you headed?"

"Hearts of Fire sculpture," Diane said.

"You're a long way off," the man said.

"Can you point me in the right direction?" Diane asked.

"Sure," the man replied, then pointed. "Head in that direction. See the Temple? Keep it on your right, then look for the blinking red lights."

"Thank you," Diane said gratefully.

"No worries," the man said, then turned and walked into the darkness.

Using the lights of the Temple as a guide, Diane found her way to the sculpture and parked her bike. The small red lights were the only illumination in the quiet dark.

"So you decided to come out, then?" The deep voice, almost at her feet, made her jump.

"I . . . I . . ." Diane stammered in confusion until she finally managed to say, "Want a beer? Pizza?"

"Sure," Malcolm said, standing up.

Diane was blushing, grateful for the darkness. She was very aware of Malcolm's presence as he stood over her, taking the beer from her hand. He opened the can and took a drink.

"Want to sit with me a while?" Malcolm asked, gesturing to the blanket he had been lying on.

"Sure, yeah, great," Diane said, inwardly mortified about her lack of eloquence.

The two took a seat, Malcolm lounging on one arm, observing her between bites of pizza. Diane's eyes had adjusted better to the darkness. She could make out more of his shape, his face, those eyes.

"Couldn't sleep?" Malcolm asked.

"A bit," Diane replied. "You?"

"Kind of reveling in getting it done," Malcolm replied. "It was a long time coming. It's a victory of sorts." His eyes glowed. Something about the moment.

"Being an artist?" Diane asked. "That sort of thing?"

"I guess I can call myself an artist now," Malcolm said, twisting his head, then wincing.

"Does your neck hurt?" Diane asked.

"Everything is sore," Malcolm replied.

"I could—I could rub it if you want," Diane said. "Your neck, I mean."

"That would be a very kind gift," Malcolm said. "Thank you."

Diane took a big gulp from her beer and set it down carefully on the playa. Standing, she moved behind Malcolm where he was sitting cross-legged. She sat down behind him but realized he was too tall for that to work. Coming up to her knees, she placed her hands softly on his broad shoulders.

The heat from his skin was intense. Diane's stomach was fluttering, and she could feel her excitement building as she started to knead the muscles of his neck, her fingers sliding up under his long hair to slowly squeeze with each hand. Malcolm made rumbling noises with each release, the noise deep in his chest.

"Is that okay?" Diane asked.

"Fantastic."

Diane began to work her way down his back, pushing her thumbs around and then under his shoulder blades, searching for and finding knots in the thick muscles. She began to lose herself in the task, working her way into the ridges of muscle along his spine.

"Mercy," he said, laughing, after she had pressed on a particularly stubborn knot.

"Is it still good?"

"Yes," Malcolm replied. "Just want to take a break for a bit."

He turned to face her.

"You could do more to my neck from this angle, maybe," he said.

Diane leaned in. She couldn't reach his neck or back at this angle. She stopped, looking into his eyes, which were sparkling in the moonlight. Their faces were close together.

Diane leaned forward, pressing her mouth to his, feeling his thick beard part to reveal soft, full lips, reveling in the sensuous feeling of his mouth on hers. Malcolm responded, lightly pulling her lower lip into his mouth. Their tongues touched, flicking at each other's lips.

Malcolm's strong hands grasped Diane at her hips, pulling her forward onto his lap, her legs wrapping around his waist. Their kissing intensified, Diane's breathing becoming deeper as she squeezed his body between her thighs. She felt high, the moment, her desire building.

Malcolm ran his hand up underneath her shirt as he nuzzled his face into her neck, suckling on her earlobes, his lips and beard tickling. Diane's fingers were entwined in his thick hair. Feeling her breasts exposed to the night air, Diane guided his face closer, feeling him lightly lick the lower curve of one before sucking the hard nipple into his mouth. The feeling was so overwhelming that Diane began shaking, a small orgasm blindsiding her. She tensed against him in his arms as she shivered.

"Is this okay?" Malcolm asked. "Do you consent to continue?"

Diane felt bewildered. Then, as her head cleared, she looked at him.

"Hell, yes," she said. "Is this okay for you?"

Malcolm nodded.

"Well, I love the idea of the consent and the checking in," Diane said, "but from here on out, just assume I'm into it. If I'm not, I'll let you know. Good?"

"No," Malcolm said, pulling back.

Diane was surprised. Hesitation and excitement were battling in her mind.

"No?" she asked.

"We have to be able to check in," Malcolm said. "You need to communicate consent with me, and I need to be able to communicate and consent with you as needed. Understand?"

"Yes," Diane said. Somehow, this unusual exchange was very sexy. "So does that mean you consent?"

"Yes, please!"

Diane stood, laughing and happy. Pulling the condom from her pocket, she shucked off her leg bag and shorts. Clambering back onto Malcolm's lap, she tore the condom from the wrapper, reached between them under his kilt, and grasped firmly. Diane was not disappointed as she slipped the condom onto his tumescent member. It throbbed as it was sheathed. Malcolm's breathing quickened.

Placing one hand on his shoulder, she used the other to guide him into her, whimpering as the head aligned and penetrated. She shivered as she slowly took him into her body, his girth stretching her. Her sensory receptors going into overload, she grabbed his head again and kissed him deeply as she began to ride him. His strong hands were on her hips, assisting with the rhythmic pulse and dancer's undulation.

Eyes wide, gasping for air, Diane threw back her head, and Malcolm again took his mouth to her breasts. Details became crystalline in her mind as she began to have a series of orgasms, her whole being shuddering as wave after wave of pleasure shook her to her core.

Malcolm slipped his arms under her knees, his hands on her ass cheeks. He stood abruptly, supporting Diane easily. Her hands were tightly clasped around his neck. Slowly, he slid Diane up and down against him, on him. The pace was building. Diane could feel his muscles tighten and writhe under his flesh as he thrusted deep inside her. Diane's orgasm shook through her body yet again in response.

Malcolm suddenly gave three hard thrusts and held himself deep inside her as he shuddered and came, gasping in the starlight. Slowly they sank to the earth and slipped apart as they lay together on the blanket, both panting.

The moments slid to minutes as they lay there in postcoital bliss. Diane finally stirred, sitting up to find her clothing. Malcolm dozed beside her, his breathing even and deep. Dressing, she grasped a blanket and draped it over Malcolm's sleeping form. Leaning close to his face, she gave him a light kiss on the forehead.

"Good night, sweet prince."

Diane walked on weak legs to her bike. Switching on her lights, she took one last look at the art and the artist, then began her journey home.

CHAPTER 21

Wednesday, September 2, three days until the Man burns

Opening her eyes in her tent, Diane was surprised how normal it was becoming not to wake up in a bed. Her dreams had been intense, though she could only recall whispers of them. The coffee on, she took care of nature. It was fairly early in the morning, the dawn had not yet broken. As usual, no one else in the camp was stirring.

The false dawn light was clear as she returned to pour a cup of coffee. On a whim, she climbed to the top of the container and looked around. The city was full, all of the camp spaces had been filled. Diane noticed a tower a few blocks away, at least four stories high.

Climbing down from the container, she grabbed her gear and her phone from the carport and walked down the road to the tower. It was only a few blocks. Standing at the base, she looked up. The camp it stood in was quiet. Circling it, she saw a series of ladders. Diane began to climb, moving up through the tower until she reached the top platform and looked out over the city.

The view was spectacular, the height dizzying. Diane

snapped photos in all directions. She could see the Man, and further out the Temple, glowing in the morning light. There were various other structures and art out on the playa. The mountains ringing the desolate valley were stark and in shadow, the sunlight just clearing the peaks. Lights and neon glows were on the playa from people who had partied through the night. Art cars, some standing, some moving, were dotted about the dusty plain.

How would you ever explain this place to someone who hasn't been? Diane wondered. *How would you explain what the experience is truly like? I'm here, and I can't even begin to understand it. How it came to be, how it keeps going.*

Diane was so glad she had come to this magical place. The break was unlike any she had taken in her adult life. One last look at the wonder that was the Burn, and then she climbed down and walked back to camp.

Diane took care of the chores, then changed clothes for yoga. She was enjoying the easy morning access to the teachers. TK put her mat down beside Diane, causing a puff of dust. She looked tired.

"Late night?" Diane asked, stretching.

"Hmmph," TK said, lying on her back.

The class was taught by a new man, not from Dead Presidents. It went well, and Diane was glad for the exercise and stretching.

"What's on the agenda today?" Diane asked.

"Wanna get your hair washed?" TK asked. "I'll get Sequoia."

"Do I?" Diane replied. "Hell yeah!"

The showers she had taken had been too quick for real hair-washing. She hadn't wanted to waste the water on shampooing and rinsing.

"Let's head out to my friends' camp, then," TK said.

TK, Sequoia, and Diane grabbed their stuff and moved out into the morning sun, soon to arrive at a camp not far away.

"Welcome to Celestial Splash!" a large, handsome man boomed at Diane. "Do you hug? I'm Jupiter, by the way."

"Absolutely!" Diane said and received a warm embrace. "Diane."

"How do you know this scamp?" Jupiter asked Diane, putting his arms around TK.

"Childhood affliction, I'm afraid," Diane replied as Jupiter turned to embrace Sequoia as well. She liked this gregarious man instantly. He was broad-shouldered and burly, his attractive, expressive face framed by impressive sideburns.

"Well, we haven't opened yet. Did you guys eat? Need anything?" Jupiter asked, leading them into the carports.

Walking inside revealed multiple washing stations. Complicated tube work was piped to each station.

"We could fit you in before we open if you like," Jupiter said. "And here is Miss Fancy."

An attractive, smiling woman came up to welcome them. She hugged Sequoia and TK, then turned to Diane.

"Welcome," Miss Fancy said, opening her arms. "Your first year?"

"Yes," Diane said as she embraced the woman. "It's amazing so far."

"Let's get you guys set up," Jupiter said.

Diane and Sequoia were ushered to individual stations. TK, with her braids, went to chat with Jupiter. An incredible experience followed, with Diane's hair being gently washed and rinsed and her scalp massaged by a nice young man named

Sunshine as they talked and laughed together. Diane felt utterly comfortable and grateful for the attention. The last detail was a leave-in hair conditioner. The smell was heavenly, and Diane felt refreshed and relaxed.

They said their goodbyes, Jupiter and Miss Fancy promising to see them all later.

"What next?" Diane asked as they returned to their bikes.

"Well," Sequoia said. "It's about to be the hottest part of the day. I want to head over to the misting tent."

"That sounds perfect," Diane replied. The sunlight was relentless already. She could feel her skin heating up in the hot air.

The Cool Rain camp, a large tent, was situated directly on the Esplanade. The temperature dropped immediately upon entry. The floor was vinyl, decorated with plastic greenery, and resembled a jungle. Diane closed her eyes as fine droplets of water coated her body. Taking a seat in a chair, she leaned back and relaxed. The feeling was heavenly.

"You made it."

Diane opened her eyes to see Garrett, standing near her, smiling. Diane got up and gave him a big hug.

"You did this?" Diane asked.

"Yes," Garrett replied. "With a lot of help."

"It's incredible," Diane said. "Thank you for bringing it."

"My pleasure," Garrett said. "Enjoy yourself. I gotta go run the camp."

They relaxed in the tent for another half hour, the mist soaking in, cooling them off until they headed outside to the bikes.

"Let's take the back way in and see what's around," TK said before she started to pedal.

Diane noticed that the wind was picking up, so she stopped

to raise her dust mask and wrap her freshly washed hair with her shemagh.

"So much for staying clean," Sequoia said, then stopped, staring at something in the city. "Will you look at that?"

Diane followed his gaze. Through the building haze of dust, a defined and coalesced tube was moving through the city.

"Is that a tornado?" Diane asked.

"Dust devil," TK said. "It's coming closer. Let's see which way it goes."

As Diane watched in amazement, the air around them became dustier, harder to see through. The wind began to pluck at her clothing as the spinning tube of dust grew larger and closer. Debris was being sucked up and projected into the air by the powerful weather anomaly.

"Let's get under cover," Sequoia said urgently. "Leave the bikes."

Diane and TK put down the kickstands of their bikes and followed Sequoia under the shade structure at the camp nearest to them. As they watched, the air went from hazy beige to brown. The wind increased in speed and volume. The tornado turned toward them. Slowly moving along across the street, the maelstrom pulled a carport from the ground and launched it high into the air, until it was out of sight from their covered view.

"Shit!" Sequoia said. "What comes up must come down."

Suddenly, the carport slammed down on the street, not ten feet in front of them. As quickly as it had started, the wind suddenly died, the air clearing. A middle-aged man in shorts and shirt and a woman in her thirties walked from the direction of the camp across the street.

"Is everybody okay?" the woman asked.

Diane looked at TK and Sequoia, who were now, again, covered in a patina of dust. She imagined she looked the same. She could see the dust covering on her arms and legs.

"Yeah," Sequoia said. "Looks like it. Is that your carport?"

"Yeah," the woman said. "The tent stakes didn't work."

"Need help?" TK asked.

"If you don't mind," the man replied. "I have a bad back."

TK, Sequoia, and Diane walked to the carport and, with the woman's help, righted the structure. Aside from a bent pole, it was in decent shape. Each person taking a corner pole, they lifted the frame. Two more people passing by grabbed the center poles and helped the group carry the carport to the camp.

"Do you have lag bolts?" TK asked the man after the carport was positioned.

"What are those?" he asked.

"Great big honking screws that go into the ground," Sequoia said. "Stop by our camp and I can hook you up. Three-thirty and E, Dead Presidents. Looks like you could use a drink after this."

The group departed with waves and hugs. As they walked back to where their bikes had fallen to the ground, Diane looked around the camp. Debris was everywhere.

"See why we use the lag bolts?" TK said to Diane.

"Again," Diane said. "this place is intense."

"My vacation could kill you," Sequoia replied.

They made their way down the road and were back to camp in a bit. Pulling up, Diane realized that after the disaster of the tornado, everyone had just gotten back to what they were doing. The air was clear and the sky was blue, just like nothing had happened.

"I'll catch you guys later," Sequoia said, heading back into the carport village.

"Dust cutter?" TK asked Diane, indicating the bar.

"Sure, it must be two o'clock," Diane replied, following her.

They each sipped a whiskey, chatting at the bar, soaking their feet in buckets of ice water. Diane felt her head bobbing, her eyes closing.

"Going to the tent for a bit," Diane said. She wanted a little quiet.

"Okay," TK said. "Remember, we wear white tonight. For the Happy Times Party."

Ducking inside her carport, Diane took off her equipment and shoes and sat in a chair. Closing her eyes, she let her mind wander, napping. Then she heard Sheba's voice just outside.

"*Mon ami*," Sheba said, "may I enter?"

Diane opened her eyes and looked up to see Sheba outside the door of the carport.

"Please," Diane replied.

Sheba walked inside the carport clad in a long blue silk robe, her hair wrapped in a towel.

"Tonight is the party," she said. "We must get you ready!"

"Oh, I'll get a quick shower—"

"No, not for you tonight," Sheba said. "I have a gift for you. Gather your toiletry items and come to my RV."

Diane watched Sheba depart and shrugged her shoulders. Doing as she was bid, she gathered up her things. As she crossed the camp, she could see TK in the kitchen, so she walked in.

"Good nap?" TK asked. "Hungry? Here, have some."

"Starving," Diane said, grabbing the proffered quesadilla.

"Where are you going?"

"Sheba said to come by her RV to get ready."

"Oooh, fancy," TK said. "Don't get spoiled."

"I won't," Diane said. "See you in a bit."

Diane finished the quesadilla in three quick bites. She hadn't realized how hungry she was. Then she walked through the meandering pathway between tents and carports until she got to the large RV Sheba had arrived in. It was white and easily thirty feet long, with windows covered in a reflective material. A sitting area with three chairs and a table was just outside the front door.

There was a doorbell on the front entrance, so Diane pushed it. She heard a chime inside the vehicle. The door swung open, cool air spilling out. A young woman and young man, the pair she had seen arrive with Sheba but had not yet met, walked out. They were both bursting with healthy energy and smiles. They were dressed in matching tight red satin onesie outfits that looked like Santa elf costumes, with curly shoes.

"Hi," the girl said. "Are you Diane? I'm Debbie."

"Hi, Debbie," Diane replied. "Is Sheba here?"

"Yes," the young man said, smiling. "I'm Dale, by the way. Go on in, we will meet later. Leave your shoes on the table."

Slipping out of her sandals and placing them on the table, Diane climbed the steps up into the RV, closing the door behind her. A heavy satin curtain was strung directly behind the driver's and passenger seats.

"Hello," Diane said.

"Hello, hello," Sheba's voice said behind the curtain. "Come in."

Diane stepped through the curtain and stood there, stunned. She had seen the slide-outs from the side of the vehicle, but the space they provided seemed much larger than she would have expected. The room looked about twelve feet across.

Diane thought the place resembled a cross between a Bedouin tent and a gypsy caravan. The interior had no natural light, only cleverly placed indirect lighting. The walls were draped with burgundy silk cloth. The ceiling had a rich blue drapery attached at several points, stretching from one wall to the next.

Yellow crystal bangles and baubles lined the edges of the room where the walls met the ceiling. Multiple thick sheepskins were on most of the floor, and a dark, polished wood floor could be seen in the kitchen area. A large refrigerator was on one wall, while a sink, multiple cabinets, stove, microwave, and coffeepot were on the other. A small humidifier was running in the corner. Soft music, a woman singing in French, played from hidden speakers.

Diane breathed in the cool air, smelling lemonwood and other scents she couldn't identify. Sheba sat a small table, applying eye shadow while looking into a lighted mirror. Her dark blue hair was up in curlers and wrapped with a scarf. A glass of sparkling wine was at her elbow on the table.

"You've arrived," Sheba said. "Prosecco? Set those down on the counter."

"Yes, please," Diane said, accepting the flute of wine. "Thank you."

"Through the door, there is the bathroom and shower. Go ahead and take a hot shower—just a quick one, water is precious—and we will get ready for the evening."

"Oh my God," Diane said. "That is so nice of you. This place, Sheba, it's amazing!"

"Nothing is too good. I give you the gift of self-care. It is critical to making it here," Sheba said, waving her hand dismissively. Then, turning back to her mirror, "Now go refresh yourself. There are a fresh towel and washcloth set aside for you."

Diane picked up her toiletry bag and walked farther into the RV. Sliding a wooden door open, then closing it behind her, she stepped into a room with a sink, a shower, and a closed door to the right. Peeking behind the door, she saw a toilet. Diane undressed and used the bathroom, then brushed her teeth and flossed.

After putting her hair into a ponytail, she opened the shower door. Standing in the shower, she turned the handle. The water was cold, then gloriously hot. The feeling, after lukewarm showers, was ecstatic. Diane found herself gasping at the sensation, reveling in the moment.

Turning off the water, she soaped herself down with the washcloth, noticing that her body seemed leaner and fitter than usual. Switching to her razor, she quickly shaved her legs and did some touchup grooming. Turning on the water again, she applied apricot scrub to the washcloth and deeply cleansed face, neck, and ears.

"Use the robe on the hook," Sheba's voice said through the wall. "Don't put on your soiled clothing."

Diane turned on the water again to rinse off. Suds dissolved on her skin and slid down the drain. She turned to rinse her back, reveling in the hot water and steam. It was with regret that she turned off the water and stood dripping in the shower. Drying herself, she slipped on the robe and went to where Sheba was sitting on the floor atop the sheepskins, rubbing lotion on long legs.

"That was amazing!" Diane exclaimed, coming out and taking a seat.

"It is nothing. You are welcome. Here is a moisturizer to take care of your skin."

Diane took the bottle and squeezed. More came out than she expected, and Sheba reached over and swiped some from her palm. Her touch was silken from the cream.

Diane rubbed the lotion on her arms. Surprisingly for the amount, it was gone quickly, her skin drinking it up. She pumped the bottle again and continued with the other leg. Sheba was running an orangewood stick around her toenails, trimming when necessary.

"You can do your ears," Sheba said, indicating the cotton swabs. "Something about the heat out here will melt the wax in your ears. The astringent will help."

Cleaning her ears, Diane was surprised to find Sheba was right.

Looks like I could grow potatoes, Diane thought, looking at the tip, then completing the other ear.

The mood was light and refreshing. Diane was comfortable just existing in the moment, enjoying the prosecco, the air conditioning, the absence of dust in the luxurious sweet-smelling space. It was calming and soothing. The French singer murmured a light melody.

"You've quite the setup here," Diane said, watching Sheba trim and file her short fingernails.

"There's no need to chat," Sheba said. "Unless you want to. We can just exist together. Use more lotion. Actually, on second thought, I will ask you the most important questions."

Diane felt very comfortable with that answer. Squeezing out

more lotion, she slathered her arms, followed by her face and neck.

"When did you last rest?" Sheba asked.

"Just took a nap."

"Good. When did you last eat?"

"Grabbed a snack on the way over," Diane replied.

"Would you like some fruit?" Sheba asked, raising a bowl of cut melon.

Diane raised her hands, which were covered with lotion. Sheba chose a piece of melon and placed it into Diane's mouth.

"When did you last hydrate?"

"Drank three quarts of water when I woke up."

"You are doing well, then," Sheba said. "Would you mind putting some lotion on my back? I can do yours if you like."

"Of course," Diane said.

Sheba turned her back to Diane, loosening her robe and letting it drop off her shoulders to her elbows. Her shoulders were well defined but not overly muscular. Diane took some lotion and rubbed her hands together, then placed her hands on the long line of Sheba's neck, rubbing down to her shoulders. Her skin was smooth and warm under Diane's touch. Sheba sighed as Diane applied more lotion to her tapered lat muscles.

Diane came to her knees, rubbing more lotion in. She couldn't help but notice Sheba's breasts were exposed. They were large and extremely firm, perfectly formed, with dark areolas and even darker hard nipples. The woman's body was a masterpiece.

Diane was struck by the thought of how attractive Sheba was and felt her own body responding to Sheba's presence. Diane shook her head. She had never been attracted to women, aside from some drunken kissing of girls at parties in a brief exploratory stage of her life.

What the hell is happening? Diane thought, sitting back.

"Wonderful," Sheba said, putting her robe over her shoulders. "Now, you."

Diane sat, flustered by unfamiliar feelings, then turned and slid her robe off her shoulders, letting the front cover her breasts. Sheba's hands were warm as the lotion was rubbed into the middle of her back, then spread around. One hand slid down her spine as the other massaged her neck. Diane groaned at the pleasurable feeling. Sheba was working the muscles in her back, teasing apart knots in the muscles she hadn't known she had.

"You work at a desk?" Sheba asked, coming to her knees.

"Yes, long days," Diane replied, then gasped as Sheba's fingers found a particularly tight spot on her shoulder blade. "Are you a masseuse?"

"I was a massage therapist in another life. We prefer to not be called masseuses."

"Whatever you call it, it's working," Diane replied.

Diane could not put her finger on it—the setting? the lighting? the music?—but she was as relaxed as she had ever been. Sheba finished rubbing her shoulders and sat back. Diane turned to face her. Sheba came up on her knees again and began to take the curlers from her hair one by one, the thick, dark blue tresses dropping down. Diane realized the color matched the robe exactly.

What happened next happened naturally, and if she'd been asked about it later, Diane would not have been able to explain. She felt as if someone else were in her body in that moment. Someone else's hand reached out to stroke Sheba's robe where it lay over her thigh, someone else felt the smooth material. Sheba said nothing, but a small smile played over her red-lined lips. Amusement was in her mascaraed eyes as she reached up with both hands to take the final curlers out of her hair.

This motion caused the silky robe to shift, and Diane watched it slowly part, her fingers trembling on one smooth, muscular thigh. Diane could not tear her eyes away from the blue silk edges of the robe, just holding onto Sheba's breasts.

Diane's eyes found the smooth cleavage valley and tracked it down to the trim, defined six-pack abs. The upper abs stretched and defined, connecting to the lower, longer abs. Diane couldn't stop her eyes moving to Sheba's now-visible labia majora, smooth and beautiful. A small clitoris peeked from between the folds of the labia minora. Lean, muscled thighs led away.

"You are supposed to ask for consent, my dear," Sheba said playfully, finished with the curlers, her hair falling and framing her face.

Diane removed her hand. It was trembling.

"I'm sorry," she stammered, looking up at Sheba. "I don't know what hap—"

Sheba placed her finger softly on Diane's lips, stopping her.

"You may touch me if you like, or not," Sheba said. "But first we must talk."

"Okay," Diane replied breathlessly. Her mind was spinning. The woman was intoxicating.

irst," Sheba said, moving closer, still on her knees. She took Diane's hand and placed it on her stomach. "I consent to you touching me. May I touch you?"

"Yes!" Diane said, louder than she'd meant to.

The two women shared a laugh. Diane stroked Sheba's stomach. It was like silk poured over steel. Sheba put a hand on Diane's chin and raised her face to look into her eyes.

"We are adults and will talk as adults," Sheba said, her blue eyes gazing at and holding Diane. "Before we go forward there are some things we need to discuss, chiefly our STI status. Have you been exposed to or carry any STIs that I should know about? I myself carry HSV-1, the oral form of the virus, though I have never had an outbreak. The overwhelming majority of society carries HSV-1."

Diane's touch lingered on Sheba's stomach. Mesmerized, slowly she reached up, brushing the lower curve of Sheba's right breast with the back of two fingers. Diane traced the rigid nipple, feeling it roll beneath her fingers. Sheba's breath quickened until she pulled Diane's finger slowly away.

"Focus my dear," Sheba laughed and continued. "I had a full

course of STI testing before leaving for the Burn as a matter of healthy choices last week and all were clear, I have not been with anyone sexually for two months before the testing.

I also want you to understand that I will always treat you with kindness and understanding regardless of STI status, you should not be afraid or embarrassed to share with me. I hold this honesty between us sacred and whatever we share will never leave this space. There are many ways for us to be intimate that keep us both safe. I want to give and receive with you all of the information possible so that we both have the agency to decide what is best for each of us physically, spiritually and emotionally.

"No, I have been checked," Diane said, snapped from her daze. "My annual exam was last month and I had all the checks done on a whim. I only have had sex with one person, once, in well, forever it seems. It was last night." Diane cringed a bit.

"Was it the artist?" Sheba asked. "Did you a condom? The whole time?"

"Yes," Diane replied. "The whole time. It was still on him when we finished."

"Then we should be fine," Sheba said, stroking Diane's hand. "Now, have you been with a woman before?"

"No, not really."

"It is no matter," Sheba replied, looking into Diane's eyes. "I consent to be with you, but there is something you must understand. I will be with you once. There will be no more, just one perfect moment. There will be no moving truck in our future. We will share this and remain friends. No jealousy, no hurt feelings, nothing. Do you, as an adult, consent to this?"

Diane considered the questions, never before having had

such a frank and open discussion with an intimate partner. Looking into Sheba's smiling face, taking in her exquisite body, she felt slightly scared, slightly confused, and massively turned on.

"I consent," Diane said, breathlessly.

Sheba sank onto her haunches, sliding her hands to go beneath Diane's robe to reveal and then stroke her breasts. Sheba leaned in, bringing their faces closer. Diane's stomach was quivering as Sheba softly kissed her lips, tracing them with a wet and warm tongue.

Diane lay back, hands finding Sheba's full breasts, gripping and caressing them, pulling Sheba forward. Their lips touched, tongues exploring each other, Sheba's hand cradling the back of Diane's neck. Diane felt Sheba's thigh slip between her own, firmly nestling close to her vagina. She could feel her own wetness.

Silky skin slid against silky skin. Diane felt their breasts touching, their stomachs. She wrapped her arms around Sheba, nuzzling into her neck, suckling on her earlobes. The sensations were overwhelming. The firm body, the incredibly soft sheepskin below, a moan of desire slipping from Sheba's lips.

Diane slid her hands down Sheba's back, gripping her firm buttocks, pulling her body closer, squeezing her thighs around Sheba's and grinding, luxuriating in the feeling of pleasure. Sheba's breath quickened as her own warm wetness pressed against Diane's leg.

Sheba abandoned kissing Diane's neck, throwing back her head and arching, her hair cascading down her back, pressing herself more tightly against Diane's leg. Diane grasped Sheba's waist, pulling herself up to suckle at Sheba's breasts, an exquisite sensation on her lips as she sucked in the nipple and fluttered her tongue against it.

Sheba let loose a deep, ragged breath as she cradled Diane's head, pressing it gently toward the other breast, Diane happily complying, switching back and forth between the two incredible globes. All the while, their legs were intertwined and writhing against one another on the sheepskin rug.

Sheba, eyes blazing with passion, lay Diane's head down and kissed her deeply on the mouth, moving down to kiss and suckle at Diane's breasts, slipping her hips between Diane's thighs. Diane buried her fingers in Sheba's dark blue hair, her nipples aching, vagina sopping wet as she moaned.

Sheba began to kiss lower, brushing her hair and her lips across Diane's stomach before diverting and brushing her lips against Diane's inner thigh.

"I'm checking in," Sheba said, pulling back. "You still consent?"

Diane was confused by the question, then had clarity.

"What? Oh, oh, yes. God, yes!"

"Good."

Sheba's hands lifted Diane's thighs, spreading them. Diane's blood was roaring as blue hair tickled her inner thighs and pubis. Diane didn't know what to do with her hands, running them through the thick sheepskin. Sheba took them and placed them on Diane's own legs. Deftly slipping a small pillow under Diane's tailbone, Sheba bent her head.

Diane could feel soft lips kissing her thigh crease, first one side and then the other. Eyes widening, she took a deep, ragged breath when the tip of Sheba's tongue slowly found and separated her labia minora, her inner lips. The slow travel up was an excruciating, torturous pleasure as the tongue found her clitoris, slowly brushing ever so lightly the taut pleasure center.

Diane could feel her juices flowing from within her. Pulling her legs up, she spread her thighs further, willing Sheba deeper. A small shudder went through her body as her pleasure circuits were overloaded.

Ever so slowly, Sheba licked and grazed with her lips. Diane's breath was mixed between ragged breaths and moans through gritted teeth. She shuddered again as Sheba slipped a finger inside, slowly penetrating, sliding deeper.

Sheba's breath was hot on Diane's clitoris as the finger curled, caressing her G-spot. Waves of desire ran through Diane's body as Sheba's mouth applied a slight suction, her tongue slowly caressing in long up-and-down strokes. A guttural sound escaped from deep in Diane's soul. She couldn't believe such a sound had come from within her.

Without warning, Diane began to violently and ecstatically orgasm, her body shaking. She tried to drop her legs, but Sheba released her from her mouth and held them up with one hand, continuing to pleasure her with strokes to the G-spot.

Diane could hear Sheba's finger moving inside her, the rhythm changing to pulses. The orgasms began coming one after the other until Diane's body seized, then released.

"There you go," Sheba said, her voice husky. "There you go."

Sheba withdrew and now let Diane drop her legs. Lying down beside Diane, Sheba cradled her in strong arms. Diane continued to have shuddering aftershocks as endorphins flooded her body.

"Oh my God," Diane said, holding Sheba close. "Oh my God!"

Sheba leaned in and kissed Diane deeply. Diane responded, arching into her, desperately wanting to give pleasure to this magnificent woman. Breaking the kiss, Diane pulled Sheba up until she straddled Diane's face.

Grasping Sheba's hips, Diane pulled her face into Sheba's vagina. Kissing and licking deeply, she tasted Sheba's sweetness. Diane lapped up the softness, long strokes finding the tight clitoris. Sheba moaned and bucked.

Unbelievable, Diane thought.

Diane lost track of time. It and everything else ceased to exist. She had never released herself so completely so quickly. To passion, to the moment, to everything. She wanted nothing but to bring pleasure to the incredible person she was engaged with. There was no future or past.

Sheba's moans and exclamations made Diane pull harder with her arms, moving her tongue at a furious pace on the clitoris as Sheba came again and again.

"Enough," Sheba panted. "I can't take any more."

Sheba stood up on shaky legs, walked to get the bottle of prosecco, and returned to stand over Diane. Drinking straight from the bottle, Sheba shook her head.

"That was epic," Sheba said, looking down at her. "Are you satisfied?"

Diane lay back and stretched. "Completely."

"Good," Sheba said, sitting beside her, stroking her body from her legs to her neck.

Diane lay back, breathing deeply. She could feel her lopsided grin as Sheba stroked her. Sheba was sitting nude, her blue eyes observing Diane, her blue hair offset by the burgundy walls. The moment lingered, the soft music and their breathing the only sounds. Diane let it fix in her memory. It was different than anything she had experienced. Not knowing how to feel, but more importantly, not caring.

"That was wonderful," Sheba said, then leaned in and kissed Diane deeply. "Thank you for sharing this time and experience with me."

Sheba embraced her, holding her close, then kissed her and stood up.

"Let's get ready for the party," Sheba said.

Diane took a deep breath, then stood.

"Do you have an outfit?" Sheba asked, slipping on a white miniskirt.

"Nothing specific picked out," Diane said.

"Here," Sheba said, picking up and holding a white dress. "I think this will fit you."

Diane took the dress and slipped it on. It hung well on her.

"Thank you," Diane said.

"It is a gift," Sheba said. "It suits you. Now sit."

Diane sat down in the chair indicated. Sheba moved a makeup case, picked up a brush, and dusted Diane's face with it. She then deftly applied lipstick and eyeliner and quickly tousled and arranged Diane's hair with her fingers.

"You are beautiful," Sheba said, observing her face. "But you were before as well."

Diane looked up at Sheba, topless in her skirt. Diane's eyes traveled up her stomach and breasts to her face. Diane took Sheba's hand and looked deeply into her eyes.

"Thank you," Diane said. "For everything. I will treasure this."

Sheba smiled and wiped a tear from her eye.

"Don't make me cry," Sheba said. "I will treasure this as well."

Diane stood, sensing that the moment was ending, but not regretting it. She hugged Sheba, holding her close, then withdrew.

"See you later," Diane said as she gathered her things.

Sheba nodded.

Diane took one more look at Sheba sitting in the reflected light, a beauty surrounded by beautiful things. Then she closed the door of the RV and walked into the camp. Night had fallen, and the solar lights illuminated the winding path between tents and carports. The air was noticeably cooler. Diane felt as if she were floating, still in the grips of what she had just experienced. Music and laughter from the bar was pleasant to her ears. Sound from the city winding up for the night could be heard as well. Slipping into the carport, she deposited her bundle beside her tent. Sitting down, she felt she was smiling from ear to ear.

"Well then," Diane said to the darkness after a few minutes. "That happened."

Standing up, she slipped on her belt with all of its attachments and headed to the bar. Sequoia, bartending in a frilly shirt and white kilt, was laughing and smiling with Pepper. As Diane looked around, she saw everyone was smiling, everyone was happy. In the middle of this harsh, desolate place, cut off from the outside world, working in miserable conditions, people had found happiness.

"Diane!" TK said, walking over to her.

"Hi, you," Diane said, hugging her friend.

"Look at you all dolled up," TK said, admiring her. "Did you have fun?"

"The hot shower was amazing," Diane said. "Best I've felt in a long time. I could use a drink, though."

"You're at the right place," TK said, turning to the bar. "Sequoia, two whiskeys."

Sequoia nodded and indicated two seats where people had just left. TK and Diane sat down and held out their cups to be filled. Diane pulled a pack of cigarettes from a pouch, lit one, and took a long drag.

"Must have been a good shower," TK said, eyeing her friend.

"The best," Diane replied, then downed her drink. "Another."

Sequoia topped her up and moved to take care of other patrons. Diane could feel her friend's eyes on her. She also could not wipe the smile off her own face. TK knew Diane well, although whatever TK might have wanted to ask, she was keeping to herself. Diane did not want to share anything, even with someone as close as TK, not until she'd processed the experience a bit more. She would keep this treasure for now.

"Have you eaten?" TK asked.

"I had a nibble earlier, but I could eat," Diane said, smiling in her mind.

TK again gave her a raised eyebrow, but said nothing except, "Here, I saved you a bowl of pasta Twinkle made."

TK handed her a covered paper bowl. Diane put down her drink and stamped out her cigarette in the ashtray on the bar. She consumed the food, savoring the bites, looking out at the people chatting and laughing in the bar. It was delicious.

Everything was delicious.

Diane ate, drank, and smiled until they left.

Soon the group arrived at the massive structure they had been to on their travels the night before. Almost everyone was dressed in white as they approached. The building was even changing color, with multicolor blooms of light cast upon huge white sheets.

"What is this?" Diane asked.

"It's the Happy Times Party," TK said. "It is put on by a wealthy camp. The camp itself is a pay-to-play. Millionaires, billionaires, celebrities, that sort of thing. I expect they need the security of a central location."

Parking and locking their bikes, the group joined the party. Diane was exhilarated by dancing to the driving beats. She stopped, breathless, to fill her cup from the proffered champagne.

It was an awesome spectacle of lights, flames, music, and a mob of costumed people of all shapes and sizes, dancing and milling around. It was too much to take in all at once. Diane retreated to where they had parked their bikes. The bikes had almost disappeared into the sea of other lighted bikes that seemed to grow exponentially. Diane saw Sequoia was leaning on his bike, talking to a woman. Downing the champagne, she returned to the dance. The music boomed. An hour of dancing, and Diane had had her fill. Finding TK, she waved and walked back to the bikes. The sea of lights had grown around them.

"You good?" Sequoia asked.

"That was great," Diane said, breathlessly.

They were joined by Twinkle and TK.

"I want to go as far out as possible tonight," Twinkle said. "I haven't been to the farthest reach yet."

They unlocked their bikes and, with care, extracted them from the obstacle course of other bikes around them. As a group, they pushed off into the dark of the playa.

It wasn't really dark, though, Diane thought, not like when she had first come here alone. Bikes were everywhere, though not in as much a crush as near the Esplanade. Art cars of all sorts roamed the dark, open plain, light shows of illumination and fires belching into the air. The sound of the party was fading behind them. Diane felt like a kid on an adventure, smiling at the happy banter from the group. The pedaling had become more comfortable over the week, and she thought she must be getting stronger. On and on they rode, the lights from their own bikes flashing around them.

Diane could see the trash fence ahead in the beam from her headlamp. It was an orange plastic barrier about four feet high, stretching off into the dark to the left and the right, with only empty, dusty plain as far as the eye could see beyond it. Following the group to the right, Diane came to a place where the fence came to a corner. They dismounted and stood with their backs to the fence.

The view was incredible. Diane could see the whole face of the city. Lights, lasers, and flames streaked across the horizon— the Man and the Temple were small bits of light that could just barely be picked out. Towers with additional lighting on them stood in various points of the city. Diane knew that she was watching madness, chaos, and noise, coupled with joy and life. A flask of whiskey was passed around the group, and Diane took a swig.

"God, I love this place," Sequoia said to no one in particular.

"You're wrong," TK said. "It's not just a place. Burning Man is a living, breathing thing, alive with the people, the art, the joy and sadness. It is fed by the creativity, the drive to express and experience, to give and receive. We are its children as well as its creators. It lives in each of us, it gives us life as we give it life. We carry a spark of it out, carrying the Burn with us."

They stood in silence, absorbing her words.

Sequoia reached out and hugged TK, and then Twinkle and Diane put their arms around the two.

"I'm sorry," Sequoia said.

"You don't have to be sorry," TK said.

"I'm sorry," Sequoia said again and let out a gigantic fart which vibrated the air around them.

"What the fuck," TK said, laughing, trying but failing to pull away.

"You were going on like Ayn Rand," Sequoia said, laughing. "I've been holding that forever."

The friends laughed hysterically in the night. Then they mounted up, pointing toward the city and its possibilities.

"Where now?" Twinkle asked.

"Wherever," TK replied.

CHAPTER 23

Thursday, September 3, two days until the Man burns

Diane awoke to the smell of bacon cooking and followed her nose from the tent to the kitchen. Pepper had multiple pans of bacon cooking on the gas grills in the kitchen.

"Is it a bacon-themed day?" Diane asked, looking at the piles of already cooked strips.

"No," Pepper replied. "I always pack too much, and it was thawing out. When the Burn starts to end, you will see people cooking and giving away all sorts of food. The non-perishables can be given to DPW. They prefer beer and booze, but the canned goods can go to the local tribes. We make a big difference in their food bank each year. I like to cook breakfast one day of the Burn, and everyone likes bacon at the Burn, even vegetarians."

Diane took a healthy portion of bacon and sliced tomatoes. Slathering a piece of tortilla with mayo, she ate the sandwich slowly, relishing the flavor. Pepper poured her a cup of coffee. Other campers filtered in, partaking in the crispy goodness.

Diane busied herself with the chores. They took half the time they had at first. Soon the generators were gassed, the shower bags filled, the burnables in the barrel, and a MOOP sweep completed.

"There's a gold star Virgin," Sheba said. "Good morning, my friend."

"Are you teaching?" Diane asked, walking with Sheba to the bar area. Her stomach was flipping just from being near her.

"No, just participating," Sheba replied. "Here is the teacher."

TK was walking toward them, her yoga mat under her arm.

"Joining, ladies?" TK asked.

"Be right over," Diane said.

TK walked on to the tent, where a few early morning practitioners were laying out their mats. Diane turned to Sheba, who returned her gaze.

"Are we good this morning?" Sheba asked.

"Thank you," Diane said. "I'm good."

"You always were," Sheba said, leaning forward to give Diane a hug.

Disengaging from the embrace, Diane felt happy, lighter. She was good, and the day awaited. The pair of women joined the group and began a much different, but still challenging, yoga routine from the day before. Diane was impressed at how proficient a teacher her friend had become. Upon completion of the class, she stowed her stuff with TK in the carport.

"There's a talk at center camp on time travel in a few minutes. It might be interesting," Diane said.

"I could use a coffee, and center camp is always interesting to check out," TK said. "Let's do it. We just need to be back in time to see the Schoolhouse burn."

"I thought the burn was on Saturday?" Diane asked as she gathered her things.

"It is," TK said, "but more burns happen throughout the week. An art piece went up last night. The Schoolhouse burns tonight. Other pieces will burn tomorrow, and then the Man on Saturday night. The Temple is on Sunday night, and then it's over."

Following TK down the street, Diane watched people streaming around her. The pure mass of humanity was amazing. She noticed one woman coming off a side street, wearing no top. Another followed the first, and then more topless women on bikes followed. Diane pulled up where TK had stopped.

"Free the nipple!" one of the women yelled.

"It's the 'Free the Nipple' parade," TK said. "I forgot it was today. Want to join?"

Diane considered it. She had never been one to be nude or topless in public, but she had done so many things so far at the Burn that were out of character. The desire for a new experience won out over her fear. The women looked like they were having a blast.

"Why not?" Diane said, pulling off her T-shirt and bra to stow them in her saddlebags. After adjusting her shemagh around her head with her goggles in place, she joined the now-topless TK, both of them blending in with the other riders.

Laughing at the ridiculousness of it, Diane enjoyed being a part of the flow of carefree bare-breasted women. Bystanders along the route clapped and cheered as the women rode by. They were awash in sounds of bike bells and honking horns, added to the cacophony of laughter, yells, and general sounds. Diane felt happy and free, riding a bicycle topless for the first time ever. She enjoyed the feeling of the sunshine and the breeze.

The center camp talk was forgotten as the bike ride went on

throughout the city, then down the Esplanade. The weather so far was clear, no dust storms or winds spoiling the ride. Diane estimated over a thousand women were in the parade of topless freedom.

The parade headed back into the city from the Esplanade, the group pulling up in front of a camp. Diane tried to get close to where TK was. As she balanced on the pedals of her bike, a woman suddenly swerved in front of her.

Diane wasn't sure how it happened. One moment she was maneuvering her bike, the next she went down, hard.

"Son of a bitch," Diane said, lying on the ground, her eyes squeezed in pain.

"Diane!" TK exclaimed.

Many hands lifted the bike off Diane.

"Stop!" a woman shouted. "Her foot is caught."

Diane opened her eyes to see a topless young woman helpfully holding her bike up while an older woman, wearing only a tutu, gently extracted her foot from the wheel.

"Ow, ow, ow," Diane said, reacting to the pain in her ankle.

TK and the older woman crouched over her, looking concerned. Even though she was distracted by pain, seeing herself surrounded by a bevy of topless women struck Diane as incredibly strange.

"Are you okay?" TK asked.

"My ankle, it's hurt," Diane replied.

"I'm an orthopedic surgeon," the older woman said. "Would you like me to look at it?"

Diane nodded, wincing as the woman probed and touched around the ankle. After studying a bit, the woman pulled back her hands.

"It doesn't appear broken. Probably just a sprain," she said. "Can you stand up?"

Several helping hands steadied Diane as she rose. The women around her applauded. She felt embarrassed.

"Put a little weight on it," the woman said, feeling the ankle. Diane did as she was told and was able to put some weight on the ankle, though she winced at the discomfort.

Then a man in khaki Ranger clothing, with a khaki boonie hat, walked up. He had a trim frame and white hair around a deeply tanned face.

"Is everything okay, Mary?" he asked the woman examining Diane's ankle.

"Probably a sprain, Marty," Mary said, and then turned to Diane. "You should go to Medical to make sure."

"I can take her," TK said. "It's not far."

"Do you need transport?" the Ranger asked. "Are you able to make it?"

"Let me get my top," Diane said, feeling embarrassed. "I should be able to get there."

"I'll get it," TK said, taking the item from the saddlebags.

Diane put on her shirt, TK brought her bike over, and Diane leaned against it. TK then got her own bike and slipped on her own shirt.

"You ready to go to Medical?" TK asked. "You're getting the full tour."

CHAPTER 24

Limping down the road, leaning on her bike. Diane gritted her teeth against the dull throbbing pain in her ankle. They were only a few blocks from the medical center. Diane parked and locked her bike, then accepted TK's shoulder to limp into the shade-covered area and took a seat.

"Hi, I'm Noah. What's the issue?" a young man in a logoed shirt asked, a clipboard in his hand.

"Bike accident, ankle injury," TK said.

"Pain?"

"Yeah, it's pretty tender," Diane said.

"Okay," Noah said. "Fill out this form, and I'll get you set up."

"I don't have my insurance card," Diane said to TK as Noah walked over to a large, modern, military-style tent directly behind the shaded waiting area and entered it through a wooden door.

"It's covered under your ticket price," TK replied. "All of it. Unless there's an evacuation. That's why I had you get the medical evacuation insurance. You'll be fine."

Presently, Noah returned, pushing a wheelchair. He loaded Diane into it and directed TK to wait outside while he took

Diane into the tent for treatment. The clinic was well lit, clean, and blessedly cool. Diane was wheeled across the wooden floor to the reception desk, where a woman in medical scrubs smiled at her.

"Bike accident? Ankle?"

"Yes," Diane replied, embarrassed.

"Hi, I'm Joan. We will take care of you," the woman said.

Diane looked around. After the dusty days she had spent on the playa, this clean medical facility seemed surreal. She didn't know what she had expected. A dirty tent with a witch doctor?

Diane was pushed from the reception area to an adjacent room set up as an ER. A few beds and medical devices were around the room. There was one young girl on one of the beds, hooked up to an IV, softly weeping.

"The doctor will be by in a minute," Joan said, parking Diane near a bed. "Would you be more comfortable in the chair? We will probably have to X-ray you in a bit."

"Yes, it's fine," Diane replied. "If I could elevate the leg, that would help."

Joan made an adjustment to the wheelchair, raising a support so Diane could rest her leg, then went about her business. Diane relaxed, noticing how dusty she was in comparison to the clean medical surroundings. The weeping girl on the bed next to her stirred.

"You get in an accident too?" the girl asked.

"Bike crash," Diane replied.

The girl looked very young, maybe twenty years old. She was brunette and thin. One skinny leg was bruised all up its side.

"I fell off of a sign I was climbing on. It said AMOR," the girl said. "Typical."

"Are you okay?"

"It's just—it's just—I didn't know it would be so dirty!" the girl said with a sob.

She began to cry and explain her story. It was an ugly cry, complete with a snot bubble.

"Jared, my boyfriend," she burbled. "He said I would love it here, that it would be something we could share. I said yes, cause he's hot and he's a DJ. He said it would be magical and transformative. But it's not, it's scorching, and you have to work, and the food sucks, and there are weird people everywhere, and—and you can't sleep with music blaring all night.

"Jared told me about it, and I researched it, and there were pretty people having fun, and I thought we would have an RV or something, but no, it's a fucking tent, a dirty tent with all his stuff all over. I haven't had a shower in four days. Why aren't showers provided? I never went camping before. I thought it would be better. And then Jared and I had a fight, he called me a sparkle pony, I don't even know what the fuck that is. So I kicked over three of the water barrels. And now everyone in camp hates me. I have friends at home, they love me, we go to clubs and dinner, so fuck these people.

"And then I wanted a picture like you see on the internet, I climbed on some artwork, and this dirty guy yelled at me to get off his art, and I said no, I want a picture. He said I was a dumb bitch, how could he say that? So I went to the AMOR word and climbed up and tried to do a jump shot selfie. Then I slipped and hit the ground. Fuck this place, I want to go home. No one said you would be dirty all the time."

The girl rolled over on the bed and continued sobbing. Diane raised her eyebrows at the girl's story. It hadn't occurred to Diane how lucky she was to be in a good camp.

"Diane?" a woman asked, approaching. "I'm Dr. Miller."

The doctor had Diane slip off her boot and then probed the ankle with her fingers.

"Doesn't seem broken," Dr. Miller said. "We will X-ray you to make sure it's not a spiral fracture and then get you on your way."

The X-ray went quickly. The ankle wasn't broken. Joan gave Diane a bandage wrap and instructed her to rest for a few days.

"Do you have a brace?" Diane asked.

"No, sorry," the nurse said. "Ask around at your camp. The playa will provide."

"Ummm . . . alright."

"Rest, ice, and elevation," the nurse said. "Take whatever you need for the pain. You should be good in a few weeks."

"Thank you," Diane said as she was wheeled out of Medical to the shaded waiting area. TK was waiting with a tall man wearing a top hat and a kilt.

"You good?" TK asked.

"No break, just a sprain," Diane replied. "Who is this?"

"This is my buddy Diego," TK replied. "He was driving by, so I flagged him down. He is going to give you a ride back to camp. I'll bring your bike."

"How you doing, girl?" Diego asked.

The man was handsome, tall, with long, dark hair. He had a gypsy pirate sort of vibe about him. Diane blushed a little at his kind gaze.

"You ready?" Diego asked.

"Yes," Diane said, getting unsteadily to her feet.

"You mind if I help?" Diego asked.

"No, I would welcome it," Diane said.

Diego stepped forward and lifted her easily in his arms. Carrying her out to the street, he walked up to a fantastic art car. It sat on wheels over which a flat, thick cushioned platform was covered in multicolored furry fabric. Four five-foot flowers were placed around one taller flower in the center of the car. When Diego placed Diane on the cushion in the front of the car, she could see that the flowers were steel frames with fabric stretched over them.

In the front seat of the car was a very pretty young woman. Her hair was done in fabric braids like TK's, and her eyes were expressive and mysterious. She gave Diane a friendly smile.

"Diane, this is Cassandra," Diego said, getting into the sunken driver's seat. "Cassandra, Diane."

"Did you hurt yourself?" Cassandra asked as Diane stretched her leg out in front of her.

"Unfortunately, but I should be fine," Diane said. "Thank you for the ride."

Diane waved to TK, who was riding her own bike and guiding Diane's alongside.

"We will see you at your camp," Diego said to TK, and then started to drive.

Aside from the pain in Diane's ankle, the drive was fun. Though the sun was scorching, the innovative placement of the flowers gave them good shade. Music played through an impressive sound system as Diego steered the car across the playa toward Dead Presidents.

Diane chatted with the couple and once again was struck

by how comfortable she felt with people she had just met. As they drove, she noticed new artwork had gone up, even some honest-to-goodness buildings.

"That's the Schoolhouse," Diego said, pointing to a structure. "It burns tonight. Have you seen a burn yet?"

"No," Diane replied. "I was planning on going tonight, but . . ."

She indicated her ankle.

"Billy is camping with you, right?" Cassandra asked. "Did he bring the Starfish?"

"Yeah, he brought it," Diane said. "He had some trouble about lights or something with the DMV, but I think he got it resolved."

"Fucking DMV," Diego said, shaking his head. "A ton of the art cars out here aren't even inspected. When you build a good one, they still bust your balls. So, you adjusting well to the Burn so far?"

"Pretty much," Diane replied.

"If it ever gets too much, head out to the furthest point in deep playa at night, where the trash fence joins. Look back at everything going on. When I do it and see that seventy thousand people having fun don't care about my problems, I probably shouldn't either."

"Here we are," Cassandra exclaimed as they pulled up to Dead Presidents. "You know, Diane, Robot Head is playing at the trash fence tonight. You should check them out."

"Diego! Cassandra!" Sequoia said, coming up to the car.

"Sequoia!" Cassandra said, jumping down from the car to give the big man a hug.

"What's up, man?" Diego asked, giving him his own hug.

"Did you break our Virgin?" Sequoia asked, noting Diane's foot.

"Just transporting," Cassandra replied.

"Bike accident," Diane explained, moving to the edge of the cushion. "TK is bringing the bikes here now."

"Sounds like a job for whiskey," Sequoia said, lifting Diane in his arms and walking into the bar. He called back to the others, "Join us?"

"Sure, can't say no to that," Cassandra replied.

CHAPTER 25

Y ou just needed to be a princess a little bit," Sequoia said, teasingly. "Your drink, madame."

Sequoia had deposited Diane into a lounge chair in the bar area, where she sat with her foot propped on a small, cushioned stool.

"Pepper!" Sequoia yelled. "Time for you to earn your bread."

A smiling Pepper came walking from the direction of the carports into the bar.

"What are you whining about now?" Pepper asked Sequoia jokingly.

Sequoia pointed to Diane's wrapped foot.

"What did you do, girl?" Pepper asked, coming over. "Who left you unsupervised?"

"Bike accident," Diane said, taking a sip of her whiskey. "Medical did an X-ray. No break, just a sprain."

"Alright, we can deal with that," Pepper said. "Let me get you some ice and a bucket."

"Do you have medical training?" Diane asked.

"Basic," Pepper said and wandered off.

"He's a doctor," Sequoia said from the bar.

Diane thought about it. It was interesting how many people at the Burn had very respectable professions in the real world. Being able to shed the expectations and strictures of their real-world personas must be freeing.

"Here we go," Pepper said, bringing a bucket full of ice water. "Soak as long as you can take it, preferably fifteen to twenty minutes at a time, with the same amount of time in between soaks."

Diane slipped her foot into the icy water, flinching at the cold.

"How's your pain?" Pepper asked, sitting down next to her.

"Better," Diane said, letting her foot soak. "More of a dull throb."

"Normally I would advise acetaminophen," Pepper said, "but I wouldn't want you to drink with that. Here is some aspirin. It will help with the swelling some."

"Thanks," Diane said, taking the tablets.

"Keep drinking water as well," Pepper said. "Let me know if the pain or swelling increase. I'll look for our resident witch doctor, she may be able to help."

Diane relaxed, sipping her whiskey and soaking her foot. The heat of the day had increased dramatically. Still, it was pleasant under the shade of the bar, especially with her foot in the icy bath in the bucket. She sat back and closed her eyes, listening to the banter at the bar between Diego, Cassandra, and Sequoia.

"You made it back alright?" TK said, walking up to her.

Diane opened her eyes. She must have dozed off. Diego, Cassandra, and the flower car were gone. Slipping her foot out of the ice water and resting it on the stool, she sat up.

"No problems," Diane replied. "I heard Robot Head was playing by the trash fence tonight. I love them! Could we go?"

TK laughed at her. Diane looked back quizzically.

"It's a running joke," TK explained. "Someone famous is always supposed to be playing in deep playa somewhere."

"Well, is there a plan for tonight?" Diane asked. "I'm kind of immobile for a bit."

"All good," TK replied. "At least you should be able to give hand jobs."

"What?" Diane asked, choking on her drink.

"Hand jobs," TK said, grinning. "Twinkle has an event today giving hand jobs for whoever wants them."

Diane fixed her with a wary look.

"No, it's not what you think," TK said. "You'll see. I'm going to make lunch. Chicken and salad sound good?"

"That works for me," Diane said.

TK went back toward the kitchen, passing Jeremy.

"Hey, stranger," Jeremy said to Diane. "What happened?"

Diane explained the bike accident.

"You need anything?" Jeremy asked.

"I could use a top-up," Diane said, indicating her glass.

Jeremy went to the bar to fill the glass. Returning it to Diane, he sat down.

"How has your Burn been?" Diane asked, taking a sip.

Jeremy sat back, shaking his head. He smiled. "Unbelievable. You could talk about this place for a year to someone and never be able to communicate it to them. I helped with an art project, helped build a camp. Made arts and crafts. I've been fed I don't know how many times, all over the place. And the kindness, it's been . . ."

"Overwhelming," Diane offered.

"Yeah," Jeremy said, looking at her. "You never know when something is going to happen, something amazing. Everyone is so cool here."

"Not everyone," Diane said. "I met a sparkle pony today who wasn't happy at all. We got very lucky where we camped."

"Agreed," Jeremy said. "Oh, and I went to this place where everyone gets nude, outdoors in a line, then gets sprayed down with soap and rinsed. So refreshing but different, and men and women together. There wasn't any sex vibe, just a light-hearted, party one."

"I had my hair washed," Diane said. "So very nice."

"Here you go," TK said, placing a bowl in front of Diane.

Diane dug into the salad. The fresh vegetables were delicious.

"Are you the wounded camper?" Twinkle asked, coming over.

"Guilty," Diane said.

"I do acupuncture and Reiki," Twinkle said. "Do you know about them?"

"Acupuncture I've heard of," Diane said, chewing. "What's Reiki?"

"Basically, energy work," Twinkle said. "If you're comfortable with it, I'll get my things."

"Sure," Diane said. "Why not?"

"Soak your foot," Twinkle said. "Get it good and numb. I'll be back."

Diane did as she was told and finished her salad. Twinkle came back with a basket in her hands and sat down at Diane's foot, with Pepper trailing behind. Pepper carried a pair of crutches and an ankle brace.

"The playa provides," Pepper said, placing his items on a table. "Is it time for the witchcraft?"

"He teases," Twinkle said. "Last year his back locked up and he refused to take any medication. My needles and Reiki had him up in a few hours."

"Can't explain it," Pepper said, taking a seat. "But it worked."

Twinkle unrolled a bundle, took out a couple of small bottles, and placed them on a stool. With the group watching, Twinkle took Diane's foot from the bucket and put it on a clean towel. The ankle was puffy and slightly discolored. Twinkle cleaned it with fluid from one of the bottles. She then selected a couple of very small needles and a thin metal tube. She cleansed the needles and her hands, then turned her attention to Diane's ankle again.

"Do you have any needle triggers?" Twinkle asked as she slipped a needle into the metal tube.

"Not a huge fan, but I don't faint or anything," Diane said.

"Here is the Xiaojie pressure point for your right ankle," Twinkle said, taking Diane's left hand in her own. Twinkle cleaned Diane's hand, then massaged the point in the web between her thumb and forefinger.

Picking up a needle, she lined it up on Diane's skin and gave it a couple of taps. Diane jumped a little at first, then relaxed. The tiny needle stuck out from her hand but didn't hurt.

Moving back to Diane's foot, Twinkle tapped five more needles into the flesh. Two in the top of the foot, one in the ankle, one in the sole, one in the calf. A group surrounding them stared, fascinated.

"Does it hurt?" TK asked, looking at Diane's leg.

"No," Diane replied. "It feels fine."

Resting Diane's heel on the towel-covered stool, Twinkle began rubbing her hands together swiftly and breathing deeply. Twinkle's hands felt hot near Diane's skin as she moved them over and around the ankle.

"Where did you learn this?" Jeremy asked.

"Tibet," Twinkle said, continuing to breathe deeply. "Ten years."

Diane relaxed back into her seat, she could feel more heat and something else in her ankle and leg. Energy? Was that what she felt?

"You should be good for a while," Twinkle said. "Let the needles stay in for a few more minutes. Who wants to help set up for hand jobs?"

Jeremy and TK both raised their hands and followed Twinkle to begin gathering chairs and tables and placing them into the yoga tent.

"My back injury should have taken weeks to heal," Pepper said. "I know the timeline precisely for skeletomuscular injuries, even for a person who heals quickly. I thought I would have to leave the Burn mid-week, so I figured, why not try it?"

"Did it help?" Diane asked.

"I was up and moving the next day," Pepper said. "It was amazing. In three days, I was terrific. Another four and it was like nothing had ever happened. It made me start to take alternative medicine seriously. Started a whole new path of research for me."

"Let me get those out," Twinkle said, coming over to them and sitting down. She quickly removed the needles from Diane and put them away. Diane was not sure, but she believed the swelling had already gone down some.

"Leave off the wrap for a bit and use the ice," Twinkle said. "Then we can move you over for hand jobs. Your hand isn't hurt."

"I'd love to," Diane said and started to rise. Twinkle stopped her with a hand on her shoulder.

"Don't put any weight on it yet," Twinkle said. "We got you."

Twinkle rounded up Jeremy and Sequoia, who carried Diane bodily in her chair over to a table in the yoga tent. The table had lotion and bowls that TK was filling with water and a drop of vinegar.

"So, a hand job is the care of the hand and then a lotion massage," Twinkle explained. A woman was at her shoulder. Twinkle directed her to sit across from Diane.

"You soak their hands in the water, then clean the nails with these orange sticks," Twinkle said, demonstrating. "Once that's done, you apply lotion."

Diane spent the rest of the afternoon taking care of people's hands, chatting with a wide variety of people and personalities. Everyone was very grateful and friendly. Diane alternated soaking her foot in the bucket of ice water throughout the experience.

Wrapping up the event, the campers began gathering up the materials and putting away the table and chairs. Diane's ankle was feeling much better.

"Would you like to try and walk?" Twinkle asked, coming over to her.

"Sure."

Twinkle brought over the ankle brace, crutches, and a sock. Slipping on the sock, then the brace, she held the crutches as Diane stood. Diane tested her weight on her foot and found that, while it was tender, she could manage with the crutches.

"Take it easy for a while," Twinkle said. "When you go to the porto, wrap your foot in a plastic bag. Same for the shower."

"Will do," Diane said, maneuvering to the bar. "Thank you."

The Starfish car rolled up with Billy and Sheba on board.

"Diane?" Sheba said, getting off the car. "What happened?"

"Bike accident," Diane said. "Twinkle took good care of me."

"You feel alright?" Sheba asked, her face concerned.

"So far, so good," Diane replied.

"If you're feeling up to it, we can see the Schoolhouse burn tonight," Billy said, coming over to them.

"I would like that," Diane said. "What time?"

"Mostly playa time, but it's scheduled for eight," Billy replied. "If we want a spot, we should get there by seven."

"I'll be ready," Diane said.

Sheba and Diane sat down.

"You are having all of the adventures," Sheba said.

"Looks like," Diane said.

"Can I get you anything?" Sheba asked.

"More water and whiskey would be good," Diane said.

Sheba grabbed and filled a couple of glasses from the bar and topped up Diane's water bottle. Then she sat back down. The two women chatted and laughed for the next hour. Sheba fed Diane dinner from a vacuum-sealed bag she heated up in boiling water in a pot.

"This is delicious," Diane said.

"Throughout the year, I make a little extra at some meals, then vacuum-seal it and freeze it. That way, I have plenty of good food when I come out."

Diane enjoyed the rest of the meal. As she looked at Sheba, some part of her thought she should feel romantic interest or, well, something. It just wasn't there, other than a comfortable feeling of friendship. Diane suspected that anyone who wanted to pursue a long-term relationship with Sheba would have to be able to grab the wind.

"Now, my love," Sheba said. "I will get cleaned up for this evening. Do you need anything else?"

"I'm good," Diane said, standing.

The two women shared a hug, Sheba gathered the utensils and went back into the camp. Diane hobbled to her carport, where she found TK getting ready to shower.

"Shower?" TK asked.

"Yeah," Diane said. "If you could help a bit, I can do it."

"No problem," TK said.

Diane undressed and put on a light robe. With TK's help, she was able to get to the shower. While a bit uncomfortable with the plastic-wrapped brace on, she was able to balance and get clean. *Each shower in this place is better than the last*, she thought.

While the water rinsed her off, the sun must have begun to set. Howling sounded around her, and she joined in. Diane felt an immense gratitude at being cared for by her friends.

CHAPTER 26

The ankle made getting dressed a challenge after the shower, but with TK's help, Diane managed.

"I'll get all the things," TK said. "Meet you in the bar."

Diane hobbled, getting used to the crutches. Sitting at the bar, she sipped water from her bottle and accepted a drink from Steven.

"Enjoying your stay?" Steven asked her, pouring a dram of whiskey into her cup.

"So far so good," Diane said, propping her crutches against the bar.

"Twinkle work on you?" Steven asked. "She fixed up my shoulder last year."

"Yes," Diane said. "It seems to be helping."

Jeremy and Sequoia sat down beside her. Diane realized that a naked elderly man was standing five feet from her, talking to another man in a tiger onesie. She hadn't even registered it.

TK walked past, taking their things to the Starfish. Diane noticed that there were a lot of people in the bar, both from their camp and others. Night had fallen, and a fire was burning in the burn barrel. The bar was well lit, music playing, everyone talking and having a good time.

"Let's saddle up!" Billy said.

Diane made it to the art car, noticing that quite a few people were getting on their bicycles. In moments, a parade of people were biking behind the Starfish. Laughing and joking, they made a mob, turning down the street toward the Esplanade. The city around them was in full stride, the party ramping up. Overhead, Diane could see powerful green lasers reaching from the back of the city to deep playa. People filled the street, streaming toward the playa.

Reaching the final street, Billy steered the car left. As they drove along the Esplanade, Diane could see even more people out on the playa zipping around. Art cars were driving, lit up, in the darkness. Music boomed from art cars, bars, and even individuals with speakers mounted on their bikes. Diane could see the Man lit up, people under it.

A concert was going on at one of the camps along the road. Hundreds of people were gathered, watching others dance onstage under spotlights. Another camp had a long line of people being served soup from a giant kettle. Going farther down the road than she had been before, Diane could see a substantial domed cage structure with the word BATTLEDOME in flames on top. People were sitting on the rails, multiple levels up. Diane could see people lined up to get in. She glimpsed someone swinging on something inside.

"What's that?" Diane asked TK, pointing at the structure.

"Battledome," TK said. "Put on by Chaotic Good Cabal. My friend camps with them. They're awesome. You fight each other on bungees, like in the movie."

"Really?" Diane asked, trying to see more as they passed. "Is it dangerous?"

"Very," Billy said.

"It's pretty intense. We will check it out later," TK said.

Soon they passed people skating at a roller rink set up in front of a camp.

"Oh, that looks like fun," Diane said. "Maybe next year I'll bring my skates."

Sheba turned to her. "Next year, huh? And they have skates for you there."

"Maybe," Diane laughed.

Billy steered the car off into the playa. Diane could see the Schoolhouse lit up. A crowd was gathering.

Pulling as close as he could, Billy parked the Starfish in a sea of bicycles.

"I think I'll stay here," Billy said.

"I'll keep you company," Sheba said, settling in.

Diane and TK joined with the rest of their group, who parked around the Starfish. They weaved their way through the bikes and art cars ringing the perimeter, music and lights blaring from many. One car they passed, a postapocalyptic escape vehicle, let loose a giant blast of flame over their heads as they went by.

"Shit!" TK said. "Watch it!"

The woman standing on the back of the truck did not even acknowledge them as she let loose another blast of fire, uncomfortably close. Diane and TK hurried past, finding a spot on the ground with their friends and campmates. The crowd ended abruptly, with a khaki-clad Ranger standing alone in front of them. Other Rangers were spread out at intervals in front of the crowd.

"They're the outer perimeter watch," Sequoia said to Jeremy

and Diane. "They keep people back. There are inner perimeter Rangers called Sandmen who stop anyone crazy enough to run past the outer perimeter toward the fire."

"People run into the fire?" Jeremy asked.

"It's happened," TK said.

"So tell me, why are they burning this?" Diane asked.

"It's built to burn," Sequoia said. "The inside was a school-house, with little wooden desks, a chalkboard. An old-time schoolhouse. It was an interactive art piece, built for one time only. There are a few more art pieces, different kinds, that will be burnt. The flames symbolize endings, rebirth. A clearing away of the old to make way for the new. Also, it's fun to light shit on fire."

They arrived just in time. Soon after finding their seats, they saw flames starting to lick the sides of the building. An explosion suddenly bloomed from inside the structure. Fireworks popped off again and again, arching into the sky.

The crowd oohed and aahed appreciatively, applauding when the structure was fully engulfed in flames. As Diane watched, small dust devils began spinning, one after the other, from the schoolhouse. The small, thirty-foot-high tornadoes slowly started to travel across the dirt, lit up from behind by the fire.

After about fifteen minutes, the entire structure collapsed on itself. People clapped and cheered. The crowd started getting up and dispersing. With Sequoia and Jeremy flanking her, Diane made her way on her crutches back to the Starfish through the mass of people.

"Where to now?" TK asked Billy.

"Thought we would find the Aztec Princess," Billy said.

"Great, let's go!" TK said.

After waiting for the bikes to clear around them, Billy pulled out onto the playa, weaving around art and bicycles. Diane noticed more flames, more lasers. Even a giant buzzing Tesla coil was reaching bolts of electricity out into the sky. It was pure chaos everywhere you looked.

"There it is," Sheba said, pointing.

Billy steered to where she was pointing. Diane could see a large building with a massive number of flickering and glowing lights. Flames kept popping off on top of it. Art cars and bikes were dwarfed by it. Music was booming, a techno dance beat.

Pulling up, Diane realized what she had thought was a building was, in fact, a giant mobile stage, easily three stories tall and very long. The thing must have been mounted on the bed of a semi, but she couldn't see one.

Sheba and TK jumped off the Starfish, heading toward the dance area. Sequoia, Pepper, Twinkle, and Jeremy followed them. Diane had to resign herself to sitting on the edge of the Starfish, having a beer with the quiet Billy. He seemed content to people-watch without saying much. As her friends danced to a dirty, thumping beat, Diane took in all the sights and sounds. She looked back toward the city. There was all manner of activity around her, an overwhelming sense of freedom of motion unrestrained.

A groan from the crowd made her look back. The huge stage was pulling away. People were running for their bikes and cars. The group came back to the Starfish, where Twinkle said goodbye and went off into the night with a friend. Sequoia wandered off on foot. Everyone else agreed a bathroom break was in order.

Billy steered toward a distant blue light. Arriving at the line

263

of dark portos, Diane finagled her way in with the crutches and was able to relieve herself with a minimum of fuss. As if the day hadn't brought enough of an encumbrance, she discovered to her dismay that her period had started more than two weeks early. Diane asked Billy to take her back to camp.

The Starfish dropped her and headed back out. Having taken care of what was needed, she sat at the bar. Pepper was bartending. Old, scratchy blues music was playing on the speakers.

"Whiskey, sir," Diane said, placing her cup on the bar. "Is this your event?"

"Starlight Blues," Pepper said. "I love the old blues musicians. Blues history is a passion of mine."

"Where's everybody at?" Diane asked, taking a taste.

"It got left out of the book," Pepper said. "No one knows about it."

"Bummer," Diane said.

"Yeah. I got it in on time, even though the event registry is only open for a short while, but it didn't make it in. You go through so much trouble to put something together, then it doesn't get out. The book used to be better, it had all the events. This year it has a bunch of useless bullshit. People want to *do* things, not look at pretty pictures. They should just have a map, the principles, and then the events."

"So what's it about?" Diane asked.

"My event?" Pepper asked. "The deep appreciation of the old blues and its influence on modern music. Robert Johnson for Delta blues, Blind Boy Fuller for Piedmont blues, Big Bill Broonzy for urban/country blues, and Frank Stokes for Memphis blues. There are a lot more, but we only have so much time."

"Let me hear it," Diane said. "How many do you need for the event?"

"You're enough," Pepper said. "And here come my DPW friends."

Diane turned at rowdy talk behind her. An art car had pulled up and disgorged a motley band of people.

"Pepper!" a tall blonde woman yelled to the bar.

Pepper came from behind the bar and hugged her and her friends.

"Diane," Pepper said, bringing the woman over, "meet Galactica. She runs a DPW crew."

"Hi," Diane said, standing up. "Hug?"

"No," Galactica said, putting up her hand. "DPW doesn't hug."

Diane looked at her quizzically.

"I'm just fucking with you," Galactica said, hugging her.

The group of men and women mobbed the bar. Pepper poured them healthy measures of whiskey. Diane looked at Galactica. She was young, probably mid-twenties. Blonde hair in dreadlocks, wrapped in a black scarf. Black cargo pants and black boots, all worn and dusty. A black, long sleeved T-shirt pulled up to reveal heavily tattooed forearms.

"Pepper tells me this is your first Burn," Galactica said, sitting beside Diane as Pepper served whiskey and played music.

"Yes."

"But not your last, right?" Galactica said. "What do you think so far?"

"Pretty amazing. How long have you been here?"

"Coming to the Burn or on the playa?"

"Both."

"Sixth Burn, on the playa six months," Galactica said, taking a sip of her whiskey.

Diane choked on her own drink. "Six *months?*"

"Yeah, we build the city structure," Galactica said. "We build the thing that gets built on. I got here in March."

"How do you do it?" Diane asked.

"One day at a time," Galactica said. "Pepper, play some Little Walter."

Pepper waved and played a song.

"Think you'll come back?" Galactica asked.

"I think so," Diane replied. "Can you explain more about DPW?"

"Sure," Galactica said. "DPW, Department of Public Works, makes all the streets, builds Medical, the Ranger HQ, and Information, sets up the trash fence, moves supplies, and aids artists with heavy equipment, cranes and such. We drive the tow truck, Captain Hook, and other heavy machinery. We are one of the things that make this place run. A lot happens behind the scenes."

"How did you get into it?"

"My first Burn," Galactica said. "I met a crazy desert carny guy. He invited me to the DPW bar. It felt like home. I joined up the next year, dropped out of Yale. That was five years ago."

The night wound on. Diane took turns bartending, which was a new, fun experience. Diane found the DPW crew to be rough diamonds. They were loud, brash, and fun-loving. Galactica and Pepper took turns singing songs.

The night became a blearily fantastic blur of experiences. At some point, Diane was aware that TK was perched on the lap of and making out with an extremely tall man at the bar.

Sequoia wandered in from in the night with a friend, then back out. Sheba, by turns, danced and tended bar, holding court, breaking balls, and laughing.

Diane didn't know exactly what time she hobbled off to bed, but it was late. Helped by Pepper to her carport, she made it halfway into her tent before darkness took her.

CHAPTER 27

Friday, September 4, one day until the Man burns

D ead Presidents!" a drunk voice shouted. "Is this Dead Presidents?"

Diane winced at the loud noise. Her head was splitting.

"Dead Presidents?" The drunk's voice came again, right outside her carport.

Diane opened gummy eyes. Her mouth tasted awful from cigarettes, booze, and playa.

"Dead—" the voice shouted again.

"Shut the fuck up!" TK interrupted from her tent.

"TK!" the voice shouted happily.

Diane came to her knees and retched. Gritting her teeth and willing herself not to vomit, she crawled backward out of her tent to sit on the carpet, looking though one eye toward the dusty path outside the door flap.

Sequoia stood there, weaving and staring at her.

"Diane!" he exclaimed.

Diane winced again at the loud noise, waving her hand to keep him quiet.

"Does he belong to you?" a voice asked.

Diane looked up to see a young woman, dressed in the khaki of a Ranger, staring in at her. Diane was confused at the question.

"He was wandering into camps, lost, shouting at people for Dead Presidents, so we brought him here," the Ranger explained.

"Yeah," Diane said in a croaky voice. "He's mine."

"Great," the Ranger said. "We're off."

Diane looked up to see Sequoia blearily grinning at her, weaving unsteadily in place, his eyes at half-mast. Judging by the light, it was very early morning. Diane blinked as she looked. Sequoia, who had left the camp fully dressed, was now wearing only a silver lamé G-string and was covered in glitter. No shirt, no shoes, one hairy testicle hanging out of the pouch.

Diane sighed and got to her feet, unsteady herself. Taking Sequoia by the hand, she led him through the paths to his carport, propelling him toward the queen-sized blowup mattress until he fell facedown. His massive, hairy white ass, split by silver lamé, pointed to the sky and shook at the eruption of a colossal fart.

"'Scuse me," Sequoia mumbled.

Diane retched again, leaning against the carport pole for support, as the smell hit her.

"Pepper bag," Sequoia mumbled.

"What?" Diane asked, leaning outside to get fresh air.

"Pepper bag!" Sequoia roared.

"Oh shit," Diane said, holding her head.

"Pepper bag," Sequoia mumbled again.

Diane weaved away from his carport and made her way to

the kitchen. Pepper was sitting with closed eyes, a cup of coffee in front of him. Twinkle was frying something in a skillet.

"Bacon?" Twinkle asked brightly.

When the smell of grease hit her, Diane leaned over and vomited into the large kitchen trash bag. Holding onto the bag, she spat out the remnants in her mouth.

"Sorry," Diane said.

Pepper cracked a beer and handed it to her.

"Rinse your mouth," Pepper said.

Diane took a sip from the cold can. Swirling the liquid in her mouth, she was able to spit out the remaining bits. The beer tasted surprisingly good. She sat down across from Pepper.

"You too?" Pepper asked.

"Ugh," Diane said in response. "Sequoia is asking for a pepper bag. Do we have one in here?"

"Is he drunk?" Pepper asked. "Was that him shouting?"

"Yes," Diane said, taking another sip. "Epically."

"He wants an IV," Pepper said, standing up to leave. "I'll take care of him."

"Here," Twinkle said, placing a paper plate in front of Diane. "Breakfast sandwich. It'll make you feel better."

Diane blinked at the English muffin sandwich next to her elbow.

"Thanks. Give me a minute," she said.

Diane sipped her beer, the cold brew somehow easing some of her queasiness. Then she began taking small bites of the sandwich. Chewing slowly, washing down each bite with a sip of beer, she ate the whole thing.

"Your ankle better?" Twinkle asked.

Diane considered it, flexing her ankle. It was still sore, but the swelling had gone way down. She hadn't even thought about it when walking.

Twinkle went out of the door and was back in a moment. She set down a stiff plastic shoe with straps as well as an acupuncture roll.

"A friend of mine had this walking boot that should fit you," Twinkle said. "Wear it for a while until you are better. Would you like me to help with the hangover?"

"Thank you," Diane said. "After the ankle, how could I say no?"

Diane slipped her foot into the shoe, tightening the Velcro straps. It fit perfectly. Meanwhile, Twinkle cleaned her face, popping two needles into one of her earlobes and one between her eyes.

"Give it five minutes," Twinkle said. "It will be as good as it can get."

Diane waited, relaxing against the table. After the time allotted, Twinkle removed the needles. Standing, then testing her weight in the boot, Diane was able to walk easily. She tossed a wave to Twinkle, then swung by her carport to grab her mask, goggles, and sunglasses. A pair of long legs and two giant feet were sticking out of TK's tent.

As she walked to the portos, the sun seemed brighter than usual. She put on her sunglasses. The food had helped, but she was still feeling delicate. After using the just-cleaned portos, she felt better. But then, as she took a deep breath of the morning air, a honey wagon suction truck drove by, and the sewage smell drove her back into the porto. Diane deposited her breakfast where her dinner had gone.

Eventually, Diane stepped from the porto and walked back

to camp. Her ankle was doing well in the walking boot. Pepper met her at her carport, an IV bag in his hand.

"You looked pretty rough yourself," Pepper said, then looked inside. "Them some big-ass feet."

"Will it help?" Diane asked, indicating the bag.

"Yeah," Pepper said. "It's my business back in the world. I'll get you set up. Have a seat."

Diane sat back in the chair. Pepper hung the bag on the carport support, wiped Diane's arm with alcohol, and inserted the needle. It was relatively painless. Diane could feel the fluid going into her, her body drinking in the liquid. She tasted citrus in her mouth.

"Orange?" Diane asked.

"There are some vitamins," Pepper said. "Leave it in, and I'll be back."

Diane sat back, the IV in her arm. Pepper came back, handed her a cup of coffee, then left. She sat for a while, letting the IV do its work, sipping the coffee.

A rustling near her feet made her open her eyes. The giant feet moved. A man crawled out of TK's tent, then stood up and then more up, towering in the carport. He was naked, his chiseled body lean. Diane tried to avoid looking at his package hanging in front of her.

"*Dobro jutro*," the man said unselfconsciously, stretching.

Diane nodded, trying not to stare. The man scratched himself, slipped on shorts and shirt, bent at the waist under the door, and walked out of the carport. After a moment, TK stirred in her tent.

"Is he gone?" TK asked.

"Yep," Diane replied.

"Good," TK said, crawling out of her tent. "I hate long goodbyes. Not that I could have understood it. He is a Croatian, apparently a basketball player. That's as far as we got."

TK held her lower stomach as she spoke.

"That was a lot," she said.

"A lot to drink?" Diane asked.

"A lot of cock," TK replied and rummaged in a backpack.

"What's that?" Diane asked, looking at the package in TK's hand.

"Plan B," TK said, opening the package and swallowing a pill. "Plan A exploded."

Diane laughed despite her hangover.

"Pepper hook you up?" TK asked.

Diane looked at the IV.

"He runs a business back home, he's extremely successful," TK said. "I'll see you in a bit."

TK walked out of the carport. Pepper came in a moment later.

"How's the patient?" Pepper asked, looking at the bag.

"A lot better," Diane said, amazed that it was true.

"This is my hangover mixture," Pepper said. "A little pain relief and anti-nausea, along with other things. I figured I would test-run it out here."

Pepper slid the needle out of her arm, placing a piece of gauze with tape. He put a cap on the needle and lifted the now-empty bag.

"Let me know if you need anything else," Pepper said. "Drink lots of water and take it easy."

Diane sat sipping on her water bottle. While tired, she did feel much better. Eventually, walking out into the camp, she brushed her teeth in the sink by the evap pond, then brushed the water to help it evaporate. Gassing up the generators, she then strolled around the camp picking up MOOP of all sorts.

The water bags had all been filled, so she walked back to the bar. A new teacher was conducting a yoga class. Diane just wasn't up to it today, so she watched, drinking water, basking in the morning sun. Waiting to see what the day would bring.

ell, that was a wasted pill," TK said, sitting down beside her. "My period started."

"When?" Diane asked.

"Right then," TK said. "Didn't you hear the bell?"

Diane smiled at her friend's teasing.

"Anyone want a bacon-wrapped hot dog?" Twinkle asked, holding a tray.

"Why does that sound so good?" TK said, taking a dog. "Thanks, Twinkle."

Diane waved her hand, her stomach roiling from the smell.

"Don't think I'm ready yet," Diane replied. "Thank you, though."

Twinkle wandered off, dispensing the dogs until she came to the street. She handed out dogs to three people walking by, then returned to the camp with an empty tray.

"You're missing out," TK said, wolfing down her dog.

"What's the plan for today?" Diane asked.

"Up to you," TK said. "Anything you want to do?"

"I thought I might go over to a camp I heard of," Diane said. "Creative Destruction. Nine o'clock something."

"Let's swing by Information," TK said. "We can leave in ten. I want to check on Sequoia."

"Sure," Diane replied. "He was pretty wrecked. Pepper is taking care of him."

"Dumbass says he took off his clothes for a foot race, then couldn't remember where he'd left them. We can check the Lost and Found when we are at Information," TK said, joining her at the bikes.

The trip to center camp was smooth. The sun was warm but not hot. When they arrived, Diane went to Information and TK went to the Lost and Found.

"Hello, may I help you?" the woman at the desk asked Diane.

"I'm looking for a camp," Diane said.

"The map on the wall is the best resource for you to use if you know the name," the woman replied.

"Thanks."

Diane walked over and studied the large map of the city. She found Creative Deconstruction and noted the location. Walking back to the bike, she saw TK with a bundle of clothing in her hands.

"Dumbass left his ID, kilt, car keys, and boots," TK said. "The woman said someone dropped it off twenty minutes ago. He is going to owe me big. Where we headed?"

"Nine-fifteen and G," Diane said.

"Great, we can pass by and drop off the clothes."

Diane looked up and pointed. "Parachutes."

"Yeah. Apparently you need three hundred jumps to qualify to jump at Burning Man," TK said. "They take off from the airport."

"I keep forgetting there's an airport here."

The trip back to the camp was uneventful. People were still partying, trying to entice Diane and TK into their camps. TK took her bundle and threw it into Sequoia's carport. They moved along the street, taking in the sights.

They pulled up to a camp with sun shelters in front. Bicycles were mounted inside on stands. Diane poked her head in to see Badger working on a bicycle, a young woman standing near him listening. TK wandered off to check out the Burner boutique across the street.

"Badger?" Diane said.

"Diane, right?" Badger said, handing a wrench to the young woman. "From the plane?"

"Yes," Diane said, opening her arms.

Badger gave her a hug. "Well, you didn't die."

"Not yet," Diane replied. "It's been great so far. Completely not what I was expecting."

"You think you'll come back?" Badger asked.

"I could see it happening," Diane said. "So, you repair bikes?"

"Yes," Badger replied. "We teach people how to repair their own."

"Mine had a problem with the chain," Diane said.

"Well, bring it in," Badger replied.

Diane wheeled her bike into the shade structure. There were three bike stands and tables with tools. Vinyl sheets lined the ground. Badger lifted the bike onto the stand and clamped it into place.

"Clogged with playa," Badger said quickly. "Happens a lot."

"What do I do about it?"

"You just spray it off and then lubricate," Badger said. "Like this."

Badger took a bottle and sprayed the chain and gears with it while rotating the tire. The runoff was caught in the tray beneath. He then sprayed it liberally from another bottle.

"There, good as new," Badger said.

"Thank you," Diane replied.

"Looking forward to the burn tonight?"

"Wouldn't miss it."

Diane took her bike outside as Badger helped another man mount his bike on the rack. TK walked up with a couple of items of clothing.

"Lucky?" Diane said.

"A few neat things," TK replied. "How's your head?"

"Feeling pretty good," Diane asked. "Why?"

"I figured we could explore a bit," TK said. "Make our way back to camp for lunch. It's probably gonna be a late night."

"Lead on," Diane said.

They stopped at bars and viewed art in camps along the way, traveling to streets Diane had seen before. The camps had similarities, but each had its own flair. Extra time and effort had obviously been put into some camps to make their plots of land an offering to the other participants. Some appeared just to be a place for people to sleep, with no art or interactivity at all.

"What flag is that?" Diane asked, seeing a large banner of a heart and infinity symbol intertwined.

TK regarded it. "Oh, that's for a poly camp," she said.

"What do you mean?" Diane asked.

"People who are polyamorous, who are open to having more than one romantic or sexual partner at once."

"You mean swingers?"

"No. I mean, there are swingers at the Burn, but being poly is different. It's about relationships, not just sex."

"How do you know all this?" Diane asked.

"I don't know," TK said. "Guess I picked it up on the way. Want to head in? They're usually really nice, very big on consent."

"Not really," Diane said. "Another time, maybe."

The sun was warming up, the wind starting to whip up dust around them. Diane knew enough to get her goggles and face mask ready. They continued on their ride. Turning down a street, they saw a line in front of a large complex of white tents.

"Sheba," TK said, riding up to the line.

"Hello, my lovelies," Sheba said, standing in a light cloak and wide, fashionable sunhat beside a handsome man.

"What's happening?" Diane asked.

"I've been invited to an orgy," Sheba said unselfconsciously. "I hadn't been and thought I would give it a try. Sven here was nice enough to invite me. You interested in going?"

Diane gawked as she realized what Sheba had just said.

"I—I—" Diane stammered.

Sheba smiled at her and laughed.

"I am only teasing you, *mon ami*," Sheba said, then turned. "It looks like it is our time, Sven?"

TK and Diane watched Sheba and Sven enter the tent.

"Someone's got a grumpy face on," TK said.

Diane said nothing, then started to pedal. She felt hurt. She knew she didn't have any right to be, but still, there was a sting in her chest. Diane pedaled harder, cruising at speed down the road. She didn't plan her direction, she just rode away.

"Slow the fuck down," TK said, catching up to her.

Diane applied the brakes to slow, then stop.

"What the fuck was that?" TK asked.

"I don't know," Diane said, upset. The emotions had come out of nowhere.

"Okay, okay," TK said. "Let's take a break. There's a seating area under that shade cloth. Let's have a seat and talk."

Diane followed her to the cushions under the shade. They sat down, and Diane drank from her water bottle, avoiding TK's eyes.

"Okay," TK said. "Spill it."

"I don't know," Diane said. "I got upset."

"Bullshit," TK said. "I've known you for twenty years, and you can't trust me?"

"Bleh," Diane said, then nodded, shaking her hands nervously at her sides. "I was with Sheba. Somehow it just happened."

"Whaaat?" TK asked, her eyes wide.

"Yeah," Diane said, blushing. "Oh my God, it was wonderful."

Diane was grateful to be able to share with her friend an event this large in her life. She spilled the whole story.

"So, what now?" TK asked. "You in love? You have an expectation?"

"No," Diane said. "We discussed it thoroughly—the expectations, I mean. No, right now I don't, but when I saw her with that guy, I don't know, logic wasn't working in my brain."

"Fair enough," TK said. "You feel better now?"

"Yes, I think so."

"Look, you can make all of the agreements, consent, and compromises you want, but people who pretend they can have sex with each other without emotions being involved sometimes are fooling themselves," TK said. "Anyway, shit gets weird out here. You got to ride it out sometimes. You probably are just projecting past stuff on today's stuff. That happens too.

"I will tell you this. Just because she doesn't want to be with you again physically, or is with someone else, that doesn't change your worth as a person. Sheba and I talked about you. She really, really likes you and is grateful you are here. Now it makes more sense, actually. You've been acting a little strange. I noticed, but I figured it was just the Burn, and I didn't want to pry . . ."

Diane felt better at hearing this, like a weight had been lifted.

"So, good now?"

"Mostly. I still kind of want to take out some of this emotion. Is that terrible of me?"

"Really?" TK said. "I got the perfect place."

CHAPTER 29

After a bite to eat and the sunset howl at camp, Diane and TK headed out on their bikes into the early night.

BATTLEDOME, the sign said in flames. The massive metal geodesic dome was literally crawling with people lined up on the bars, some twenty feet off the ground. Diane and TK parked amongst the sea of bicycles surrounding the dome. It was lit brightly from within. Hard, intense rock music was pulsing from speakers.

Finding an open space, they peered into the madness within. The center of the dome held quite a few people. Men and women in various shades of black clothing, with fantastic masks and hats, were working the event. They looked like space-cowboy-biker-gang meets industrial-rock-concert meets apocalyptic film. They looked intimidating, sexy, and competent. They looked like they were having a great, if chaotic, time.

The focus of the dome was two sets of thick bungee cords attached to the top of the structure. As Diane watched, two men were strapped into waist harnesses with bungees on both hips. The participants were about twenty feet from each other, taunting and gesturing. Each held what appeared to be a plastic bat wrapped with padding.

A man with a skull mask was holding a skull-topped staff. This ringmaster strode into the middle of the participants, gesturing to each one. Receiving ready nods from them, he swung the staff around in a circle, then brought it down in a stroke.

Burly men pulled each participant back, lifting them off their feet and stretching the bungees far back and up. The music was a driving force of its own. The crowd was chanting and cheering as the combatants were released and flew through the air at each other, colliding with a crash in midair.

"Holy shit!" Diane said, watching the melee.

The men had grabbed each other's bungee straps and were pummeling each other with the bats. They were swinging back and forth, unsteady in the air, each trying to gain the advantage and land a solid shot. The swinging bats were a blur, the crowd was screaming and cheering. It was a gleeful madness.

The combatants were pulled apart by the same men who had launched them, then returned to their own sides of the dome, panting but still gesturing at and taunting each other. The man with the staff walked into the center again, held up the skull-topped staff, and brought it down.

The blows exchanged were, if anything, more furious and fast this time. One combatant lost his bat and clung to his opponent, trying to shield himself from blows. After a bit, they were again pulled apart and brought back to their sides.

The man with the staff gestured again. The crowd cheered. The combatants crashed into each other, grabbing the bungees and trading blows. They were pushing hard against each other, landing strikes, but Diane didn't see any real damage, no blood.

The last fight was desperate and flailing. Both combatants appeared winded. The skull-masked raised his staff, then pointed to the combatant on the left. The crowd cheered as the victor raised his hands. Then both combatants were taken out of their harnesses.

"What do you think?" TK asked.

Diane had never seen anything like what she had just witnessed. It had been a violent, chaotic spectacle, completely unhinged. Anyone who would volunteer for such a thing couldn't be right in their minds.

"Let's do it," Diane said. "Do I fight you, or . . ."

"Yeah, you have to bring your own opponent," TK said. "I've never done it before, though."

They made their way to the front of the dome, where there were only a few other people in line, nervously talking to one another. Diane felt a flutter in her stomach but shrugged it off. Each pair of combatants in front of them went into the dome through a metal archway. The music drove up the tension, the anticipation. Diane looked at TK, an intense focus on her face.

"You scared?" TK asked as they stepped up to the door. They were next.

"Not really," Diane replied. "Why?"

TK turned to her as the gatekeeper beckoned them in. "Because I'm gonna beat your skinny ass flat."

TK turned to the left as Diane went to the right.

The process involved stepping into a harness that enclosed Diane's legs and hips.

"Are you fucking ready?" The woman helping her screamed in her face, cinching Diane's harness tight. She had dark hair and wore heavy black mascara and black lipstick.

"Uh . . ." Diane said. She could see TK screaming back and forth with her own helper, a muscular man with dark designs drawn on his bald head.

"'Uh'?" The woman yelled in her face. "'Uh'? You want that girl to beat your ass?"

"No," Diane said, then yelled, "Fuck that! Yeah, I'm ready."

"That's better," the woman said. "Make sure you grab her bungee, there's no way to win unless you do."

The combatants before them had finished. Diane saw with some trepidation that both were limping. Strong hands moved her into position, and the bungees were snapped onto the D-rings on each side of her harness. She bounced, her legs barely touching the ground. A man handed her a foam-wrapped bat.

TK's face was animated as she pointed and yelled, taunting. Diane looked at her friend. For some unknown reason, Diane felt fired up, awash with adrenaline, captured by the moment. The music growled a fast guitar rage. The crowd was screaming, cheering for TK's antics.

The ringmaster from hell lifted his staff and brought it down, and Diane was raised from her feet by the men at her side. The pressure of the bungee on her harness grew taut around her pelvis. Across from her, TK was in the same position, held by a man and a woman, her bat up and ready.

Released from restraint, Diane flew to meet TK in midair. They crashed together in a tangle of arms and legs, though for some reason Diane barely felt the impact. She managed to grab TK's bungee, but she had the slightest feeling of restraint toward hitting her friend until TK caught her full in the face with a swing from her bat.

Diane and TK exchanged a furious flurry of blows with the

padded bats, both screaming like banshees. After a moment, they were pulled apart, Diane landing a lucky late hit to TK's head as they parted.

Diane was winded and exhilarated, not having much experience in physical conflict. Adrenaline was pounding through her veins. The hands at her sides pulled her back, the ringmaster stood in between them and brought the staff down. Diane flew through the air at her friend again.

This time TK thrust out her knee at the last moment, catching Diane in her chest. It didn't slow Diane at all. She grabbed TK's bungee and began chopping at TK with short strokes of the bat. The crowd was roaring, the music driving them on.

Diane and TK were separated, both women howling, reaching for each other to continue. Once more, the ringmaster stepped in between them. He looked from side to side, the crowd holding their voices. Down came the staff again. There would be a third round.

Lifted up by strong hands, Diane was eager and leaned into the flight. TK looked like a homicidal fairy, shouting and gesturing with the bat. At the last moment, Diane switched positions in midair, coming in with her knees up, crashing into TK. Diane grabbed the bungee and swung with abandon. TK was landing as many blows as she received, but both women were tiring. Diane could feel her arm aching but strove to give one last blow after one last blow.

Finally, mercifully, the women were pulled apart. The ringmaster strode between them and raised his staff in the air. The crowd waited. Diane struggled to get her breath. The staff came down and pointed toward Diane as the crowd roared its deafening approval.

Diane was stripped of her web harness. She stepped out and walked to TK, and they fell into each other's arms, smiling. The crowd cheered their hug. They walked from the dome arm in arm. Diane was pulsing with adrenaline, her body shaking from exertion.

"You're bleeding," TK said. "Good."

Diane touched her face. She had a bloody nose that hadn't even registered.

"It's good that I'm bleeding?"

"Makes me feel better," TK said, wincing but smiling. "You kicked me in the box."

"You guys did great," the dome gatekeeper said as they left.

Limping over to their bikes, they extricated them from the sea of blinking bikes and stood upon the road.

"I don't know about you," Diane said, her legs shaking, "but I could sure use a drink."

"Yeah, but let's walk a bit," TK said. "I don't think I want to sit on my bike yet."

CHAPTER 30

TK and Diane made their way back to camp. Diane was still buzzing with the adrenaline rush, but it was starting to fade. In its place, she could feel at least two spots where she would surely have spectacular bruises tomorrow. Her ankle was beginning to protest.

Sheba, Sequoia, Billy, and Jeremy were at the bar when they returned.

"Drinks for the winner of Battledome," TK said.

"Holy shit," Jeremy said. "Did you do that? Who did you fight?"

"TK," Diane said, smiling as she sat down. "I kicked her ass."

"Fuck you, I was sick," TK said, reaching out to get her cup filled.

"Congratulations on your victory," Sheba said, clinking glasses with Diane.

"Thanks," Diane said, noticing that whatever jealous emotion she'd had before was gone.

"What haven't you seen yet?" Sequoia asked.

"I saw a lit-up building on the playa, somewhere past the Man," Diane said. "It looked interesting."

"The Temple," Sheba said, turning to the left, her tone lower.

"Oh, I didn't recognize it. Is it worth seeing at night?" Diane asked.

"Definitely," TK said.

"Billy," Sheba said, "we should take Diane to the Temple. She hasn't seen it at night."

"You sure?" Billy asked.

"Yes," Sheba said, finishing her drink.

The group gathered their things and mounted the Starfish. Sequoia and Pepper decided to ride their bikes.

Pulling up to the Temple, Billy parked the car. They all looked up. Lights both subdued and cleverly positioned set the structure off to dramatic effect.

"Wow," Jeremy said.

"Yeah, they did well this year," Pepper said.

TK, Diane, Jeremy, Sequoia, and Pepper walked into the side entrance of the Temple. Again Diane was struck by its size. It was huge, easily the size of a cathedral. Somehow it seemed both bigger and smaller at night, in the shadows.

As the group walked in, the pace was languid. Many people were walking through the structure. Drawings, memorabilia, pictures, letters, and signs lined the walls. People were still bringing things in, putting things up. The mood was solemn. People spoke in muted tones and moved slowly through the hallways, some meditating, some just lying down in soaking in the quiet vibe.

"It's so different than everywhere else here," Jeremy said softly.

Diane nodded in agreement. Apart from the rest of the chaos, the Temple seemed different.

A place made sacred by people who need a sacred place, she thought.

"Oh man," Jeremy said, stopping in front of what appeared to be an art piece.

It was a combat helmet, perched on the end of a rifle pointed to the ground, with a pair of desert combat boots side by side at the base. A couple of dog tags were looped around the handle of the rifle. A small wooden box with a metal clipboard was to one side. A glow came from within the helmet.

Jeremy seemed frozen in one spot. Diane looked to the wall and saw a printed sign. There was an emblem for each branch of the armed forces.

"I didn't think anyone out here cared," Jeremy said softly. Diane began to read the sign.

THE SOLDIER'S CROSS *consists of a rifle inverted between a pair of combat boots and topped by a helmet. This simple symbol is a powerful image to those persons who have served in the armed forces. This practice evolved to mark a burial place of a soldier who had fallen in combat. This was used when the body could not be extricated because of the remoteness of the location or the requirements of battle.*

Armed forces members sacrifice to serve. Whether in times of war or in peace, those persons who volunteer to protect their country give up the comforts and security of civilian life to keep family, friends, and countrymen safe.

This project was not designed with the intent to celebrate war, violence, or the loss that results from it. This project was placed in the hope that even one person's suffering would be lessened. That even one person could leave behind the memory of comrades fallen, the trauma endured.

You are invited to write whatever you choose and place it

in the box provided, whether it is the name of a lost comrade, an event you wish to no longer be affected by, or any other thing you have been carrying and would like to release.

Every note will be burned with the Temple.

When she finished reading, Diane turned to see Jeremy sitting on the ground, his arms wrapped around his bent legs. Looking at the art piece, she leaned over to him.

"Would you like me to leave you alone or keep you company?" Diane asked him softly.

Jeremy glanced at her.

"I wouldn't mind it if you sat with me a bit."

Diane sat beside him. Jeremy reached out his hand, and Diane took it in her own. They sat quietly for what seemed like a long time. Jeremy looked up, apparently reading the sign again and again. People milled about them. Some stopped to look. Occasionally, after reading the sign, someone would write on the paper pad in the clipboard and slip a note into the box. One woman came to attention and saluted, holding the salute with tears in her eyes.

"I can never go to heaven," Jeremy said. "That weighs on me."

"Why not?" Diane asked.

"Too many sins," Jeremy said, and was silent.

Jeremy reached into his pocket and pulled out a chain on which six dog tags hung. Holding them in his hand, he flipped through them one at a time. A stoic look was on his face.

Eventually, he seemed to come to some sort of decision. While Diane watched, he released her hand and rose. Sinking to one knee, he closed his eyes, tightly gripping the dog tags in his hand. He held the pose for a moment, then looped the chain around the trigger of the rifle and let them hang. As he stood up again, Diane joined him.

"I think I would like to be alone a bit now, if you don't mind," Jeremy said, turning to her.

Diane reached out and hugged him. She rubbed his back, then released him.

"I'll be around if you need me," she said.

Walking away from the cross, Diane came to the large center room of the structure. She spotted Sheba standing alone, staring at something on the wall. Billy was standing back from her, quietly keeping his distance.

Walking up, Diane could see Sheba was looking at a framed picture of a smiling family outdoors. Two little boys joyfully played on the sunlit grass in front of their father and mother. The mother was brunette, smiling in a yellow sundress, visibly pregnant and holding a baby girl in her arms. The photo looked like an advertisement for conservative Christianity.

"I was fucking perfect," Sheba said in a whisper.

Diane looked at Sheba, taking in her beautiful blue hair in ribbons, her lipstick a deep maroon, her eyelashes long and full, her face shape accentuated by artful blush. Sheba wore thigh-high black leather boots and leather shorts, a black velvet cloak, and a black ribbon around her neck, held there by a carved figure of a woman's face. She looked as fierce as always . . . but her body was trembling.

"He was the best I could ever have dreamed of," Sheba said, her voice low.

Diane looked closer at the photo and realized the smiling woman was Sheba, as different in appearance from today's Sheba as night and day, but the same person.

TK, Sequoia, and Pepper walked up to them.

A young, slim, beautiful woman, dressed in a feather headdress and fringed leather outfit, slipped by Sheba to lean against the wall beside the picture and struck a pensive pose. Diane turned and saw a man in flowing pants and a sleeveless shirt with a shell necklace fiddling with a camera. Sheba looked at the man and then the woman and leaned forward.

"If you take a picture beside my dead family, you sparkle pony cunt," Sheba said, her voice a menacing growl, "I will gouge out your fucking eyes and make you eat them."

The woman's eyes widened in alarm. She began babbling in some European language and scuttled away. Sheba took a deep breath.

"I did everything right," Sheba began again, a tear glistening in her eye as she stared at the photo. "I went to church every Sunday. I made lunches, dinners, clothing, cleaned the house, hosted play dates. I used to sing to my boys, read them to sleep. I never spent one night away from my children from the moment they were born. I read book after book on how to raise happy, healthy children. When one of them was sick, I stayed up all night, slept on the floor to be near them. I gave them kisses every day. Every chance I got, I told them I loved them. And you know what? It worked. It was perfect."

Diane watched her, this woman trembling in the power of her memories. She realized that Sheba's voice had changed, was wavering.

"Bill was my first and only lover and then my husband. We met in grade school, stayed together in college, and started our life. It was perfect. We were perfect."

Sheba stopped, pulled a red silk handkerchief from her

pocket, and dabbed her eyes. A pained, halting laugh slipped from her lips. Then she shook her head and raised her chin. Touching the photo, she continued.

"Marie was a blessing. She slept through the night from the second day I brought her home. She was the sweetest baby."

Sheba smiled as she moved her fingers to the two boys, smiling.

"Timothy and Paul were twins, twin terrors. From the same womb, but they were as different in personality as oil and water. Always so serious, my little old man Timothy, oldest by a minute. Paul was full throttle from the moment he was born, though for all his wildness he was a complete little momma's boy. They both thought Marie hung the moon and couldn't wait for the next sibling," Sheba said, smiling with memories, until her eyes grew sad. "We were coming back from a church dinner. There was rain that night, the roads were wet. The boys were fussing in the back. Marie was sleeping in her car seat. Bill was singing along with the radio."

Diane was enraptured by the story. She did not even dare to breathe.

"The semi ran a red light," Sheba said, tears now flowing and voice cracking. "It hit on Bill and Marie's side. I don't think she ever woke up. I must have blacked out, but when I did wake up, there were lights in my face from the rescue team coming down the hill. I'd been thrown from the car. My legs didn't work, they were broken.

"The boys were gone. I could see them with their arms wrapped around each other. Bill was gasping, so I crawled to him. Held his hand as he took his last breath. The baby inside me didn't make it. My womb didn't, either. And then I was alone."

The moment was broken when a gray-bearded man with a large belly, dressed in a khaki uniform and boonie cap, walked up to Sheba and Diane. A woman, similarly clad, stood with the couple from before, the couple looking indignant. Sequoia and TK stiffened beside Diane. Billy watched calmly.

"A Ranger," Diane thought, her own eyes tearing up as she imagined what might happen to Sheba now.

"I heard someone was threatening violence over here," the man said, his gray-bearded, tanned face concerned, his voice low.

"There was not a threat," Sheba said, her voice wavering. "There was a promise. I said if she took a picture beside my dead family, I would do her violence."

The Ranger looked at the picture on the wall for a long time. He then looked at Sheba, her mascara running, her eyes filled with tears. The Ranger turned to face the couple.

"If I were you, I would take your pictures somewhere else."

The couple walked off in a huff. The other Ranger came closer to peer at the photo. The bearded, big-bellied Ranger turned to Sheba.

"I'm very sorry for your loss," he said in a low voice, looking into her eyes.

Sheba dropped her eyes, her shoulders shaking. The Ranger stepped forward, wrapping his big arms around her, pulling her against his big belly.

"My babies . . . my babies," Sheba keened into the man's chest, wrapping her arms around him.

Diane was crying now too. The pain from Sheba's story was palpable. She could see other people in a ring around the Ranger and Sheba, many also crying. Sheba's sobs became wails, her sorrow painful to watch and impossible to turn from. Diane stepped forward, embracing Sheba from behind.

"I'm sorry!" Sheba screamed. "I'm sorry! Momma loves you. Momma misses you. My babies, oh, my babies . . ."

Diane could feel arms from TK, then Sequoia and Billy, then the other Ranger, and then multiple people surrounding her in a group with the big Ranger and Sheba in the middle. The air was electric. The hairs on Diane's arms and neck were standing up.

It must have been twenty or more people, all with their arms around one another. Strangers, all moved by Sheba's agony, a deep reflection of their own internalized pain and trauma. They held one another, slowly rocking, some weeping, some being quiet, all together at that moment. Sheba's deep, primal wails continued as she grieved for her family.

Minutes went by as the emotions poured out of the woman in the center. Nobody moved, nobody left. Everyone just held on, to each other, to the moment. Slowly, quietly, someone started humming. The low, comforting noise began to build in the group as other people picked it up. Somewhere close, Diane could hear Pepper's voice as he started to quietly sing. His voice was rich and beautiful. Words from an opera, from another time, another place, filled the Temple. Anguish, love, and loss in a language Diane didn't recognize but could understand with startling clarity. Pepper's voice intertwined with the humming of the people around him, the noises of grief, emotion, and support blending perfectly. The powerful expression of emotion was tempered by the sublime humming, both masculine and feminine voices blending together to form something more, something healing, something calming.

More people joined the humming. Diane could see Pepper being embraced by a woman who was crying and singing. Diane was humming with everyone else. It seemed as though the whole Temple had joined. Looking around, she saw faces in sorrow, faces releasing suffering, tears streaming from eyes, mirrors of her own. The mixture of Pepper's voice, the humming of the crowd, and Sheba's keening reached a crescendo, made a music out of nothing but shared sorrow, loss, and love.

The energy in the Temple was indescribable. Diane saw her friends' faces shining. She could feel the coming together of the crowd, seconds ago strangers, now shared souls. Diane felt despair, loss, and then an unimaginable joy flood her body.

Pepper held the last note, letting the song disappear as quietly as it had begun. The group slowly swayed in their embrace back and forth. Sheba's cries slowly turned to weeping and then soft breaths in Diane's arms. Still, the group held together, not moving from the tight circle. Minutes passed, then more minutes. Sheba stood with her head on the Ranger's chest. Diane rested her head on Sequoia's shoulder. She could feel Billy pressing his head to her back.

"I'm good now," Sheba said at last, in a steady voice. "I'm good. Thank you."

The group relaxed, releasing one another from the embrace, from the shared experience. Sheba hugged both Rangers and thanked them. Different people hugged one another as they made their way out of the Temple.

Sheba walked over to the photo. Diane watched as she kissed each face, letting her fingers linger on the frame.

"Momma loves and misses you," Sheba said softly.

Sheba wiped her eyes and blew her nose. Taking a deep

breath, she shook her head and held it high as she turned and walked out of the Temple alone. The group of friends followed behind her in silence, walking to where the Starfish waited, glowing in in the darkness. All of them climbed on board, not saying anything, as Sheba stood, looking out to the dark emptiness of deep playa.

Sheba took a last look at the Temple, lit from within, then turned to Billy, who sat quietly in the driver's seat.

"Take us home, Billy," she said, and then nestled tightly between Diane and TK.

Billy turned the Starfish and headed into the night. Back to camp, back to home, they rode in silence.

The Starfish pulled up to Dead Presidents, parking near the bar. It had to be around midnight. The lights were off, the camp was quiet. The surrounding camps were mostly dark and quiet, a contrast to the chaos of the playa. The bar was dark and deserted.

Everyone sat on the car together after the quiet ride back from the Temple. The experience was still fresh, vivid, and raw. They all sat on the car, not yet wanting to break whatever spell had grabbed them, pulled them into something more than a group of friends. Forged them together in a perfect moment of magic.

Sequoia and Pepper pulled up on their bikes a moment later. Sequoia dismounted, looked at the group on the car, and then walked into the camp. A moment later came the sound of a generator firing up, and then all the lights on the bar came up, bathing the area in a homey glow.

Diane watched Sheba next to her, her head coming up with the lights. Sheba smiled and stood up off the car, walking to the bar, where she unlocked the cabinets and placed a bottle of whiskey before her. Everyone took seats as Sheba poured shots, then distributed them. Raising her glass, she spoke.

"To all those we love, let them know that we have loved them," Sheba said. "Let them know that they are worthy of that love, and may love find them all of their days."

Diane downed her shot with the others, the warm whiskey slowly burning its way to her belly. Sheba set down her shot glass and looked at the quiet people lining the bar.

"You're not going to get *that* at a fucking *music festival*," Sheba said.

The friends laughed, welcoming the release.

"Sequoia," Sheba said, "play something good. I wanna dance."

Songs began to pump from the mounted speakers, driving, sexy, hard-rock beats, shattering both the quiet of the night and residual somberness from the Temple. People wandering by joined the celebration. Sleepy Dead Presidents campers came out to see what was going on.

An impromptu party ensued, with laughter, drinking, and dancing. At one point, Pepper brought out pizzas from somewhere. They were delicious and hot. Sheba sang along on the bar microphone, belting out song after song. The music genres played were wildly swinging from old rock ballads to rap to goth favorites.

Diane sat back on her barstool, tapping her foot. She knew she was drunk because three times, she had lit a cigarette when there was already one burning in the ashtray.

Fire spinning started at some point, the flaming sticks and chain pots throwing light in the night. Electric, bright LED hula hoops were spun incredibly artistically in the darkness. She watched the group of friends and strangers celebrating life, banishing sorrow and worries, enjoying a shining moment of joy in the desert night. Art cars and bicycles came and went, the crowd surging and falling in number.

Diane watched the assemblage of human beings coming together in celebration. She realized the emotional journey this place could put you through was powerful. The Burn threw people into common shared hardship, scouring away the clinging norms of society with freedom to explore, to love, to grieve, to celebrate and experience. It confronted you with your own judgments in a place of freedom and safety. It let you see others as humans and, in doing so, discover your own humanity. It tore you away from your ordinary, compartmentalized life to be a part of something amazing, something whole.

It was late when Diane called it a night. The air in her tent was still. She slipped in earplugs and crawled into her sleeping bag. As she drifted off to sleep her last thought was, *What is it about this place? What is the secret ingredient?*

CHAPTER 31

Saturday, September 5, the Man burns tonight

Diane opened her eyes to the sound of the wind gusting against the carport walls. Taking a moment to orient herself to where she was, she sat up and blinked. Slipping out of the tent, she put on the walking boot and stood. The ankle was not swollen, and she felt only the mildest discomfort from it. The rest of her body had aches from the Battledome, but she could deal with that.

The percolator on boil, she set out to the portos. There was some wind, but the dust was not a problem. Stragglers from the previous night's festivities weaved down the road. A few cars crept along. The people inside looked clean.

People are still coming in, Diane thought.

Having brushed her teeth, she sat in the empty bar, drinking her coffee. She realized she hadn't checked her phone in three days, had not thought about the office or the world outside.

"Morning," Jeremy said, walking up to her.

Diane rose and gave him a hug.

"Good morning," Diane said. "How are you?"

"Good. I partied at the bar, then walked a lot, went on an adventure on an art car, crashed with some people I met. They just took me in, no questions. They fed me and sent me home. It was good, I'm good."

"That makes me happy to hear," Diane said, sitting down.

"No worries," Jeremy replied. "I was just going to head over for the *haka*. Want to come?"

"I'll get my stuff," Diane replied.

The trip to the camp was slow, both of them taking their time. The early morning sunshine showed people just getting up and people just going to bed. A double-decker art car passed by, decorated like a fish, as they pulled up to the camp. A sign placed by the road read "Haka at Esplanade."

They followed the road down to the Esplanade, where they saw Tane and Ahora speaking to a group of at least three hundred people. Tane was on a small stage looking at the assembled people. He nodded as he saw Jeremy and Diane join the group. Tane had a microphone headset, and there were large speakers nearby.

"Good morning, my friends," Tane said to the crowd, his voice amplified. "I am so pleased you could join us for our mission of cultural sharing."

The crowd clapped appreciatively.

"We are here to introduce the *haka*, a Māori traditional dance. Specifically, we are going to do the Ka Mate. Te Rauparaha was the composer of the Ka Mate. He was chief of the Ngāti Toa Rangatira in the northern part of New Zealand. The Ka Mate is a celebration of life over death. Te Rauparaha created it after enemies nearly caught him. Nothing seems to bring out the creativity like almost dying, it seems."

Diane laughed with the crowd. She was intrigued by how much charisma Tane had. His storytelling style was excellent.

"The *haka* is a call and response. The leader is seeking to inspire his fellow tribesmen, to raise them up, raise their spirits, for the tasks and challenges ahead. As a celebration of life over death, the *haka* brings us together in focus and action.

"We did not know what we would find here, on the other side of the world, amongst people and things that are new and different. In our short time here, we have met many wonderful people. We have been embraced and thanked for sharing our culture, and we in return have experienced other cultures and given gratitude to others. And we have experienced dust. A bunch of dust."

The crowd laughed.

"Now we will go step by step through the *haka*, the Ka Mate. In doing the Ka Mate, it is important to achieve perfection in speech and execution. It is a goal for a lifetime. It calls on your *mana*, your essence. In working and accomplishing greater skill, you raise your own *mana*, your own spiritual force. As our language and pronunciation are difficult for people to master quickly, we will walk you through it."

The five other Māoris distributed themselves in the crowd.

"*Taringa whakarongo*," Tane shouted.

"Ears open," Ahora translated into the megaphone she was holding.

"*Kai rite! Kai rite!*" Tane said.

"Get ready, get ready," Ahora said.

"*Kia mau!*" Tane shouted.

"Stand fast," Ahora said.

"*Hi!*" The Māoris and some of the crowd members shouted, striking poses with their feet in wide stances. Their arms were held up, their forearms parallel in front of them.

"Yeah!" Ahora translated.

Diane noticed that an ever-larger crowd was forming, observing. Tane saw it too and waved the group to join. The people now facing him had to be a thousand people strong.

"*Ringa ringa pakia!*" Tane shouted. "*Waewae tahahia kia kino nei hoki!*"

The Māoris and some of the crowd began slapping their thighs. The beat was taken up by the rest until everyone was slapping in rhythm, stomping their feet.

"Slap the hands against the thighs," Ahora said. "Stomp the feet as hard as you can!"

"*Kia kino nei hoki!*" Tane, the other Māoris, and people in the crowd chanted.

"As hard as we can," Ahora said.

"*Ka mate, mate ora, Ka mate, mate ora!*"

"I am going to die, die. No, I'm alive! I am going to die, die. No, I'm alive!" Ahora shouted.

"*Tenel te tangata, puhuruhu. Nana ne i teke mal whaka whiti te ra!*"

"A fully grown man!" Ahora said. "Who can bring back the sun, so it will shine on us again."

"*A Upane. Kupane!*" The crowd chanted, slapping their forearms and stomping.

"Rise now! Rise now!"

"*A Upane. Kupane!*"

"Take the first step!" Ahora shouted.

"*Whiti te ra! Hi!*" The crowd shouted, cheering and applauding.

"Let the sunshine in. Yeah!" Ahora said with a flourish.

"Thank you, my friends! You are not dead, you are all alive!

Remember that you participated here at this moment with us. And we thank you," Tane said.

Diane and Jeremy walked to Tane and Ahora and exchanged the *hongi* with each of them.

"That was great, Ahora," Diane said. "Are you happy with it?"

"Ecstatic," Ahora said. "We already have plans for next year."

"You are going to the Man burn, yes?" Tane asked.

"Wouldn't miss it," Jeremy said.

"Hope to see you there," Diane said.

After exchanging hugs with Tane and Ahora, Diane and Jeremy departed, heading back to the camp. More people were awake than usual for the time of day. The yoga class was wrapping up.

"What's up?" Diane asked TK at the bar.

"Teardown," TK replied. "That's the last yoga class. When they are done, we break down the structure."

Diane stood dumbfounded. She had known that the Man burn was tonight, but as she looked around at the camp she had helped build, had lived in for the week, a certain sadness struck. She felt both that she had been here forever and that the time had been way too short.

"You alright?" TK asked, looking at her.

"Yes. I . . ." Diane said, shaking her head. "I guess I got used to being here."

TK gave her a hug, holding her close.

"It hit me my first time like that too," TK said, and then released her.

"I'll change and help," Diane said.

The disassembly of the yoga structure was easier than putting it up had been, with so many more people to help. Some of them Diane didn't even recognize. They must have arrived recently. The poles were laid out near the shipping container, the fabric folded and neatly stacked.

Dusting herself off, she walked over to the bar, then stopped when she heard an engine fire up. It wasn't a generator, it was the diesel motor on an RV. Walking to the shipping container, she saw Sheba's RV was running, and the sitting area and table on front of it were gone. Quickly, she walked to the door of the RV and looked inside. Sheba was sitting at the wheel. Sheba looked at her and smiled, then beckoned her in.

"Are you leaving?" Diane asked, closing the door behind her. "You're skipping the Man burn?"

"My Burn is here already, my love," Sheba said, touching her heart and then smiling. "You're spoiling my Irish goodbye."

A tear formed in the corner of Diane's eye.

"Don't do that, my love," Sheba said, handing her a silk handkerchief. "You'll get me going."

"I don't mean to," Diane said, dabbing her eye. "I just . . . wanted . . ."

"Wanted what?" Sheba asked.

Diane took a deep breath. "I've never met anyone like you, never imagined anyone like you. I want to ask but don't think I have the right to."

"You're asking for consent to ask something?"

"Yes, I guess I am."

Sheba looked at her, amused.

"Then you're learning. Go ahead."

Diane paused, shaping her question.

"After your family . . . I mean . . . how did you . . ."

Sheba took a deep breath, blew it out, looked through the dusty windshield, then turned to face Diane.

"Survive? Evolve?"

Diane nodded.

"Okay, okay," Sheba said, nodding her head. "This is between you and me and no one else, agreed?"

"Yes."

Sheba lit a cigarette.

"After I buried my family, I went home in a wheelchair. I cried it all out, almost all of it. I ate, I slept, I woke up. I signed paperwork. I slept. I slept like a dead person. I had a bottomless hole in my heart. I couldn't taste anything. All joy was gone.

"I didn't know it yet, but I had died in that wreck too. That woman you saw that was me? She followed all the rules because the rules worked for her, right up until something that had no rules blew it all away. I used to think I had it all under control. I was a fool.

"My legs healed, but my body was a wreck. I started to go to yoga, went after it like a thing possessed until I could teach it, trying to fill the hole. I then did a massage school. I didn't need to, not financially. Bill had insurance, he took care of me even after he died. I just couldn't stay in that house and do nothing.

"Everything I did, filling every day and night, was me trying to fill the hole where my heart used to be. I yearned for what I lost, ached for it. Wanted something that could never be. I was cut off and alone. I had built my world around my family, I didn't know what to do without them. So I decided I wouldn't live without them. I decided that I would join them . . . by killing myself."

Diane widened her eyes.

"And then someone told me about this place, Burning Man. Gave me a ticket and a car pass. I had a date set in my mind. I would attend, and then I would take a long sleep."

"What happened?" Diane asked quietly. "To change your mind?"

"I loaded up my mommy minivan with some camping gear, food, and water, and drove out here, to open camping. I slept in the dust the first night, the van was so full. When I awoke, I sat up and blinked my eyes. A young woman was passing by on a bike. She had colored hair, wore a yellow sundress, and had a smile that could light up the sky. She stopped, said good morning to me, and handed me an apple, then drove off, ringing a little bell. And I bit into that apple, and it tasted sweet, the first taste of anything in a year."

Sheba smiled at the memory.

"I wanted what she seemed to have. To smile, to be free. It gave me something to strive for, to live for. So I dusted myself off and walked to where some people were setting up an art project, and I told them I was there to help. And then I didn't stop working for three days straight, from camp to camp, project to project. I slept where I fell, I ate what I was given.

"One day I just started walking, out into the playa, no direction in mind. I stopped at the trash fence, staring out into the emptiness beyond. It must have been hours.

"And then an art car pulled up, the Starfish. I met Billy. He stopped and asked me if I wanted a ride. I said I had nowhere to go. He asked if I had been to the Temple, so I went. I sat in that Temple for the rest of the afternoon and then through the night. Billy watched me, brought me food and water, gave me a coat, asked nothing. I cried in that thing, cursed everything and everyone.

"In the morning, I stood up and walked out of the Temple. Billy was sleeping on the Starfish. Someone I'd met the day before, who didn't know me from anyone, had waited for me. He woke up as I walked up. The sun was behind me, and he said I looked like a queen, the Queen of Sheba.

"So Sheba was born, and that woman you saw, she was laid to rest to be with her family. I visit them once a year now. My husband, my babies. In the emptiness, I was filled."

Diane was crying, from the story, from the strength it must have taken.

"Alright," Sheba said. "Go on now, you've had your story."

Diane stood up. Sheba did as well, giving her a long embrace.

"Goodbye, Sheba," Diane said.

"Until next year," Sheba replied.

"What about your roommates?" Diane asked. "Who are they, anyway?"

"They have their own ride out," Sheba said. "As to who they are, that's a story for another time."

Diane stepped out of the RV, closing the door, and stood back. The big machine idled out of the spot it had rested in, took a left, then turned slowly onto the road. Diane watched it go and walked back to the front of the camp.

"Was that Sheba leaving?" TK asked, meeting her.

Diane nodded, blinking away tears. TK slipped her arm around Diane's shoulders and walked with her toward the bar.

"Yeah, she does that," TK said.

CHAPTER 32

The dome was unwrapped of its shade cloth, the hammocks were taken down, the playa tech beds were disassembled and staged beside the container. All the pillows and carpets were pulled out and piled. The campers unwrapped and stowed the exterior fabric. Slowly and carefully, the poles of the dome were taken apart and staged for packing.

They pulled the decorations from the bar. The bar itself they left up. Perimeter flags were taken down, the fabric slipped from the poles and stowed in labeled black storage containers, the PVC poles bundled.

"Camp meeting," Twinkle said over the loudspeaker. "Everyone to the bar!"

Diane assembled with the other campers in the bar area. There were still more faces she did not recognize. The camp had swelled to at least sixty people. Some she had met briefly, some not at all.

"Okay, campers," Twinkle began. "I want to congratulate you all on not dying so far."

The assembled group clapped and cheered.

"Tonight is the Man burn," Twinkle said. "The bar will be

closed to the public while it goes on. Make sure you lock up all your stuff. Some camps have been pilfered from in the past. I just wanted to thank each and every one of you for your help and participation in this year's camp. Have fun tonight. We will be striking the kitchen tomorrow, and the bar will go down Monday morning. Last showers are tonight, to let the evap pit dry out. Don't dump any fluid into the evap after tonight, and brush, brush, brush the water tomorrow.

"Some of you will be leaving after the burn tonight. Make sure you are rested enough, pack up your area, and do a thorough MOOP sweep. Take your trash with you, and try not to let it fly off your car. The trash littering the road is usually a disgrace. Don't be those people!

"Enjoy your day, have fun. A group of us will be leaving for the Man burn around six tonight. That's it!"

"What's the plan before then?" Diane asked, joining TK and Sequoia.

"Figured we would wander," TK said. "Take a look at some art before it's gone. Was there anything you wanted to do or see?"

"I'm up for a wander," Diane said. "Let's see where the day takes us."

They grabbed their gear and set out on the bikes, winding through the streets. Diane could see camps doing their own teardowns.

"Why did we take down the dome?" Diane asked. "It could come in handy for people to rest in."

"We used to leave it up longer," TK said. "But a three-day build and a three-day teardown works better. Less exhausting. You'll see. After being out here for so long, you have to push and push to get torn down and packed up. A lot of people hit the wall and get tired out. Some of the people in the camp have been living in tents for eight to twelve days, people can make it one night."

Diane noticed that some of the wooden street signs were missing. It also appeared that cars were still coming in. Clean people were walking around. She hadn't realized how much she had gotten used to being dusty since being here.

"Those people look new," Diane said.

"Yeah, some weekend partiers show up just for a few days," Sequoia said.

Diane couldn't put her finger on what she was feeling. After being here for what felt like forever, and experiencing what had happened, she felt that for people just to show up for a weekend party and photos felt wrong. Galactica had told her that DPW had been out here for months, and other people had also been working to bring this to life. It had to mean more than just a party.

"You smell burgers?" Sequoia asked.

Not waiting for an answer, he was off following his nose. TK and Diane walked after him. They arrived at a camp with a line of people waiting their turn, and they each received a gift of a hamburger, dripping and delicious.

After eating, they wandered back through the city, arriving at the camp where they'd met Dust Granny. Diane could see Maybelle and Rayleen being loaded onto an art car, which left before she and TK arrived. It made Diane feel good that people were taking care of Maybelle and her group. As they passed the camp spot, Diane saw that more tents had sprung up around Dust Granny's RV. A village of people previously unknown to one another had found a place.

The afternoon had waned into early evening when they decided to head back to camp. There were only about thirty minutes before sunset. A thorough scrubbing in the shower and Diane was dressed and ready on top of the container for the howl.

Diane looked out again over the city. Stretching out in each direction were humanity and that which humanity had brought to the desert. Tents of all sizes, RVs, shade structures, cars, trucks, everything. When Diane and TK had arrived, there had been barely anything, and in a few days, the empty space would return. Howling with her friends on the container, Diane watched the sun slip behind the dark, rocky mountains.

Now to get ready for the culmination of this madcap, difficult, and wonderful time.

It was time to see the Man burn.

Diane put on an iridescent dress over leggings. After slipping on her boots, she piled the things she would need for the evening beside her tent, ready to go. Lights, coat, backpack with food and alcohol, full water container.

A large group had assembled in the bar, listening to music, drinking, chatting, laughing.

"You're not ready," Pepper said. He was wearing a leather vest and harem pants, and his face was painted with stripes and swirls. He was holding a brush in one hand and a drink in the other.

"What do you mean?" Diane asked.

"Have a seat," Pepper said. "Trust me."

Diane sat down and presented her face. The brush tickled as Pepper applied silver stripes across her forehead and cheeks. A continuous line went across her nose. Pepper switched brushes.

"A little gold around the eyes," he said, using a fine-tipped brush. "There, now you're perfect."

Diane looked into the hand mirror he provided. A wild and fierce face looked out, hers, but not hers ten days ago. The woman in the reflection was someone new, something untamed and untethered. Diane liked her smile.

"Thank you," Diane said, giving Pepper a hug.

"You guys ready?" TK asked. "Nice paint!"

"Pepper did it," Diane said.

"Ready?" Sequoia asked. He was dressed in a clean black kilt and a leather shirt with many buckles.

"Yes," Diane replied.

A group of twenty or so Dead Presidents set off on their bicycles into the night. The feeling was something out of childhood, a group of childhood friends out on an adventure. Whooping and calling, ringing their bike bells, they turned as a group down the main thoroughfare, heading to the Esplanade. The closer they got, the more lights, noise, and people they encountered.

The Man was illuminated on its tower. Already there was a huge crowd. Sequoia and TK stopped a few hundred yards back, near a light post. Most of the group did as well.

"Isn't this a little far?" Diane asked. "We could get closer."

"You'll see," TK said. "This is about to be a giant, glorious shitshow."

"It'll be easier to find the bikes here than in the sea of bikes that will be up there," Sequoia said. "Billy is already parked on the Starfish to get a good spot."

They strode up the wide lane. Diane figured they were on the six o'clock side. All around them, people on lighted bikes, art cars, people walking illuminated streaming toward the Man. The energy was palpable, a buzzing Diane could feel in the air around them.

They weaved their way through a sea of parked lighted bikes, just as Sequoia had said. It appeared as if most of the art cars were pulled around the perimeter of the Man. Each seemed to be trying to outdo the others for sound dominance. Flames blasted into the air. Everywhere was bathed in glowing and pulsing lights.

Diane's eyes widened from the onslaught of lights, colors, sounds, faces, costumes, dancing, everything moving in motion upon motion. It was the culmination of seventy thousand people who had been at least mostly spread over a vast area of plain and city for days. Now all were coming together at one focused point. Energy built upon energy. Diane could feel the vibration, not just of the noise, but of the souls existing in one another's spaces.

They arrived at the Starfish. Billy had secured a spot among the art cars ringing the area, and he and Twinkle were sitting on the vehicle. In front of them, a sea of people encircled the Man structure. The focus of their attention stood tall on its platform in a vast ring of open earth, bathed in light.

Rangers formed a perimeter along the edge of the crowd. Other Rangers were closer to the Man, in a smaller inner perimeter. Underneath the Man platform, Diane could see masses of wood piled high.

Diane noticed what must have been news crews in one section, the lights from cameras illuminating reporters. She could see a clean, immaculately dressed young Japanese woman speaking into a microphone in front of a camera as if she were covering a speech or a retail opening event. Diane could hear her speaking Japanese.

International press? Diane thought.

"Drink?" Twinkle asked Diane, holding up a bottle of champagne. Diane unhooked her cup from her belt, and Twinkle filled it.

A troupe of men and women filed into the open space around the platform. Diane could see they were dressed in shades of black and carried various items lit by flames. Staffs, chain bowls, flaming finger sticks attached to gloves. Music played, and the troupe swirled and flashed and blew fire. Their performance was choreographic and impressive.

Leaning against the Starfish, Diane took in the sights. A dance party was raging on one of the larger art cars, which appeared to have been made out of a double-decker bus. Flashing lights and music poured from it as another group of dancers performed in the open space around the platform that supported the Man. A feeling struck Diane of being absorbed into the moment, into the whole.

Diane watched as the arms of the wooden figure rose up. This was some sort of signal to the crowd, who started to cheer. The sound around them was pulsing. The Rangers on the perimeter kneeled.

Diane could see Dust Granny on an art car nearby, in her wheelchair, smiling with wonder. The crowd was too thick, so Diane didn't try to approach her. It made her happy to see the elderly woman accepted by the community and enjoying the show.

The lights on the Man went out. The crowd quieted, then stirred. Flames could be seen in the pile of wood. Diane watched as the fire hit an accelerant—gasoline, most likely—and suddenly bloomed. The crowd roared. The flames were rising to the platform and to the Man's feet. Another bloom of fire erupted, then another.

Soon the platform was fully engulfed in fire. Diane could see the crowd, across and to the sides, in the flame light from the inferno. The music on all sides of her was pounding, driving, people were jumping, shouting, and dancing. Fireworks began to shoot off from the Man, further illuminating the area by exploding in the sky. The crowd roared its approval. Diane accepted another drink, laughing with her campmates.

Flames leaped and danced around the Man. Diane danced with TK and Sequoia, an ecstatic celebration. TK dragged them behind the Starfish, where two other art cars had parked at angles, with the space between filled with people dancing, luxuriating in the moment. The fireworks continued in an endless crescendo of light and sound.

Diane looked up to see the Man fall from its perch to crash to the ground. Small tornadoes of heat and dust swirled away from the base to twist off into the crowd to her left. The dancing was frenetic and joyful. Diane had never experienced anything like it, the release and celebration.

The platform collapsed a few minutes after the Man did. Diane, panting, made her way to the front of the Starfish, grabbing a drink of water. She hugged Twinkle and Billy. People streamed around them, moving away from the burn site. There was no recognizable Man figure anymore, just a huge bonfire.

"What do you think?" TK yelled into Diane's ear, hugging her.

"It's—it's—" Diane stammered, smiling, looking into her friend's face lit by the glow of fire.

TK hugged her closer, rocking from side to side.

"Let's get a drink," Sequoia said as he wrapped his arms around them both.

They gathered their things and slowly made their way through the crowd, through the art cars and bicycles. Diane could see that the sea of bikes had grown, and finding theirs would indeed have been difficult at best. As they walked into the open playa, people and lights streamed in every direction around them.

They stopped by the camp and had a few drinks. Then, setting off on foot, Diane, Jeremy, TK, Sequoia, and Pepper explored the full majesty of the city. The night became a blur of drinks at bars, dancing in clubs, games, performances at camps ranging from small and intimate to lavish and huge.

Laughter, singing, and hugs filled their hours as they existed in the glory that seventy thousand people with aligned values could build. In the night, amongst friends, Diane became the Burn.

CHAPTER 33

Sunday, September 6, Temple burn

Diane opened her eyes. The whisper of the wind on the carport was soothing, and she lay listening as her eyes focused. She looked to her left, where Jeremy lay on his side with his head turned toward her. His eyes fluttered as she lifted his arm off and slipped out of the sleeping bag.

Diane put the percolator on and took care of her morning routine. Pouring herself a cup of coffee, she climbed to the top of the container and took a seat. It was still only warm outside, approaching hot. She didn't think she had slept for more than a few hours. Jeremy had asked if he could just lie beside her, and she had let him. He had been a gentleman, sleeping on top of the covers, his arm around her as they slept, peacefully.

Diane noticed a few dusty cars and RVs moving slowly down the roads, all packed up. She thought they must be people leaving after the Man burn, slipping out in the morning hours to avoid the traffic. A steady stream of bikes and walkers went by the camp. The day's activities had just begun.

Diane noticed a group from the camp starting to take the kitchen apart. She climbed down and pitched in. The disassembly took less time than she would have thought, since there were many more people to help than when they had set up.

As she finished stowing the poles in a pile on the ground by the shipping container, the heat and lack of sleep were starting to get to her. She took refuge in the bar, where a wide array of food and snacks was laid out on the bar top. As she nibbled on crackers and hummus, Steven and Twinkle joined her.

"That's a wrap for the kitchen," Steven said, sitting down on a stool.

"We are in good shape for Exodus," Twinkle said, taking a drink from her water bottle. "You still drinking enough water, Diane? The last days can make you forget."

"Guilty," Diane replied, and she went to get her water bottle from the carport, filling it from the jug on the table. TK was still sleeping, and Diane did not want to disturb her. Jeremy had left, presumably to sleep in his own space.

She returned to the bar, where Steven was fitting a screen tightly over the mouth of the burn barrel.

"Why are you doing that?" Diane asked.

"So people don't keep putting things in it," Steven replied. "It has to have a minimum of a day to cool before we empty it."

"Going out?" Twinkle asked Diane.

"In a bit, maybe," Diane replied. "I'll wait for TK. I was wondering about how the ticketing works? Like, if I wanted to come next year?"

"Like it that much, do you?" Twinkle replied.

"It's growing on me," Diane said.

"To just get a ticket, you register on the Burning Man website with a profile," Steven said. "Then, when the ticket sales come up, you apply. It's tricky, and it gets harder every year. Our camp will get the opportunity to purchase tickets if we are in good standing. We work hard to clean up our site because it gets inspected when we leave. We also offer a lot of interactivity."

"You can get access to the tickets through volunteering," Twinkle explained. "But that is for the following year. I could see you getting invited back to Dead Presidents if you were inclined to."

She smiled and glanced at Steven, who nodded his head, saying, "You're one of us now."

Hearing this made Diane happy. The camp had become more than just a place to lay her head. It was easy to see why many people came back to the same camp year after year.

Cradling her water bottle, Diane reclined in a camp chair, dozing in the shade. After the past ten days, she didn't feel inclined to do much of anything. Most of the campers seemed to be in the same frame of mind. There was a definite change in energy after the burn. Diane felt good but wrung out. Her body simply was not used to this level of stimulation and emotion.

"You doing okay?"

Diane opened her eyes to see TK looking down at her.

"Yes," Diane replied. "Just relaxing. You?"

"I needed the sleep," TK said, stretching her arms. "What time is it?"

"Around one, I guess?" Diane said.

"Too hot to do much," TK said, taking a seat. "I thought we could load some things in the trailer so there would be less to do tomorrow. Not really motivated though."

"When do we leave?" Diane asked, feeling both sad about the end of this adventure and hopeful about getting back to the real world.

"Depends," TK said, taking a drink from her cup. "Most of what's left is to tear down the bar, wrap up the evap pond, then pack the container. If there are enough people, it will go well. If not, it's a slog. Packing the container takes a good amount of time."

"So the Temple burn is tonight?"

"It's a different burn," TK said. "You'll see."

"Well," Pepper said, walking up, "I'm all packed up."

"You're leaving now?" Diane asked with alarm.

"No," Pepper replied. "Right after the Temple burn. I have to be at work in two days, though the decompression will make it hard."

"What's decompression?" Diane asked. "Isn't that a party?"

Pepper and TK shared a laugh.

"Yes and no," TK said. "There are usually parties called Decompression, in various cities, a few weeks after the Burn."

"The decompression I'm talking about is what happens to you personally. Though it doesn't happen to everyone," Pepper said. "Have you noticed how intense things are out here, like living at eleven?"

"Yes," Diane replied.

"Your brain is not used to what happens out here, so while you are in it, you compartmentalize in order to keep moving forward." Pepper said. "Afterward . . . well, for me, it's like a low-level PTSD. I have extremely intense dreams about being here on the playa. Reentry into the real world is tough too, like getting used to paying for things again. My decompression usually lasts five days or so. I need extra time to reenter the world. Other people don't have any aftereffects."

"I didn't know it would be like that," Diane said.

"It might not be, for you," TK replied. "But it's good to know about. Now, I think we should put some things up so the teardown tomorrow will be easier."

"Let's do it," Diane said, getting up from her chair.

Together they walked into the carport and surveyed the interior. Everything was covered in the fine white dust. TK started by selecting the food they would need for the night and the next day and setting it aside. Then the decorations came down and were folded and stowed, with breaks for them both to sneeze and drink water. Diane put on her dust mask to continue.

"You're learning," TK said, donning her own mask.

In a couple of hours, all of the nonessential clothing, shoes, and various other items were gathered, packed in the black and yellow plastic bins, and staged by the trailer. Diane left out some toiletries and clothing for the evening and the next day.

The carport that had been her home for the Burn felt empty, stripped down. Diane noticed other campers doing their own packing and teardown. She began to truly realize that her first Burn experience was coming to an end.

"Should we take down the carport?" Diane asked.

"I leave it up. We could still get rain or a dust storm," TK replied.

As they finished, the sun was dipping closer to the ring of mountains. Diane and TK were handed huge bacon sandwiches by Twinkle.

"We are cooking everything we can," Twinkle said. "Eat up. We have about five more pounds of bacon."

Grabbing their water bottles, Diane and TK climbed to the top of the shipping container to eat their food. Diane looked around at the city. Many people in the camps surrounding them were also making preparations to leave.

"Any thoughts?" TK asked.

"It's been incredible," Diane began, soaking in the last rays of sun. "More than I would ever have expected. Words can't do it justice."

"Think you will come back?"

"Yes, definitely."

Sequoia, Pepper, and Jeremy joined them on the container as the sun touched the mountains. Diane felt both sad and happy to be there with her friends and howl the last howl of the Burn.

Climbing down, Diane gathered her things for the night. The temperature was cooling rapidly. Putting on her leg bag, goggles, face mask, and shemagh and gathering her coat into her arms, she walked to her bike and turned on the lights. Billy maneuvered the Starfish to the street in front of the bar. He glanced at Diane and gave her a wink.

"You ready for the Temple?" Billy asked.

"I am," Diane replied. "When are you setting out?"

"Couple of minutes. I want to get a good spot. It will fill up fast."

"I'll see you there."

Diane went to the bar and placed her cup in front of Twinkle, who dutifully filled it. The whiskey was both harsh and sweet as she sipped it. It was interesting to her that she had never drank straight whiskey before the Burn and now it was second nature.

"You about ready?" TK asked her, sitting at the bar.

"Good to go."

"As soon as Sequoia gets his ass in gear, we will head out."

More people joined them at the bar. The mood was both

light and heavy at the same time. The music was subdued and muted. The falling darkness and the reduced lighting in the bar threw shadows on everyone's faces. Diane felt at peace and in the place she was meant to be.

"Let's do it," Sequoia said, mounting his bike.

A mob of people was in motion on the street as thirty or so people from Dead Presidents set out on their bikes, one after another. Diane pedaled beside TK, Jeremy, and Sequoia. A raucous, laughing group of twinkling lights and rowdy humor wound its way through the streets toward the playa. Bike bells tinkled and horns honked as they passed slower riders and people walking along the road.

Reaching the playa, Diane could see lights and people from every direction headed to the Temple. The air was cool but not cold. The taste of playa was in her mouth, its smell in her nose. The Temple ahead was lit up, an encircling mass of humanity forming around it.

They stopped the bikes a good stretch from the gathering and locked them together. Sequoia led the way to where the Starfish was supposed to be. As with the Man burn, they wound their way through a sea of bikes and art cars. This time, though, in definitive contrast to the Man burn, there was no loud blasting of music, and the crowd quietly murmured instead of singing and shouting.

Finding their way to the Starfish was easier said than done, but they located Billy, who had found a good position for viewing the Temple. Diane found a seat on the corner of the Starfish beside Pepper and Sequoia. The mood around them was quiet. Twinkle opened a bottle of champagne, and Diane filled her cup.

Sipping, she looked at the mass of people shuffling into place, row upon row sitting on the ground in front of the Starfish. As with the Man burn, Diane could see Rangers in a perimeter row, with open ground behind them.

A hush fell over the crowd as the last light from the sunset died away. A flickering light started deep in the Temple. There was no preamble to the burn. It just started. Fire was flickering up amongst the piled wood and licking the Temple structure.

Diane could see her friends' faces reflected in the glow of the fire. Sequoia picked her up, sat down, and deposited her on his lap, his big arms encircling her and TK. Pepper stood facing them, wrapping his arms around them as well. Diane could see Jeremy's face as he stood near them. Tears were streaming down his face. She beckoned him over to the group, which absorbed him too. Sequoia laid his head against TK's face. Diane could hear him softly weeping. She watched as TK ran her fingers through Sequoia's thick beard, stroking his face, holding his head.

"I'm sorry," Sequoia said softly through sobs. "I'm sorry."

"Shhh, baby," TK said gently and kissed his forehead, dismissing his apologies for weeping in this perfect moment. "I'm here."

Tucking her head over Pepper's shoulder, Diane could see couples kissing, a young man quietly playing a guitar to a nameless melody. People were hugging, smiling, crying, or just peacefully watching.

The glow from the flames played across all of them. Diane looked to TK's face. One eye was hidden by Sequoia's hair, the other bright and shining with tears, making dusty tracks down TK's cheek to her gleaming smile.

Their eyes met and held. Diane felt grateful, wanted, and loved. She was exactly where she was supposed to be.

The fire fully consumed the Temple, its structure outlined in flames, as Diane slowly rocked in her group. Small tornadoes of smoke and dust spun away from the structure. The crowd collectively held its breath as the first spire of the Temple collapsed. Some scattered cheering quickly subsided. No one, it seemed, wanted to break the spell.

The moment was crystalline in Diane's eyes, the glow from the Temple etching each line of the crowd in warmth. Light played upon the faces of friends and strangers, each lost in the moment of reflection. The burning Temple light was the culmination of something completely different from the world not here, not in this moment. Diane was filled by a feeling of both loss and rebirth as the last frame of the structure collapsed, and with it, a delineation of what was yesterday and what would be tomorrow. The group was held there, transfixed by the flames, by the consummation of so much work, effort, and emotion gone to embers.

"Well then," Billy said as the crowd around them started to shift and dissipate. "Ready?"

Without another word, Billy turned on the motor for the Starfish. Diane linked arms with Sequoia and TK as they navigated the sea of people, bikes, and art cars until they found their own and set off back to camp.

CHAPTER 34

Monday, September 7, Exodus

Diane awoke. Sitting up, she grabbed her water bottle and took a long drink. The sound of a vehicle of some sort passing the camp resonated from outside the tent walls. Taking a deep breath, she sighed.

The air was cool as she slipped on her clothes and turned on the heater under the coffee percolator, reflecting that it was the last time she would do so, at least for this Burn. So many last times came to her mind as she gathered her things in the now emptier carport. The last porto visit, last bag shower, last night drinking at the bar and carousing. Diane did not remember when she had spent so much quality time with friends. She'd certainly never had as much fun as she'd had here. Easy access to great people and good times would be hard to leave.

TK was up and dressed when Diane returned. They shared a hug.

"Ready to pack it up?" TK asked as she poured two cups of coffee.

"I guess so," Diane said, taking a sip.

"We can get a jump on our stuff before we tear down everything with the camp," TK said. "Make sure you eat enough. It's a long day."

Diane followed TK's lead and pulled out her sleeping bag and air mattress. With the sound of the air hissing from the mattress valve, she rolled up and stowed the sleeping bag. With TK's help, the two mattresses were stowed in the black and yellow bins. Hanging items came down next and were carefully packed and stacked outside the carport.

The two women unwired the extension cord from the chandelier and wrapped it up. They carried the chairs, table, and cooler outside, along with the dusty carpet. The tarp on the ground was unstaked, untaped, and folded. Undoing the bungees connecting the side panels brought an unexpected tear to Diane's eye.

Wiping it away and laughing it off, Diane folded the long vinyl material sections with TK and placed them into the black and yellow bins. This place, which had been her home for the past twelve days, was now being packed up, ready to be loaded.

"Ready to take the lag bolts up?"

Diane saw Sequoia standing with the power tool in his hands.

"Good to go," TK said, hugging him.

The long bolts came free from the ground with an industrial noise from the tool.

Diane could see the rest of the camp packing up around them. RVs, trucks with trailers, cars packed to the gills with dusty people and things drove by on the road as they slipped the long poles from the frames and deposited them, taped together, by TK's trailer. Everything was soon laid out in a neat row, ready to be loaded. Diane and TK assisted Sequoia with his carport as well, the disassembly process going as smoothly and as quickly as their own.

"Let's muster up!" Twinkle said from the bar.

The trio joined their fellow campers in front of the bar. Diane spotted Jeremy and gave him a hug, which he returned.

"Congratulations!" Twinkle began. "Nobody died . . . yet."

Laughter rippled among the campmates.

"Virgins no more with Steven," Twinkle said. "Everyone else in their teams."

Diane and Jeremy helped Steven, depositing the remaining whiskey bottles into bins, carefully stacking them by Twinkle's truck. The bar was untethered and lifted with its steel poles and straps, carried by four people, disassembled, and then loaded into the container.

An efficient and orderly breakdown and loading of the remaining items followed. With Steven directing, the shipping container was rapidly filled from floor to ceiling, back to front. Diane stopped to drink deeply from her water bottle. The land was quickly becoming empty again, and not just their camp. Surrounding camps were rapidly breaking down their own structures.

Hot, dusty, and tired, Diane helped get the last of the camp items fitted into the container. The doors had to be physically pushed closed, with much groaning and grunting. The lock inserted into the crosspiece and snapped shut. Diane then joined Sequoia and TK in folding up the black tarp that had served as the evaporation pond. Coated in rotten food scraps, dust, and God knows what, it was easily the most disgusting thing she had seen at the burn. They got it folded and stuffed into a lawn trash bag.

"Get something to eat," Twinkle said. "Find shade where you can. Then we'll load the camp trailer."

With the bar gone, Diane and TK sat in the shadow side of the shipping container with Sequoia and Jeremy. Between bites of vacuum-sealed stew, Diane laughed as Sequoia told joke after joke.

The short rest having restored some of her strength, Diane helped pack the trailer attached to Twinkle's van. With Jeremy and Sequoia helping, TK's trailer was loaded and attached to her truck in no time.

"MOOP sweep!" Twinkle said, bring the remaining campers together. "Let's form a line on one side of the property and move forward. Nothing is too small to pick up. Our score for cleanliness will determine our placement next year, so let's make sure we get all dark green on the map this year."

"Dark green?" Diane asked TK as they lined up and started walking with the others, occasionally stopping to grab any material on the ground.

"After we leave," TK said, gathering a piece of glitter into her hand, "there will be an inspection. The color of the MOOP map published later will determine placement. Camps that don't pick up after themselves can be put on probation or not asked back. If the inspectors have to stop and pick stuff up, the color goes from green, to yellow, to red, with red being the worst."

Steven walked opposite them, pushing a piece of metal with wheels attached slowly across the ground.

"What's he doing?" Jeremy asked.

"It's a magnet," Sequoia replied. "Grabs anything ferrous, such as nails and staples. Twinkle and Greebo use the leaf rakes to turn over the dust and find more MOOP."

"There is so much more than I would have thought," Diane

said, stopping yet again, picking up a bottle cap and an earring.

After two more sweeps, the trash was deposited and loaded into the trailer. After trading hugs with everyone, Twinkle and Steven left. Diane spotted Jeremy and Sequoia standing by two tents up and went over to them.

"How are you doing?" Diane asked.

"Pretty good, considering," Jeremy replied. "Think I'm going to stay a little longer with Sequoia. Apparently, you don't have to leave for a few days. I kind of want to process a bit."

"You have my information," Diane said. "I want to keep in touch."

"You got it," Sequoia said, stepping forward to hug her.

With Sequoia's huge, strong arms around her, Diane beckoned to Jeremy for the last group hug. Lingering in the moment, Sequoia kissed her on top of her head.

"I miss you guys already," Diane said, stepping back.

"Stay gold, Ponyboy," Sequoia said, blinking away tears. "Stay gold."

Diane wiped away tears of her own as she walked to join TK by her truck and helped her load a bike onto the rack. Rubbing the fur on her playa cruiser, she had a thought.

"Do we have to leave right away?" Diane asked.

"We have some time. Why?" TK asked.

"Thought I might take a last ride."

TK stepped forward and hugged her, laughing.

"After twelve days in the dust, and when you're hours away from a hot shower, you want to stay a little longer?" TK said, smiling. "I knew you would love it."

"Thank you again, Stacy," Diane said. "Can I call you Stacy again?"

"Yeah, the Burn is over," Stacy said. "Go on your ride."

Diane picked up her gear and mounted her bike.

"Back in a minute," Diane said as she pedaled into the street.

Biking by the center camp, she saw people filing in and out. She turned at a familiar street until it took her by Dust Granny's camp. Her RV was gone, but some tents remained.

The shipping container where the pub had been was gone. An imprint in the dust was all that remained. People in camps waved at her to join them, but she pedaled on. Passing by the Celestial Splash camp, she saw the stalls had been taken down and the plot was bare. The Cool Rain tent was disassembled and lying ready to be packed.

Leaving the city behind her, she headed out onto the playa, no destination in mind. A small, swirling dust storm was off to her right. She slipped on her mask and goggles and continued. As she biked, visibility became restricted to about five feet in front of her. Diane didn't mind the dust that surrounded her, caressed and coated her. Pulling her shemagh down around her neck, she felt her hair fly in the wind. She stopped and stood, stretching her arms in the air, lost in the dust but knowing she would be fine. Everything would be fine.

As the air cleared, Diane slipped her goggles up onto her forehead. Another few minutes brought her to the orange plastic trash fence, the place where the playa ended. Diane stopped and stared into the open white plain beyond, which stretched out as far as the eye could see.

It felt as if she were looking at another world, a world only accessible after you passed through the Burn—through the toil and triumph, the beauty, joy, and heartache—and then beyond it. A place where the principles of kindness, redemption, healing, love, and acceptance existed as the primary goals, not as secondary attributes.

Diane thought of Sheba, her wildness and her pain. Of Sequoia and Pepper, two new friends who felt closer to her than people she had known for years. Of Jeremy, a young man struggling with his past of pain and violence and finding a peace he hadn't known in the other world. Of Steven, a man of war and religion, profoundly changed by a random stranger's kindness. Of Maybelle, a fierce, deeply spiritual woman who did not listen to hate and rumor, bravely setting out to see for herself.

Diane smiled as she thought of Stacy, her beautiful friend, who had known that Diane needed something and gifted her with the chance of a lifetime. Diane thought of all the people she had met at the Burn and of the kindnesses she had received. She thought of all the stories of people who had been here and who would come here, looking for something, anything.

Diane looked back on the playa and the city beyond. It was a rare place, where those who fit in, those who didn't fit anywhere else, and those who only appeared to fit in belonged. Where the broken parts of people could be soothed and healed. Where joy and hope existed side by side, blended by the dust. A place where love and friendship could blossom, where hate and prejudice could not thrive.

A place for all of them.

A place to call home.

Diane stepped over the trash fence and began to walk.

THE END

AUTHOR'S NOTE

Diane walking over the trash fence and into the open desert is an allegorical symbol, depicting that she has passed through to a new life, one she could only have reached by going through the Burn. If you go—and I hope you do—don't step over the trash fence and walk into the desert. You will probably die.

The goal of this book was to present an informative and entertaining story both for people who have been to Burning Man and for people interested in going. Many representations of Burning Man in media have focused on the more salacious stories. There is so much more to it than that. The Burn is where a lot of people keep their hearts, as well as find them.

Still, there is no way all the stories and experiences of Burning Man could be captured in one book. It is a place where the possibilities and experiences are endless. It can be as wild or as mild as you want. But remember, if you do experience things that make you uncomfortable, that is a good thing. It means your boundaries and beliefs are being pushed. Growth can be painful and sometimes confusing. Embrace it.

Burning Man has been and continues to be transformative for me, as it is for many people. If this book does inspire you to go—and everyone should—it will be with more knowledge than most Virgin Burners have, and maybe that will help you along the way. If there is one thing I suggest you take to Burning Man, it is kindness, both for others and for yourself. And always remember:

YOU DON'T EXPERIENCE BURNING MAN,
YOU ARE THE EXPERIENCE.

See you in the dust.